Praise for K.A. Mitchell's *Collision Course*

"...brilliantly written, with strong, witty dialogue, distinct characters, sharp descriptions, emotional depth and breadth and interest, and scorching sex."

~ *Dear Author*

"The remarkable K.A. Mitchell has produced another winner with Collision Course. The emotional plot touches your heart."

~ *Literary Nymphs*

"Collision Course had me cracking up and crying, and I love books that are so well written and filled with wonderful characters that I can really feel what they are experiencing."

~ *Fallen Angel Reviews*

Look for these titles by *K.A. Mitchell*

Now Available:

Custom Ride
Hot Ticket
Diving In Deep
Regularly Scheduled Life
Chasing Smoke

Print Anthology
Temperature's Rising

Collision Course

K.A. Mitchell

A SAMHAIN PUBLISHING, LTD. publication.

Samhain Publishing, Ltd.
577 Mulberry Street, Suite 1520
Macon, GA 31201
www.samhainpublishing.com

Editing by Sasha Knight
Cover by Anne Cain

First Samhain Publishing, Ltd. electronic publication: December 2008
First Samhain Publishing, Ltd. print publication: November 2009

Dedication

For my readers. Thank you.

Thank you, too, Bonnie, for helping me with my look at "the system". And the title. Phew.

Chapter One

Eighties dance music blasted through the Yaris's speakers as Joey Miller flew down the passing lane of I-10, dancing in his car. A quick glance at the clock on the dashboard put a little hitch in his rhythm, so he cranked the volume up even higher as if the vibrating beats per minute could make up for lost time.

Car-dancing kept him focused, the thump of the bass bouncing his gaze from mirror to mirror to windshield, so he was able to react quickly when it happened.

The cars in front of him slowed. The truck flying up behind him didn't.

A split second to react, and with the gift of clarity from the blast of adrenaline, Joey was able to squeeze his Yaris into the right lane, just as the truck barreled into the dark blue minivan that had been in front of him.

The brown pickup lifted the minivan, flinging it into the guardrail and over. Joey swung back, grinding to a halt on the left shoulder as the minivan flew across the opposite lanes, a final clip on the driver's side sending it rolling over the far edge, down an embankment.

He didn't think. Didn't wait for his heart to stop hammering all the way up to the base of his skull. He rode the adrenaline wave right into rescue mode.

Even as he started to sprint across the road, Joey had his cell out and was dialing 911. The driver of the pickup seemed conscious, and other people were stopping. But Joey knew he'd seen a kid in a car seat in that minivan, and he had to get there now.

He spat out the information to the dispatcher. "Three car accident. I-10." He even knew what exit, since he'd been clocking them to try to make up time. "I don't know how many injuries. There's a child involved."

He reached the minivan, which was now back up on its wheels, windshield gone, driver's window gone, back and front ends crumpled like paper. The driver's door wouldn't open, and the side curtain airbags were blocking his view so he leaned in the window.

The kid was about two or three, not even screaming, just making weird gasping sounds. The woman—mother?—was in bad shape. Unconscious, unresponsive. She had a pulse and was breathing, which he reported to the dispatcher still on the line as he checked.

"Hey, little dude, how're you doing back there?"

The kid took a shuddering breath. "Mommy?"

"Mommy's going to be fine."

"Mommy?" The voice got a little shriller.

"Hey listen, dude, Mommy's asleep because she doesn't feel too good right now. We don't want to get too loud, okay?"

The kid stopped mid-whine. "Oh, okay. Like when she has a headache?"

"Just like that." Joey hoped he wasn't lying too much to the kid. Part of the car's front end had become part of her right leg. On the left one, a huge gash through her jeans was pouring blood. Not arterial bleeding, he was pretty sure. The first-aid videos were kind of graphic on that subject. Feet lifting off the grass as he leaned in, he reached over and grabbed a fistful of napkins from the center console. He slapped the wad over the gash and applied pressure.

With his hands full, the phone was slipping out from under his cheek. He warned the dispatcher, not wanting to add too much about the bleeding in front of the kid. "I'm applying pressure but at this angle, I'm going to end up dropping the phone."

He managed to turn his head and lock eyes with the kid. The boy was a lot calmer than Joey felt.

A giggle escaped the boy's exaggeratedly pursed-shut lips. "Cotton candy."

"How's that, dude?" The blood had soaked through all of the napkins. Joey pressed harder, reaching up to check the pulse.

"Your hair. Yellow cotton candy."

Yeah. The kid had a point. When he'd changed jobs and towns, he'd tried to get the purple bleached out of it. He'd had to cut most of it off, and it did kind of look like fluffy cotton candy. Blue or pink would have been much more fun.

"How do you think it tastes?" he asked.

The kid giggled again. "Yech. Like hair. Is the car okay?" A little worry in the voice. "'Cause Mommy says we can't have a new one. I wanned one with a DVD."

"It's going to be fine. Don't worry about it. What's your name, dude?"

"Seth." Of course, it came out like Sef. But Joey could speak lisp.

"Where were you guys headed?"

"Gramma's."

"Do you know Gramma's other name?"

Seth thought about it and then shook his head. "Just Gramma."

"Okay. Do you know your other name?"

"Seth Nathan Thatcher."

Sef Nafan Fatcher. That was just cruel. With a name like that, he'd be in speech therapy for life.

"How old are you, Seth Nathan Thatcher?"

"Free."

Joey should have guessed. He wondered if he lived on Thirty-Third Street.

"Do you know Mommy's names?"

The little brow squinched up. Not even a cut on him. Thank

God for child seats and side curtain airbags.

"She's Emily. That's what Gramma calls her."

"Okay."

Joey had never been so happy to hear sirens in his life. He could feel the blood soaking into his hand, even as he pressed.

"So, Seth—"

"I want to be dude again."

"Okay. So, dude, you ready to meet some firemen and policemen?"

Flashing lights, sirens and caffeine were near the top of Aaron Chase's very short favorites list. All three gave him a rush that was almost as good as sex—which took up at least the top five on that list.

He'd just finished his fourth coffee of the day, and the sights and sounds of the accident on I-10 sent a buzz through his veins. He swung the ambulance off onto the shoulder in the spot the firemen and cops had left. As he scanned the scene, he could see that the first responders were divided into three separate clumps.

"Remember the bet," his partner Hennie said as she climbed to the back.

"One shift. No f-words," Aaron said. He could do it. Probably.

"Not even in your head."

"And how the f— how will you know?"

"Because I will." She gave him that I-was-a-teacher-for-twenty-years-and-I-have-eyes-in-the-back-of-my-head look.

A cop stepped away from the nearest bunch and came toward Aaron and Hennie as they unloaded their gear and a stretcher.

"Truck driver's got minor cuts and bruises. He's coming with us. His blood alcohol's point one eight. Lady in the Lexus is fine. Seat belt, air bag. A little shocky, firemen are handling it."

Hennie set up the tank and back-boarding gear as they lifted the stretcher down. "And the minivan?" She jerked her chin at the mangled pile of scrap.

"Can't tell 'til we cut her out. Firemen wanted to wait for you guys in case she flatlined. She's still out. Shallow pulse."

As they started down the side of the grassy slope, Aaron saw a distinctly civilian and—hey, being at the scene of an accident didn't mean he didn't still have eyes and a working dick—distinctly f— Christ—doable round ass sticking out of the driver's window.

Bonus. All his favorite things rolled into one.

"What the hell's going on?" he asked the cop.

"Witness. Said he's trained as a first responder. Been keeping pressure on a bad bleeder."

"F-friggin' amateur."

The cop shrugged. "He's doin' okay. Calm. Keepin' the kid calm too."

"Kid?" Hennie's reaction echoed Aaron's. Dispatch hadn't said anything about a kid. Hennie scrambled back up the slope for a smaller collar and board. The cop lifted the stretcher end she'd abandoned.

"He's three. Not even a scratch as far as we can see. Witness says the kid's coherent. I can't understand him."

"We'll still take him," Hennie said as she ran back. "They'll want to check him over."

The firemen standing near the driver's side had a couple of pieces of hydraulic equipment ready. Aaron walked up until he was standing next to that bubble butt. "Okay, Do-gooder. Whatcha got?"

"I've had steady pressure on it since I got here. It seems to be slowing. No change in breathing or pulse."

The cop was right. Do-gooder stayed calm. Matter-of-fact. Almost professional. And pretty—he bit his lip and swore he heard Hennie laugh—damned competent. "Why didn't you put on a pressure bandage?"

"Aside from having nothing but my shirt for it, I didn't think it was worth trying to lift her pinned leg to slide something underneath."

The little...do-gooder was right. And Aaron was even more annoyed. Probably because as focused as his mind was on that woman and her possibly severed leg, his dick was all too aware of that ass a few inches away.

Do-gooder was singing some song with the kid, probably something Aaron's baby sister Sheree would know, especially if it was based on one of those damned Disney cartoons. Aaron had let her watch too many Disney videos at an impressionable age, all the singing animals encouraging a happily-ever-after mentality, even after the crap Sheree had seen growing up.

So maybe he'd screwed up there. Sue him. He'd kept her safe, alive and sane right on up to the age of eighteen. She'd have to learn there were no happy endings in this screwed-to-hell world on her own. Of course, swallowing all that someday-my-prince-will-come crap meant that she was always trying to fix him up with some guy she'd decided was gay. At least avoiding that crap was easier with her off to Tulane.

The firemen pried open the side door, and Hennie climbed in back to hold the woman's head in line. Aaron reached over the guy's back, a nice-looking back under a painted-on red T-shirt, to fasten the cervical collar around the woman's neck, while one of the firemen slid the board between the seat and her back. Aaron's dick twitched as his body made contact. As soon as this shift was over he was going to start looking for that ass in every bar in Jacksonville. Aaron glanced back at the little boy who was still lisping along with Mr. Hot Ass.

"Okay, Do-gooder, here's what going to happen. When I give the word, you're going to back away and leave those napkins there. Davey here"—Aaron nodded at the fireman—"is going to pry open the door and see if we can get her out. You can go wash up and disinfect at the truck."

The guy broke off his song to ask softly, "What about the kid?"

"What about him?"

"Don't you think you should take him out of here before...?"

"Before what?"

"Before you cut his mom out of the car?" It was a husky whisper, completely different from the light singing voice he'd been using.

Aaron pursed his lips. "Fine." If this was the worst thing the kid ever saw in his life, he'd be doing a hell of a lot better than the rest of the world. He turned his head and spoke to one of the cops who climbed in around Hennie and started unbuckling the kid from his car seat. No point to a collar, the kid had been shifting his head side-to-side as he sang along.

As soon as the cop started to lift the kid out of the seat, the kid screeched like a siren. Finally, the kid added some words to the ear-bleeding noise. "No, no, no. Cotton-candy dude."

"Um. That's me."

Aaron lifted his head and looked. He could see where the kid had gotten the idea. A ridiculous pile of lemon yellow fluff floated around the guy's head. Lucky he had that ass.

"Okay. Go wash up and see if you can get the kid to stop screaming."

"C'mon, dude. I've gotta wash my hands. You get a ride with the policeman." When Hot-Ass-Unfortunate-Hair spoke to the kid, his screams stopped.

Sometime between the firemen getting the engine off her leg and Aaron and Hennie splinting the compound fracture, Aaron heard a song he recognized. Somehow the unoccupied police and firemen had been conned into singing "Rudolph the Red-Nosed Reindeer" to entertain the kid. Which must have taken some doing, considering it was mid-March.

They carried her up the slope and popped her into the ambulance. Aaron turned to where the Emergency Workers' Choir was performing from the back of the fire truck and said, "Let's go. We'll take him in."

The toddler shook his head and clung to his cotton-candy dude. Despite the hair, candy was a good enough label for him.

15

Eye candy. Freckles across his nose, big brown eyes, dark lashes, cheekbones in a perfect symmetry almost too pretty for a guy, but a broad, strong jaw. Face and an ass like that, Aaron bet Do-gooder didn't spend many nights alone. And then those lips. Yeah, the hair was a mess, but it would be fine for yanking on when— Damn, the rest of that sentence would definitely violate the terms of the bet.

"Wanna go wif him."

"But your mommy's in here, honey," Hennie called from the back of the ambulance.

"She's sleeping 'cause she hurts. Want cotton-candy dude."

One of the cops offered to take him. Then a fireman. Aaron would have thought the lure of riding in a fire truck would be irresistible to a boy that age, but the kid kept shaking his head. Aaron was pretty immune to tantrums from either adults or kids. He was about to grab the kid when Eye-candy shifted the kid to his other hip and dug out his wallet.

"Here." He handed an ID to one of the cops. "I work for the Department of Families and Children."

Disgust coiled like a rat snake in Aaron's gut, followed by the familiar crush of panic and guilt. The panic and guilt were stupid, a reaction from fourteen years of conditioned response. The twins and Sheree were adults now—free to screw up their own lives without the system's "help". All Aaron needed to do these days was drop some occasional cash in their bank accounts until they made it through college.

The DFC couldn't touch them now, but it was all Aaron could do not to sneer at the social worker, f—hot ass or not. "Really?"

Do-gooder looked over at the cop. "I work with Carmen Hernandez a lot. You can check in with her, or dispatch."

The cops were only too glad to have someone on hand to spare them the paperwork and the blown eardrums if that kid started screaming again.

"I'll bring him to the hospital and work on finding some family members."

The cop handed back the ID with a smile. "Thanks, Joey."

Davey the fireman went so far as to clap Joey on the back. "We'll put the car seat in your car."

"That would be great. Thanks a lot."

"His mother's stabilized." Aaron didn't know why he felt like he should tell Joey that.

Joey smiled. It almost made Aaron want to smile back, and then he remembered. DFC.

"Great work."

Like Joey was Aaron's supervisor. Like he needed the validation. Friggin' social workers.

That fugly hair barely moved as Joey turned to the kid on his hip. "See, dude? Your mommy's going to be fine." He looked back at Aaron. "I guess I'll see you at the hospital."

"Maybe." It was only a second, but as Aaron locked eyes with—Christ, what grown man called himself Joey?—he could see everything. Awareness, recognition, want, heat. All laid out right there. Joey's eyes told Aaron that ass was his if he wanted it, and despite Joey's so-called profession, Aaron still did.

As Aaron swung up into the driver's seat, he glanced into the mirror. His pants shrank around his dick at the sight of that ass swinging as Joey walked back to the car. Though Aaron could admit the swagger was probably due more to the fact that Joey was walking with a hefty three-year-old on his hip than an effort to show off.

17

Chapter Two

Seth Nathan Thatcher's mom was stable and had regained enough consciousness to check on her son and name her mother before sinking into a morphine pillow. Seth Ethan himself had managed to stay still long enough to satisfy the doctors that he had no concussion. Dad was out of the picture, and Gramma would be another two hours coming from outside Tallahassee. Oh shit. Tallahassee. The reason Joey had been speeding and dancing on I-10 in the first place.

Joey put Seth on his feet. The kid whimpered and Joey said, "Hey, dude, I've got some money. Want to see what damage we can do to the vending machines?" He pointed.

"Candy?"

"Yeah, sure." Joey hoped the kid wasn't diabetic or on some medication. The pediatric emergency doctor had quizzed the kid pretty effectively about things he had to take or what he couldn't have. Joey loved the kid's answer.

"Sometimes when Mommy has a headache"—and at that point in his longest sentence to date Seth scrunched up his face in a bang-up imitation of someone with a migraine—"I'm not allowed to have anything but bed." He nodded solemnly.

Joey followed as the kid sprinted toward the vending machines. All that damage to the car and driver and not a scratch on the kid. He was recommending that car seat to every one of his sisters—should they ever decide to give him nieces and nephews to spoil rotten. Eyes round with awe, Seth pounded on the glass, saying, "Dat dat dat."

A zillion sugary choices should keep Seth occupied for a second, so Joey dug out his cell phone and pressed three on his speed dial.

His best friend Noah answered on the first ring. "Going for a personal best?"

"Is that some kind of sports reference?"

"Don't give me that shit. You're only an hour and twenty minutes away from breaking your own record for being spectacularly late." Noah sounded amused rather than annoyed.

"Consider the record shattered. I'm sorry, hon. There was an accident. I'm at the hospital."

"Oh shit. Joey. Where? We'll be right there. I swear—"

"No, not me. It happened right in front of me, and there was this kid and now it's tied up in work."

"You did that on purpose."

"End up at the hospital?"

"Scare me. So I won't complain that you're late."

Noah had learned far too much about psychology when he lived with Joey—or maybe Noah had learned it from his lover Cameron. That guy was pretty quick to assess things.

"Maybe," Joey said, and dug in his pockets for change. He found a receipt for lunch, a paper with a phone number he didn't remember getting—and that had probably been through the wash—and two crumpled singles. He tucked the phone under his chin and started smoothing out the bill on the edge of the machine.

Still overwhelmed with possibilities, Seth slapped the glass.

"I'm going to be another couple hours at least. I have to wait for this kid's grandmother to show up."

"Shit. Did his parents die?"

"No. But Mom'll be out of commission for a bit. Can we reschedule for tomorrow night? Cameron doesn't have to fly out until Sunday, right?"

"Yeah." Noah's voice changed in a way Joey knew too well.

He could imagine what Cameron was doing to Noah right then, probably kissing somewhere while running a hand through Noah's hair. That soft wavy hair. "I think Cam and I can amuse ourselves tonight. Mmm, talk to you tomorrow."

If Joey had a Cameron or a Noah, Joey could have amused himself too. He'd had a Noah, for more than a year, until Joey had been smacked upside the head with the painful realization that Noah was always going to be waiting for Cameron.

Joey slid the phone back in its case. For a second at the accident, he'd thought the EMT was Noah. Tall, dark hair, light eyes and a confident way of crowding into Joey that made him want to climb that body like a tree. Then he'd taken another glance over his shoulder and seen that the shoulders weren't quite as broad, and the dark hair was long, but straight, pulled back in a short ponytail. And the eyes. Noah's eyes were cat-like, bright blue and full of fun. This guy—Chase according to his nametag—Chase's eyes were pale, powder blue. Flat and hard, until that moment when he'd stared at Joey right before getting into the ambulance. The heat in that stare had turned the color as hot as the heart of a candle flame.

Joey wished he had been able to meet up with Noah and Cameron at their hotel, so Noah could laugh at him for trying to arrange a hookup at the scene of a near-fatal accident. Would Joey have had the same reaction to Chase if the engine had been pinning Joey's shattered leg? He kind of thought he would. He was so confident in his gaydar that he always said he'd know if the priest at his own funeral were gay—an assertion which usually followed someone's statement that Joey would be late for the event—and if Chase had leaned in Joey's car window, he would have been perfectly willing to forget all about a carburetor on his tibia. The way Chase moved, even the sneer in his voice as he called Joey "Do-gooder", had made Joey forget the words to "Winnie-the-Pooh" as the ever-present soundtrack in his head switched over to Goldfrapp's "Ooh La La".

Joey felt a tug on his jeans and looked down at Seth. The dollar in Joey's hands was ironed flat now. He slid it into the slot and lifted Seth up again. "Okay, what do you want?"

The candy bar dropped down into the tray. If only getting what Joey wanted was as easy as hitting D-4. The annoying voice in his head which had lately been sounding a lot like Noah reminded him that he'd have to actually make a selection first.

It was after one when Joey finally finished transferring Seth and his amazingly effective car seat to his grandmother's Honda. Seth thanked Joey for the candy and for playing while Mommy was sleeping. Joey leaned against his Yaris and smiled as the two drove away. If he hadn't been on the scene, Seth probably would have ended up in emergency foster care while a search for his grandmother got buried under paperwork. Now the boy wouldn't have to deal with that trauma on top of the accident and a mom who was months of PT away from walking or driving again.

He pushed off the bumper of his car and headed for the driver's seat.

"Hey." A low voice came out of the dark on his left.

Joey's muscles tensed. He wasn't going to win a slugfest but he might be able to get away with moves he'd picked up wrestling in high school. Not that he'd been all that good; it was just that at fourteen he was small enough to get recruited when they needed someone to fill in for the one hundred and three pound weight class. He'd known he was gay forever, but rolling around on the mat with another boy draped across his back had cleared up any doubt about what he wanted to do with that information.

The emergency lot had been almost full when he pulled in with Seth four hours ago, so he'd had to park in the back corner. The only other vehicle he could see now was an ambulance. Nothing out of place for a hospital.

A shadow detached itself from the ambulance and straightened up, stepping into the misty light from one of the lamps.

K.A. Mitchell

Long black hair, tall. Joey waited, back against the roof of his car.

"All done with your good deeds for the day?"

The steady kick of adrenaline eased off. Chase, the EMT. Joey slouched, sliding his keys back into his jeans.

"You still working?" Joey jerked his chin at the ambulance.

"Nope. Finished for the night."

"Aren't you worried that if you hang around you'll get called back in?"

"It's a possibility." Still in his uniform, Chase stepped forward until he was standing right in front of Joey, crowding his space in a way that sent a thick pulse through his dick.

"So?" Joey tilted his head up. Black night, humid air thick on the tongue. Chase's eyes had none of that light color now, fully black with blown pupils. Joey's dick twitched again.

"So if I'd gone home, I might not have gotten to fuck you."

Apparently, Chase wasn't one for flirting. Much as Joey enjoyed a little banter it wasn't an issue for him at the moment. His throat went dry and his dick went from *that's interesting* to *hell yes.* But he couldn't resist. "What makes you think you will now?"

Chase closed the last few inches, bringing their hips together and sliding a hand down to palm Joey's hard-on. "This. The way you looked at me. And Do-gooder, that ass of yours was made for my dick."

The guy was an arrogant prick, but the words amped up the beat pounding through Joey, a steady thud of blood in his cock. He wrapped his own arms around the guy's waist, and Chase pulled his hand free, spreading his legs so their dicks rubbed together. And fuck, Joey got even harder. He ground the ache against the heat of that thick, hard cock, mouth watering. If they weren't in the hospital parking lot, he'd already be on his knees.

Chase grabbed Joey's neck and hauled him into a kiss.

Oh shit.

Not again.

22

It didn't matter how many times it had been wrong, he still wanted to believe it. Wanted to believe it when he kissed a guy and everything inside said *him*. It had been wrong about Mark and Noah and Jorge and Tom and the whole list going right back to kissing Eduardo under the bleachers in tenth grade. Or maybe before. When he'd been three and told his mom he was going to marry his best friend Cody.

It didn't happen with every guy, of course. Because then Joey would have a whole hell of a lot more than—shit, he was into double digits—ten ex-boyfriends. But now? The soundtrack in his head shut off, and it was quiet. Just a gasp as he met that kiss. Chase had slammed into his mouth, lips pushing, tongue forcing, and then everything changed. His mouth asked, and Joey opened to it. Chase's tongue swept in on a long groan.

Chase held Joey tight to mouth and cock with a hand on his neck and another on his ass, but his mouth was soft, tongue teasing, flicking. That same sureness vibrated everywhere inside—the whole big promise that this was different. As different as the moment under the bleachers when Eduardo had met him halfway and every hair on Joey's body had stood on end in the best possible way. Like the first time he'd gotten up on a surfboard, riding that rush of power under his feet, power sweeping him along, power becoming part of him even as it kept him high and safe.

Joey stroked Chase's tongue with his own, following it back between his lips, tasting mint over coffee, and then only the heat of Chase's mouth. Chase groaned again, and Joey knew the piercing on his tongue was having the desired effect.

When Chase lifted his head, Joey reached up to try to drag him back down. His brain spun through a dozen possibilities for where they were going to do this. After almost a month in Jacksonville, he was still living out of boxes, but he'd managed to unpack his bed. How many clothes and books were piled on it when he left this morning? He'd have to make sure he got his laptop and keyboard moved before they hit the mattress. Which Joey's dick was demanding happen sooner rather than later.

"Chase?"

The guy had been about to kiss him again. Now he pulled his head back. "Huh?"

It wasn't a *huh-what?* huh. More like a *what-the-fuck?* huh. Wrong name?

Joey tried to angle his head to look back at the nametag while keeping as much as possible of himself in contact with hard muscles. He didn't think he'd remembered it wrong. "Your nametag—"

"My last name. You want something to pant at me, try Aaron."

His last name. Of course. Joey'd been managing to steal peeks at his test scores since he was six. Despite knowing what the 98th percentile meant by second grade, he could still be pretty stupid sometimes. Chase was the guy's last name. Shame. Joey had liked the way it sounded. Different. Sexy. Aaron. Joey tried it out in his head. The guy didn't look like an Aaron.

"What the fuck does an Aaron look like?"

Oh shit. He might have better control over what came out of his mouth if there wasn't a dick pressing into his hip. Actually, what would solve all his problems would be that dick in his mouth. His apartment was about ten minutes away. And that seemed like forever. "I'm not really sure. You just look more like a—"

Chase—Aaron—pressed Joey back against the door of his car with a kiss, put both hands under his ass and lifted him, their dicks grinding hard together, while their mouths moved soft and slow. Joey didn't care if his feet ever hit the ground again. Getting off like this would be just fine. And then they could worry about making it to Joey's apartment and getting that dick into Joey's mouth.

He grabbed the back of Aaron's neck and tried to make the kiss more urgent, but Aaron kept a smooth lick inside Joey's mouth that was making Joey want to beg.

"Fuck." Aaron breathed the word onto Joey's mouth and started to pull away, this time taking Joey with him. He half-carried, half-walked him the couple of parking spots over from his car to the ambulance.

"Yeah."

The back doors hung open, and Aaron turned, dropping Joey between Aaron's long legs as he leaned back against the edge of the frame.

Joey reached up to get at that soft, hot mouth, then Ch— Aaron shifted to lick along Joey's jaw, kiss under his ear and breathe against his neck. Joey followed the program, tonguing the skin under the open collar of Aaron's shirt, tasting sweat and the thick damp night. Aaron's fingers threaded into what was left of Joey's hair.

In another second, Aaron would be urging him to his knees. Joey could feel the build, hear it in the breaths against the goose pimples on his neck. The more Joey ground his hips against Aaron, the more Joey mouthed and nipped Aaron's throat, the tighter those fingers grabbed his hair.

Joey anticipated the push and sank down onto the pavement. Of the parking lot. Of Shands Hospital. Getting picked up for lewd and lascivious his first month working for the county was probably not going to be good for his resume, but his fingers were already undoing the belt and fly in front of him.

Aaron's dick tented the black cotton of his briefs. Joey breathed in the smell and taste of him, like the scent of his neck but stronger. His fingers brushed against the fabric of the navy blue uniform pants. Definitely not cotton.

Joey licked his lips. "Should—do these have to be dry-cleaned?"

Okay. Not the smartest thing he'd ever said. Of course a paramedic's pants wouldn't be dry-clean only. And Joey had no idea what was making him hesitate. Not nerves, really. He was good at giving head, loved a cock in his mouth almost as much as he loved one in his ass. And it wasn't because he was worried about the *feeling*. He'd had his ass in the air five minutes after he met Mark, and that had been eighteen and a half months of almost forever.

The hand in his hair lifted Joey's head up. Aaron's eyes

25

were slitted, just a glitter under dark lashes, but an almost smile flickered at the corners of his mouth. "Connection 'tween your brain and mouth's pretty wide open, huh?"

At the moment it was. Joey couldn't control the random jumps in his brain, didn't even want to, but he could usually control what came out of his mouth.

Aaron pulled his head forward a little, until Joey's lips were brushing the cotton-trapped skin. "Think this could shut it down?" He let go of Joey's hair and Joey leaned forward enough to get his mouth on the damp cotton head. With a soft gasp from Aaron, the soundtrack started up in Joey's brain again. Goldfrapp's "Ooh La La" was perfect for blow jobs. If he sang along, his tongue did interesting things.

He rubbed his cheek against the thick cock as he buried his nose in the crease of Aaron's groin. Aaron's fingers stroked through Joey's hair before a wide palm covered the back of Joey's neck. The weight there reminded Joey of the weight he wanted on his tongue. Lifting the briefs off and to the side, he freed Aaron's dick.

The sight of that dark cut head made Joey lick his lips even as his ass clenched. Yeah, he was a bit of a size queen. But find a guy or straight girl who wasn't. And a cock thick enough that even getting the head in his mouth stretched his jaw made Joey groan in appreciation. As his fist followed the length to the root, Joey's dick jumped. Maybe they could skip this and get right to fucking, but then Aaron gave a soft growl, and Joey wanted him in his mouth, wanted to ride the power he'd get sucking Aaron into pleasure so high he wouldn't ever want to come down.

Long licks, then hot swirls, going at him like an ice cream on a hot day, desperate to get every drop. The song in his head curved his tongue, shifting shapes with every lick until Aaron's breath was reduced to tight, quick gasps. Joey worked his piercing around the rim, pressing everywhere he knew counted extra, laying the ball into the slit with enough pressure that Aaron jerked and offered another whispered, "*Fuck.*"

Hands spread on Aaron's thighs to anchor himself, Joey went down the silky length, bobbing and humming, a tight suck, tongue lapping the head. Aaron wasn't vocal about getting his dick sucked, but even in the silence Joey could read him. Rapid, shallow breaths, the tremble in the muscles under his fingers, and finally the jerk of hips as Joey let the head rub hard on the back of his throat.

Joey pulled off, tugging the briefs farther out of his way to get at Aaron's balls, licking and then sucking, and when Aaron's hand started yanking Joey's hair again, he dipped his tongue to lap and roll the ball across the smooth spot behind the tightening sac.

Aaron reached down and lifted Joey under his arm, pulling him up until they both fell backward onto the floor of the truck.

Joey smiled. This was where Aaron would tell him how hot Joey'd made him, how close Aaron had been to coming, how much he wanted to fuck him. But somehow Aaron didn't get the script. His mouth twitched as he scanned Joey's face and then he brought a thumb to Joey's lips. Joey sucked it in, repeating the swirl of his tongue, the tight pressure of his lips. Again Aaron's dark pink lips flickered at the corners, and Aaron pulled his thumb free before leaning up to kiss him, tongue sliding into Joey's mouth and starting the same liquid stroke that made Joey press down onto him, trying to get the hard, fast friction between their dicks that would feel so good.

Aaron pushed him off and then rolled forward to pull the ambulance doors shut. Joey'd been fucked in lots of interesting places, but the back of an ambulance was definitely going to make his top-ten list. Because he was going to get fucked. He knew that even before Aaron tossed the condom and lube onto the stretcher Joey had climbed up to sit on.

Aaron watched him for a minute, one side of his mouth lifting in as much of a smile as Joey had seen on his face. Joey unbuttoned his fly and leaned back on his elbows, making sure his shirt rode up enough to show off his flat stomach. Aaron's smile broadened as his fingers traced the skin, gliding up across the muscles.

It was dark and stuffy in the truck. Enough light from the buildings and lampposts to see what they were doing, but dark enough to hide anything but the most obvious expressions on their faces. Despite the humid air, Joey welcomed the heat of Aaron's hand on his skin as he shoved the shirt higher.

Aaron put a hand on Joey's shoulder and nudged. "Roll over."

Joey had barely managed to get facedown when Aaron yanked his jeans and briefs down his hips. The stretcher was too low to make this work. It would be easier if he sat on Aaron's lap, and easier to watch his face when he worked his muscles on that thick hard cock, to see what Aaron didn't say.

But when Joey shifted to turn and tell him, Aaron stopped him with a hand on his back. Then Aaron's body pressed all over him, shirt open, skin-to-skin where Joey's shirt had crept up.

Aaron's whisper buzzed the skin under Joey's ear. "Ass like this." A hot palm cradled the curve. "Must be busy. Bet you don't need much to get ready."

It had been over a month and getting that dick in wouldn't be easy. But Joey managed to bite his lip and keep that information to himself, even if he couldn't understand why he wanted to let Aaron think he was a slut. Aaron's hand rubbed across Joey's ass, stretching and pulling at the skin. Aaron could think Joey was a slut, but that dick wasn't getting near his ass without... "Lube," he finished the thought out loud.

It wasn't a laugh. Just a puff of breath against his ear, but Joey felt it all over his skin. He shifted his hips back and forth, nice friction on his dick while cold slick gel dripped into the crack of his ass.

"No." Aaron lifted Joey's hips off the stretcher.

With his pants bunched around his calves, Joey couldn't spread his legs very far, certainly couldn't get one up on the stretcher. Aaron grabbed Joey's hands and placed them on the cabinet above the stretcher, leaving him bent over but not touching it. Yeah, Joey got off a little on being manhandled—if he knew what he was getting into—with someone he could trust. He had no idea what Aaron had planned, beyond the obvious, and he certainly didn't trust him. Except he did.

Because of that feeling, that sureness that resonated up from the soles of his feet every time Aaron touched him.

The lightest brush of a fingertip at his hole and then Aaron slammed two fingers in right down to the bottom knuckle, twisting and rubbing, until Joey rocked his hips. The first sharp thrust had sliced into him like fire, but now the deep twist and press made him grind back for more. As soon as that sweet rub coiled in his stomach and made him moan, Aaron slipped in another finger and fucked him hard.

Joey arched his back, yelping when his head made contact with the edge of the overhead cabinet.

Aaron's fingers froze inside him. "All right, Do-gooder?"

It wasn't the kind of throbbing, seeing stars Joey had been hoping to get to, but his dick was so hard he didn't want to stop and worry about it. Endorphins were his friend. "Fine."

More lube, and then Aaron's fingers moved with a slow deliberate pressure that had Joey considering how sexy he could make a whine. He decided to try words. "Fuck me."

Aaron didn't respond with any of the quips Joey was used to hearing at this point in the proceedings for a typical fuck. Not a demand that Joey beg, not a hoarse *yeah*, not even a teasing *I'm working on it*, just a maddening slow stroke that hit every single nerve, nerves connected to every inch of his body, nerves going crazy from the rub of fingers on his prostate. If that's what Aaron could do with his hand, even Joey's scalp tingled at the thought of what the guy could do with his dick.

"Now." Joey might have repeated the word five more times than was necessary, but he didn't think Aaron needed to slip his thumb back into Joey's mouth.

"Shhh."

He wasn't that loud was he? When Aaron moved both of his hands away, Joey bit his lip and tried to remember how to breathe without feeling those fingers curling inside him. Without the other stimulation, his head started to throb again, but the sound of a condom wrapper tearing was all the reassurance he needed.

The first pressure of that head made all his muscles tighten, including a painful squeeze on his heart. Demanding *now* might have been a bit premature. Aaron didn't force in or hurt him, only pushed and took what Joey's body gave him. When the head was finally in, Joey's heart remembered how to work and he took a deep breath.

A mouth on his cock would be a big help right now. Anything to keep his mind off the deep slam of his pulse as his muscles gave around steady pressure. He didn't care if he fell over, he needed to get a hand on his dick.

"No," Aaron said again, hand trapping Joey's and lifting it back onto the cabinet. "You're going to come just from me fucking you." He put a hand on Joey's shoulder to hold him steady as he kept pressing forward.

Okay. Vanilla wasn't exactly Joey's favorite flavor. But he wasn't sure how far into the kink flavor catalogue he was willing to go with someone he'd known for ten minutes. Joey's body, however, rarely listened to his brain. Aaron's deep command had Joey's hips pushing back to get all the way down on Aaron's cock.

When his ass slammed into Aaron's thighs, they both shuddered. Aaron leaned down to lick the side of Joey's neck, setting off a buzz along his nerves, making the sting in his ass sweet. They hadn't even started moving yet, and Joey could feel the sweat making his palms slide on the cabinet, dripping from his temples, prickling on his spine.

"You can do that, right? Come just from my dick?"

"If you're any good." And he really didn't mean to say that out loud.

Another huff of breath that might have been a laugh, and then Aaron held Joey with a hand on his shoulder and another on his hip and slid back, almost all the way out. Joey wanted to follow him, didn't want to have to do the whole stretching around him again, but when Aaron drove back in, the stretch was gone. Nothing but a burning pleasure spilling from his ass, flooding his dick. After a few long deep strokes, Aaron pressed down on Joey's hip and started fucking hard, the head of his cock dragging across Joey's prostate with every thrust.

Joey squeezed his eyes shut, hands turning to fists against the cabinet. He felt so good he couldn't stand it, couldn't take it for another second, but if it stopped he was pretty sure his heart would stop right along with it. "There, right there, please, harder."

Aaron slowed, and if Joey wasn't bent over the stretcher, he'd have kicked the bastard.

"Thanks, but I really don't need directions. I have done this before, sweetheart."

That was it.

"Are you always this much of an arrogant prick?"

"Pretty much. Want me to stop?"

Without the good slam deep inside, Joey could make a coherent sentence, although he could only manage one word per stroke. "Being. An. Arrogant. Prick?"

"Sorry." But Aaron sped up again and his words weren't any less strained than Joey's had been. "Not. Gonna. Happen."

Aaron managed to push Joey's jeans and briefs down the rest of the way so Joey could kick off his flip-flops and get a leg free. He dragged it up onto the stretcher and rode back into Aaron, lifting one of his hands to wrap his wrist in the silky hair knotted at the nape of Aaron's neck. They were almost standing, Aaron supporting most of Joey's upper body with an arm angling from his ribs to the opposite shoulder. It was a wrestling hold, and Joey would remember the name of it when there wasn't a cock pounding into his prostate so hard he was going to bite through his lip to keep from screaming. Oh yeah, he could come from this.

Aaron's other hand pressed hard above Joey's dick, and he could feel it filling his balls, a hot rush, swelling, tightening in his cock. The pressure never stopped, fucking into his dick from inside, over and over, heat and power spilling through him until he shot. After a first painful jerk, there was nothing but pleasure pumping thick onto his stomach and chest.

Aaron fucked him the whole way through, until Joey's

throat and dick and balls ached. He wanted to collapse forward onto the stretcher, catch his breath, but Aaron kept him upright, driving into Joey's still-shuddering body. Joey chewed on his lip and lowered his leg to the floor, dragging up a last bit of control to tighten his muscles around Aaron's cock. A harsh grunt in Joey's ear, breath as loud as the rush of an eight-foot wave breaking on top of him, and Aaron bucked with lightning-quick strokes, balls slapping against Joey's aching ones. Endorphins were no longer keeping Joey safe from pain. His head ached where he'd hit it and the thick slam in his ass burned, but it was worth it, feeling Aaron lose control, surrender that arrogance as the pulse of Joey's muscles dragged Aaron into coming. A surprised *damn* from his mouth and then he jerked and stuttered, mouth open wet and wide on Joey's shoulder.

They fell half onto the stretcher, Joey still panting, Aaron still rocking. Joey landed halfway on Aaron, and he pulled Joey close as they got their hearts back in their chests, breath back in their lungs and the feeling back into their extremities. Aaron rolled away, slapping on a light as he stripped off the rubber.

He was staring at Joey with something Joey wasn't used to seeing after sex. Especially not sex that good. Something like disbelief in his eyes, but the wrinkle at the top his nose was a bit like disgust.

"If you didn't dye your hair orangey pink, you're bleeding, dude."

Chapter Three

Do-gooder's hands slapped up on his head, fingers moving. "Oh." A wince crossed his face. "Shit. The cabinet."

Aaron wiped his hands clean with disinfectant and brought a soaked gauze pad over. Aaron had known waiting for Do-gooder to make it back to his car would be worth it. He loved being right. Of course, he had planned to take the guy home, not into the emergency room.

Back of the ambulance wouldn't have been his first choice, but the stroke of Do-gooder's tongue stud in his mouth had made Aaron desperate to get it on his cock. And it wasn't happening in that shoebox of a car. But maybe in the car, he wouldn't have had to switch gears from calculating whether they should go back to his house for another round to patching the guy up.

"I asked if you were all right."

"I was. I am. It's fine." Joey's breath hissed between clenched teeth as Aaron cleaned the wound.

"Could've knocked yourself out."

Joey shrugged, then sat quietly while Aaron wiped the blood out of his hair.

Aaron looked down at the triangular cut. Blood still seeped out from under the flap of skin. "C'mon. Put your pants on. We'll get it taken care of inside."

"It's fine. Don't you have one of those butterfly things?"

"It needs to be stitched or glued. You're still bleeding."

Joey's hand went back up to check, and Aaron slapped it away. "I just cleaned it."

"Really, I don't need to spend the rest of the night in the emergency room for a little cut. I'm a quick healer."

Aaron watched Joey wobble as he hopped back into his jeans. Balance problems could be from a minor concussion or it could be the guy was a klutz. "This happen a lot?"

Joey met his gaze, a splash of pink high on his cheeks. "Enough," he admitted.

"Christ."

"What?"

"Nothing." What did it matter if tonight's—okay maybe he was thinking about stretching it to this weekend's—fuck couldn't manage to get dressed without knocking himself unconscious? Aaron wasn't going to spend enough time with him to have to worry about it. And it wasn't cute. And even if he'd raised three kids and was wiping the blood off Do-gooder's face, he didn't have any fucking maternal instincts.

Wide brown eyes looked up at him, all big and wet like Joey was that fucking cartoon deer, Bambi. "I really hate getting stitches."

"So maybe you shouldn't hit your head on sharp objects."

"I'll remember that the next time half of someone's hand is up my ass in the back of an ambulance."

Aaron almost laughed. "C'mon. You can sit on my lap." Though from the way Joey had slammed his tight ass down on Aaron's cock, he couldn't imagine he was worried about a quick pinch from a needle.

As they crossed the parking lot to the back entrance, Joey was still a little wobbly, and just for the record? Aaron wasn't driving him home.

He cut in behind the triage nurse and flagged down Doctor Jae Sun Kim, one of the few residents who wasn't a total asshole.

Kim arched his dark brows in an assessing stare.

"What?" Sometimes there wasn't a lot of distance between

not a total asshole and plain old asshole.

Aaron followed Kim's gaze to Joey. He did look freshly fucked, which come to think of it wasn't that different from how he looked when Aaron met him. Hair sticking up, eyes soft and wide pink lips still swollen, the guy flat-out looked like sex on legs.

Kim answered Aaron's eyebrow shrug with a smirk and led the way into one of the treatment rooms. Joey hung back in the doorway. Aaron nudged Joey through with a hip to his sweet, tight ass, and Joey stumbled in.

"What's wrong with your drunken hook-up?" Kim asked.

"I'm not drunk," Joey insisted.

"He cut his scalp."

"It's not that deep." Joey ignored Kim waving him up onto the exam table.

"Deep enough." Aaron gave Joey a look that said "Do it or I'll do it for you." It always worked on the kids. It worked on Joey. With an exaggerated sigh, he hopped up on the table and almost slid off the end.

"Sure he's not drunk?"

"Check him for a concussion," Aaron suggested.

"Okay. Lie down...?" Kim looked over at Aaron.

"Joey." Do-gooder supplied his name when it became apparent Aaron wasn't going to. He didn't know why, it wasn't like he didn't know it.

"Okay. Joey." Kim smiled. Aaron had never seen the resident smile before. In fact, his bedside manner sucked, but he at least didn't treat paramedics like they were a step up from articulate dog shit. Kim pulled on fresh gloves and peered through Joey's hair. "Yeah. That needs a couple of stitches. I'd glue it but the angle..."

"How many's a couple?" Joey asked.

"Five, maybe six? We won't have to shave off all of your hair."

"That could only be an improvement," Aaron said.

Joey looked embarrassed while Kim shot Aaron a glare from narrowed black eyes. Kim sported a basic crew cut. He couldn't be suggesting approval of whatever had happened to Joey's hair because Aaron wouldn't have ruled out exposure to toxic waste. Joey murmured something, and Kim laughed. Fucking laughed. Doctor Jae Sun Kim never smiled, and he sure as hell didn't laugh. He'd told Aaron the biggest problem he had being a doctor was interacting with people. Aaron had suggested he switch to pathology.

"Doctor Kim, please report to exam room three," the speaker on the ceiling said.

"I'll be back with the lidocaine as quick as I can. We doing this with or without paperwork?"

"I've got insurance," Joey said.

Kim nodded and ducked out.

Probably had a great benefits package with the state. Like any other devoted public servant. Aaron had managed to forget what the guy did for the last half hour. Not that it mattered. He didn't even have to like Joey to fuck that ass straight on through to Sunday.

"What?" Joey had sat up and was working those Bambi eyes again, and Aaron realized he'd crossed to the other side of the room.

"Nothing." Aaron forced himself to step back next to the table. He could check for a concussion himself, but he had a feeling that looking too long into those eyes could be dangerous to a guy's sugar level. In fact, there wasn't any reason for him to still be here. Joey had his keys, his wallet and Kim to look after him.

Joey started to feel for the wound again, and Aaron grabbed his hand. Joey didn't resist, but the muscles under Aaron's fingers were tense. He shifted his grip to Joey's wrist and found a too-quick pulse.

The liquid brown gaze dropped to where Aaron's fingers circled his wrist.

"What?" It was Aaron's turn to ask.

"I really don't like needles."

Aaron found himself rubbing the thin skin over thick, solid bones and rabbiting pulse. "C'mon. You can take my cock, you can take a little shot."

Joey grinned. "It's not the pain. It's the needle thing. Going in under my—" His face paled under his freckles, and he clamped his lips shut.

Aaron squeezed his hand. Most guys Aaron knew—straight or gay—didn't have the balls or the sense to admit there was anything they couldn't handle. Joey wasn't even embarrassed about it, just matter-of-fact. Joey being smart enough not to try to bullshit his way through deserved more respect than assholes who had to put on some macho show for everything. Aaron'd had to deal with more than one tough-guy cop who insisted he was good right until he passed out and added to the victim list.

"How the hell did you get through first-aid training?"

"Oh, I'm fine when it's other people. It's just—"

Joey's lips lost a little more color, and Aaron grabbed Joey's head and kissed him. Fuck if he knew why. After a second, Joey's mouth opened with one of his husky, whispered moans.

Joey wasn't the first guy Aaron'd had with a tongue piercing, but Joey sure as hell knew what to do with it. Especially on Aaron's dick. He drove his tongue deeper into Joey's mouth, one hand sliding up the back of his shirt. This might have started as a way of distracting Joey from fainting, but Aaron was pretty damned distracted himself.

"Jesus Christ." Kim was back, a nurse with a laptop following close behind.

With a last flick of his tongue across Joey's lips, Aaron lifted his head and turned to face Kim's scowl.

The nurse yawned and tapped her screen. "Have you been a patient here before?"

"No, I just moved here three weeks ago."

Which was why Aaron hadn't seen him before. There might be eighty-thousand queers in Jacksonville, but he'd swear he'd have noticed that ass.

As the nurse zipped through question after question on her screen, Aaron learned more about Joey than if he'd gone through his wallet. Last name, phone, address, Social Security number, allergic to penicillin and aspirin and that his parents lived in California.

"Is there any emergency contact closer?"

Joey's lower lip disappeared into his mouth. "Um. Tallahassee?"

She nodded, and Joey rattled off a number with a Panhandle area code. "Noah Winthrop."

"Relationship?"

"Friend." Joey blinked and Aaron knew Noah had been something more than a friend at one time. And maybe exactly why Joey had wound up friendless in Jacksonville.

Kim was tapping his foot, hypo and bottle in his hand. "Can't you do this while we wait for the lidocaine to work?"

The nurse set aside her computer and grabbed a pair of scissors. A hunk of yellow cotton candy got tossed in the wastebin, and she reached for a razor.

"Let me give him the shot first."

Joey wasn't particularly tan to start with, a bit of light caramel on his arms and face, an interesting V of it at his throat, but now all the color drained from his face, the freckles across his nose and the tops of his cheeks standing out like a splash of paint. Aaron grabbed him around the waist and pushed his head down.

"He'll be fine," he said to Kim.

The resident shrugged and loaded up the hypo.

"I'm not going to faint. I've never fainted." Joey's voice was a little muffled.

Aaron found Joey's hand and squeezed again. The reciprocal grip was strong.

"Stay there." Kim stepped closer. "It's easier to reach." He swabbed the area with a topical and then the long needle was sliding under Joey's skin. On a daily basis, Aaron started drips, gave shots, intubated. He was bled on, puked on, pissed on. He'd been on the scene of a fresh decapitation, but the thin needle disappearing under Joey's skin gave Aaron's stomach a quick kick of nausea. Like phobias were contagious. Thank God neither the twins nor Sheree had ever needed stitches. It seemed to take more than a minute for Kim to fully depress the plunger.

"All right?" Kim lifted the needle.

"Fine," Joey answered in a thin voice.

Aaron turned him to let him lie back on the table, and Joey flashed a grin, silver ball peeking out over his teeth. "Thanks."

"Yeah. Well, I kind of owed you." He didn't regret going fast and rough—and from Joey's reaction, Aaron was sure Joey hadn't minded—but he wished he'd thought to put Joey somewhere but under the cabinets.

The nurse stepped in with her razor, buzzing off a two-inch square. Taking Joey's insurance card and her computer, she and Kim left them alone again. Joey's eyes rolled as he strained to see his own head. "How bad is it?"

"Like I said. Not much worse than it was before."

"I tried to bleach the purple out when I changed jobs."

"From what, circus clown?"

"I was working as a counselor in a school and my hair was longer and I like purple and they really didn't care there, but working for the state I thought I'd better look a little more conservative so—"

"You think you might take a breath or should I get the oxygen mask ready?"

"Sorry."

Joey thought he looked conservative. Aaron looked at the tight T-shirt and well-cut jeans and, for fuck's sake, flip-flops.

"I didn't wear this to work. I was on my way to meet some friends and we were going to go out. How's Pulse?"

"Full of pretentious assholes." Which was exactly what he'd thought Joey was when he met him earlier. Joey was still a fucking social worker, but he wasn't one of those stuck-up assholes who thought they knew everything. "Your friends like to dance?"

"Noah does. I don't know about Cameron. I guess so."

Aaron could read the whole story right there. Dumped and replaced in three weeks. Relationships were fucked. "Try 248. The name sucks but the guys—well, some of them do too," he finished with a smile.

"We're going to reschedule for tomorrow. Do you want to come with us?"

"Gee, a double date? Seriously? What is this, high school?"

"So pretentious assholes: Pulse. Dancing and bonus blowjobs: 248. And arrogant pricks? Where do you hang out?"

"Wherever the fuck I want." But watching Joey try to summon an angry expression while the nerves on the left side of his forehead and cheek went numb had Aaron fighting another smile.

As soon as Kim and the nurse came back in, the nurse opened the suture kit.

Aaron turned Joey's head away when the needle made an appearance. "I'll hold him."

Kim pinched the cut closed.

Joey looked up at Aaron as he pinned Joey's head against the paper on the table, occasionally rubbing his thumb across soft lips. It was as much distraction as he could offer.

Staring at Joey's eyes blinking up from his pale face was a bit like inhaling a pound of rock candy while watching puppies play. Fortunately, twenty-nine years in this fucked up world had provided Aaron with a considerable immunity to both sugar and cute.

Six stitches later, Joey scored a zero on the concussion scale, and Kim signed the release.

When they'd fallen panting on the stretcher in the truck, Aaron had planned to invite Joey back to his house for as many repeats as their dicks could handle. The detour through the emergency room took more than an hour and made the post-fuck to let's-do-that-again transition awkward.

"You sure you can drive?"

"Yes," Joey answered.

But Aaron followed him back to his apartment and watched from his bike until Joey disappeared inside.

Joey tipped his head over the back of the sofa in Noah and Cameron's suite at the Airport Hilton. Noah's lifestyle had undergone a major upgrade with Cameron. Joey couldn't remember the last time he'd been in a hotel room, let alone one like the Airport Hilton.

When he'd gotten up this morning, rain and a throbbing head made him think it would be a nice Saturday to stay in bed. He called Noah as promised and invited them to his apartment. Noah's pointed silence forced Joey to confess he hadn't unpacked. After downing a couple Tylenol for the headache, he headed out into the rain, popping into their suite in time to share a room-service breakfast.

The door slammed behind Cameron, and Noah came back into the sitting area.

"I don't think your boyfriend likes me," Joey said to the upside-down Noah.

"He's just pissed because he has to go out and do an inspection in the rain." Noah peered down at him. "What the fuck happened to you? You told me—"

"It wasn't the accident, not exactly." His fingers went to the spot that the Tylenol still hadn't touched.

"*Not exactly.*" Noah came around to flop on the sofa next to Joey. Tapping Joey's foot with his own, Noah said, "Spill."

Noah was the best friend Joey had had since his dream of marrying Cody shattered when Cody's dad got transferred to Seattle during fourth grade. Missing Noah was the one thing Joey regretted about moving out of Tallahassee. Okay, sometimes he wished things had worked out between them, but he was glad Noah was finally happy with Cameron. So when

Noah said spill, Joey thought he'd be ready.

But when he opened his mouth to explain about Aaron, suddenly Joey wanted to keep it all to himself, the hot blue eyes and the way the thick cock had fucked him, the strong hands keeping him safe in the emergency room, and the way Aaron didn't laugh at Joey wussing out around needles.

Noah'd had to take him to the emergency room when a glass fell on him and sliced open his arm and been nothing but exasperated when Joey clung to his hand. Mark thought Joey was kidding when he begged him to come with him when he had to get a new tetanus shot.

"Joey? Concussion? Man, are you okay?" Noah rubbed Joey's arm.

"Oh, fine. No concussion. Six stitches. I hit my head on a cabinet."

"Maybe if you unpacked your shit you wouldn't fall over it. Who'd you get to hold your hand this time?"

Aaron. Even thinking the name made blood flash hot in his face and pulse in his cock.

"Jesus, Joey, you've been here three weeks. Not again."

It was a big mistake to tell your boyfriend about your other boyfriends, especially if you planned to stay friends, and except for Giles—what a disaster—Joey always stayed friends. But now Noah could hold Joey's bad track record over his head.

Joey shifted around to make a little room for his half-hard dick. "It's nothing. We fucked. I hit my head. He took me to the emergency room."

"He hurt you?"

"No. I really did hit it on a cabinet."

"You are so full of shit. You couldn't lie if your life depended on it."

Joey did suck at lying. Especially in front of anyone who knew him. "Okay." And the whole story spilled out of his mouth: the accident, Seth, Aaron, the ambulance, Doctor Kim, stitches, almost fainting. The only thing he left out was Aaron's cock size and forgetting to call Noah until something reminded him to do it.

"Joey..."

"I know, but not everything starts off with going for coffee." Joey could tell when a fuck was just a fuck. He knew all about relationships. He'd had enough of them, in durations ranging from eight minutes to eighteen months. He'd heard Cameron call him a dyke with a dick at one point.

"Don't you think things would work out better if you waited more than a month after dumping someone before 'falling in love' again?" Noah's voice held air quotes.

"Mark dumped me."

"Bullshit. You've never been dumped in your entire life. I talked to Mark."

Joey felt his mouth hang open in an extremely unattractive way. Noah had complained more than once that he thought Mark was scary. And if you didn't know what a marshmallow the guy was out of bed, Joey supposed the whole Leather Daddy look with beard, tats and a Harley might make Mark look pretty intimidating.

"You talked to Mark?"

"I thought he'd pushed you out of town. You just packed up and quit your job. It's not like you'd ever talked about your deep desire to move to Jacksonville. I was worried about you."

It hadn't been like that. And Joey'd liked Tallahassee. But they worked at the same school, Mark teaching and Joey counseling and it was just hard. And three exes in one town was Joey's limit. Besides, now he didn't have to drive an hour to get to the beach.

Warmth spread out from his stomach at the idea of Noah confronting Mark out of loyalty. Joey gave Noah a wide smile and nudged his foot with his own. "You went all 'I challenge thee' on Mark for me?"

"Don't go there." Noah kicked Joey's foot away, but the grin stayed.

"So, what did Mark say?"

"That it had taken him a while but he realized you

manipulated him into the whole thing."

Joey wasn't all that great at straight-up lies, but he could get people to do what he wanted. Which was kind of what had happened with Mark. The sex—God, the sex—had been everything Joey could want, but out of bed... He hated to admit it, but he'd been getting bored. And if you were in love, you weren't supposed to get bored, right?

"I manipulated him into cheating on me?"

Noah stared him down, and Joey had to look away.

"At least he doesn't have to watch you hop on the next horse."

Joey winced. "I didn't—I'm sorry." He hadn't cheated on Noah, but two weeks after he'd moved out, he was sort of moved in with Mark.

"You realize you've hit the other coast now? You can't go any farther east." The affection in Noah's tone softened the edge of his criticism.

Joey smiled. "There's always north. I hear the waves are choice off North Carolina. Speaking of waves, want to hit the beach?"

"It's raining. I didn't bring a board or a wetsuit."

"We could rent something."

"Cam will be back in a couple hours."

"Wet and cranky." Joey grabbed the remote and turned on the TV, clicking over to The Weather Channel where the current local conditions showed a nice low off the coast.

"He won't be—"

Joey dug the laptop out of the bag next to the couch and opened it up on the coffee table, high-speed internet letting him zip over to the Beach Pier surf report. He turned it so Noah could see. "Four foot swells. Regular as corduroy."

Noah stared at the surf report, eyes intent. Joey knew he had him.

He put on a disappointed voice. "Nah, terrible day to surf, forget I mentioned it."

"Fuck. You."

Noah's truck carried the boards and wet suits they picked up at Sunrise Surf Shop to the Pier parking lot. There wasn't a lot of wind, but whatever came off the waves was wet and cold, and there were only a few people out on boards, even though it was past ten.

Noah shivered as he wriggled into his suit. "Better be worth it."

A guy trotted past them with a board under his arm, headed for the parking lot.

"Hey," Joey called as he neared. "How are they today?"

The dude waved a hand in a so-so gesture. "Ledgy."

Anticipation had Joey sprinting for the water and the ledgy waves. He loved a sharp break, the moment of free-fall when the waves dropped you off a cliff. That tumble in his gut, like the way it had felt last night when Aaron grabbed his hands and pinned them to the cabinet. That no-control, you're-in-for-a-ride feeling.

The first wave Joey caught was a mushy floater, and he kicked out of it early, disappointed.

Noah's big body was graceful on his board, dropping in just right and keeping a trim ride with long cuts up and down the face of his wave. Joey wondered if Aaron surfed, pictured him riding with his long hair flying back or whipping into his high sharp cheekbones.

The tide shifted faster, outward flow slapping up against the wind-pushed waves. Joey dropped out of a wave that doubled up before it could dump him.

The few guys that had been in the lineup with them took off as the time between rideable waves got longer. Noah got a look of hesitation on his face.

"Couple more?" Joey pleaded as they paddled back out. "Look at the bumps out there."

"You always say there's a better one out there."

Shit, were they back to that again? Maybe you couldn't stay friends with an ex. But Noah was happier now than he'd ever been with Joey, anyone could see that. And maybe this time Joey wouldn't have to keep looking. He thought of Aaron mocking the idea of a double date. So he didn't see joint vacations in their future, but maybe Aaron telling him about 248 was his way of asking Joey to meet him there.

Noah nodded at the wave coming; it was going to split into an A-frame, two breaks to ride. They dropped in together, Noah sliding right while Joey took it left. A smooth slice, almost no drop, the perfect wave to end on.

But Joey cut back outside, while Noah took it in.

"Just one more, I swear," he called back. He wanted to hang on the edge and hit that break, catch one with the perfect sharp drop to its power.

Noah was far enough away that his scowl didn't work. Joey could get that Noah wanted to get back to Cameron. Noah's boyfriend would be gone for the whole week Noah had off work, and Joey and Noah would have lots of time to surf while he visited Jacksonville. But five more minutes wouldn't matter. Even less. He could see some splash on the crest of the sixth wave out.

It was a hell of a ride, water spraying up behind him as he hugged the top, hoping to skate into a nice curl. It started to break, but Joey tightened his abs and kept his balance, pearling the top of the board just enough not to fall.

Noah shouted something at him. Joey supposed he heard it perfectly clearly, but it didn't seem to make sense until he was already getting the skin sandblasted from his face. The wave tipped him facedown and then slammed him under. As the water closed over his head, his brain decided to process Noah's warning. "Gonna bomb, Joey. Bail."

Then his ears and nose and throat were full of sand and salt water, caught in a washing machine of tide and breaking wave. He tried to tuck into a ball and pop up for air, but only kept rolling. His board hit him hard on the shin and then on the back, just under his ribs. At last he managed to get to his knees and found Noah caddying Joey's surfboard. Dropping the boards, Noah braced Joey with a hand on his back as they stood in the breakers.

Joey turned away and spit up what he could get out of his mouth and nose. Noah's grip moved to Joey's shoulder, shaking him almost more than his Atlantic-filled stomach could handle.

"Didn't you hear me? Why didn't you pull out?"

There was a smutty pun there for the taking, but Joey's brain was sloshing between his ears. His face stung. Did he rip out his stitches? Because no way was he having more needles stuck in him.

"Fuck, you were under a long time. Scared the piss out of me."

Joey dragged a smile to his lips to show he was all right, though he still wasn't sure if he could speak without barfing.

The grip on his shoulder turned to a pat as Noah bent down and re-grabbed Joey's board. "Got a hell of a sand facial, Joey." Noah's fear had faded; now he just looked amused.

Joey'd be surprised if he had any skin left on his right cheek. But he checked the scalp wound first. He could still feel the knots Doctor Kim had tied.

Noah carried both their boards as they slogged through the surf to the beach. Sitting on one of the Airport Hilton's plush towels draped over the seat in Noah's truck, Joey checked out his face in the vanity mirror.

His forehead was almost as bad as his cheek, both scraped raw. "Does it make me look rugged?"

"It looks like you went skateboarding without the board."

It hurt like a bitch, but Joey could still remember the moment when the break had been so sweet. That was always the problem with a ride that good: knowing when to get off before you got hurt.

Chapter Four

Someday, Joey was going to possess the infinite cool to be able to walk into a bar or club like 248 and not make an idiot of himself over some guy. Someday, too, he would miraculously grow to six-two and be able to see over most of the crowd so the sight of the guy in question wouldn't sneak up on him before he had the time to assemble his cool. It was probably a little obvious when he dragged Noah down to his height to whisper to him while Aaron was leaning on the bar only five feet away.

When Noah straightened again, Aaron was looking at them. The guy didn't smile much, but Joey read the quirk in the corner of Aaron's lips. Joey just didn't know if it was a what-a-loser smile or a hey-nice-fuck-let's-go-again smile.

Carrying three beers, Cameron cut in front of Aaron, blocking him from Joey's view. When he and Noah had come back from surfing, Cameron had been sprawled on the couch, watching baseball on TV. A look had passed between him and Noah, a look that had made Joey feel he needed to excuse himself before he either had to run to the bathroom to jerk off or drop to his knees and beg to join them. And Cameron and Noah hadn't even touched.

God, Joey wanted that. Wanted that everyone else disappears when you see him. Wanted that thermonuclear reaction just because your eyes meet.

"Uh, pick me up at ten?" At that point, Joey had thought he might be mistaken for wallpaper.

"Uh-huh." Noah had nodded, eyes still on Cameron.

Cameron's job took him everywhere, maybe— "Hey, Cameron, do you know a guy here in Jacksonville, Aaron Chase?"

Cameron had flashed Noah an indecipherable look then, before shrugging. "I never got names."

Joey had felt the flush high up in his cheeks, burning on his scrapes, and ducked out.

Now, Cameron handed off a beer to Noah who nodded over Cameron's shoulder.

Cameron gave Aaron a long stare. "Him? Oh, I've seen him in action."

Joey wanted to shut him up, but he doubted Aaron could hear Cameron over the pounding bass.

"Joey, man, forget it." Cameron draped an arm around Joey's shoulder and steered him in the other direction. That was a bad sign. Cameron almost never spoke directly to him, certainly never touched him. The sympathy made him feel pathetic.

"What's wrong?"

"He's—"

Shit. There went another one of those looks over his head. If he jumped up could he intercept it? He felt like he was freaking three, trying to decode the words his parents spelled out so he wouldn't know what they were talking about. Just when he'd figured out the good words, his parents had switched to German.

"Definitely not boyfriend material," Noah finished.

"Who said I was looking—?"

"Joey."

"I just want to fuck him again. It was fun. God, was it fun."

Noah looked like he was going to say something else, but shut up. Joey glanced over at Cameron. It was starting to feel like a tennis match.

"Can I borrow Noah for a dance?"

"Sure. Just bring him back in one piece."

Joey dragged him out onto the dance floor. Something new was playing, slow sexy vocals over a fast beat. For a second he just let it move him, hips rolling.

Noah leaned down to yell in his ear. "Joey, I just don't want you to get hurt. You're too nice a guy to be treated like shit."

Always too nice. Joey was sick of being nice. Nice didn't win anything. Like being understanding. Aaron couldn't give a shit if Joey was understanding or nice.

He turned so he could grind his ass back against Noah's crotch, wrapping a hand around the back of his neck. The position had to remind Aaron of what they did last night. How good it felt. Because Joey knew from that surprised *damn* he hadn't been the only one having one of the best times of his life.

Noah let him go for a second and then sucked in his breath. "Jesus, Joey. Don't—" Noah's hands landed on Joey's hips and lifted him away.

"C'mon." He leaned his head on Noah's chest, trying to murmur in an ear that was still too damned far away. "Help me out a little."

"I want to but, Joey, shit, you can't keep—"

Noah probably had more to say. And Joey would have argued with him some more. But he felt Aaron's gaze on him then, and it didn't matter what boomed out from the speakers because Joey's head was singing "Playhouse" by Pretty Ricky, concentrating on the part about "eat your body out." He could feel the look like a lick on his balls, sweeping down. He turned then, putting his arms around Noah's neck and swaying.

The look rolled down Joey's spine, and he fought not to arch his back like it was a hand ready to cup his ass. One of Noah's hands slid off his waist, and Joey turned to face Aaron with a smile.

"Hey, Do-gooder." Aaron leaned in, mint and rum on his breath. "If you wanted to fuck again, you coulda just asked."

And he was gone.

Joey grinding against the tall guy's crotch might have

pissed Aaron off if Joey hadn't been so fucking obvious. Normally, that kind of bullshit was enough to make Aaron steer clear, but Joey was too transparent for bullshit. Giving Tall Dude a lap dance was just his way of saying hello.

Proof positive was Joey standing in front of him as soon as Aaron cleared the dance floor.

"And what if I did ask?"

Aaron looked down, and Joey licked his lips, making sure his tongue ring showed. Like Aaron said, obvious as the hard cock showing in Joey's jeans. Aaron's own dick remembered that tongue, and the shiny ball on it. He grabbed Joey's shirt and pinned him against the cigarette machine, kissing him until he felt the ball stroke every sensitive part of his mouth, and then chased the talented tongue back, driving in until Joey groaned and hung onto Aaron's shoulders.

Still keeping Joey where he wanted him, Aaron nosed along his jaw to tongue his neck, breathing in everything the beach was supposed to smell like, warm sand, salt and coconut suntan lotion. He was going to taste every inch of that skin. But when he reached up to cup Joey's head for another kiss, the skin flinched under Aaron's hand. And it didn't feel much like skin. So that wasn't a weird shadow from the disco lights.

He pulled back and stared down, thumb hovering over the worst of the abrasions on Joey's right cheekbone. "What the hell happened?"

Joey shrugged and smiled. "I wiped out. It was a hell of a ride."

"Surfing?" Of course. California. Flip-flops. Suntan lotion and a wet-suit tan. "So when you said this happens enough—"

"It's just been an eventful twenty-four hours."

Aaron shook his head. Joey didn't need fucking, he needed a guardian angel.

"Did your stitches tear?"

He had a hand up to check when Joey grabbed Aaron's wrist and pulled his thumb between full lips, sucking it in, swirling the ball along the whorls, gliding down to the base.

Joey's other hand reached for the waistband of Aaron's jeans, fingers sneaking in behind the top button.

Joey let Aaron's thumb slide out. "I'm asking for a repeat." After wetting his lips, Joey sucked down to the knuckle again.

What the hell. Aaron pulled his thumb free, the thick, wet sound audible even over the driving bass beat. He let Joey pull him back with that hand in his pants, knuckles brushing just low enough to make things interesting.

Aaron took in a quick breath. "Gonna do it here?"

"What?"

"Suck me off."

Joey shook his head, eyes serious. "But you feel free."

Careful to avoid the scrapes, Aaron gripped Joey's head and kissed him hard. Joey's fingers dipped a little lower, and Aaron's jeans were not loose enough for this.

He lifted his head. "Say good-bye to your ex and the guy he dumped you for."

"How did you—?"

Aaron ignored the question, turned Joey so he could wave at scowling Tall Dude and the other stud and headed out of the bar.

Joey followed. "Noah didn't dump me for Cameron. I broke up with him. Although—" They reached the street.

Aaron waited for Joey to catch up before taking off down the side street where he'd parked his bike. "Although?"

"Never mind."

They passed a dark storefront, deep inset door, and Aaron grabbed Joey's hand, pulling him off the street. "What about here?"

Joey leaned back against the opposite wall and shrugged again. "Go ahead." His fingers undid the top button on his jeans.

Aaron almost called his bluff—certain it was a bluff—even taking last night into consideration, Joey didn't seem like the type for public sex. And this was too public even for Aaron.

Especially considering that anyone from the bar might walk past and see him on his knees which—no.

"C'mon." He pulled Joey onto the sidewalk again. Another block and the bike gleamed even in the humid night. "Ever ridden before?"

"Yes." Joey's voice was soft.

"Do not make me put my bike down."

"I won't. I have— Shit, a Ducati Sport Classic?"

Joey's voice had the proper reverence. So what if even used the bike had cost more than any car Aaron'd had to take the kids to doctor's appointments. The fucker was gorgeous and Aaron knew it. And so did Joey.

He unlocked the back case, took out his helmet and a towel, and began to wipe down the seat. Joey was still staring.

"It won't bite." Aaron picked up his helmet.

"God, I'd love to, but you only have one helmet."

"No law in Florida." He tossed Joey the helmet and straddled the bike.

Joey pulled the helmet on and climbed behind him, easy, settled. Aaron snuck a backward glance. Joey's hands rested on his thighs, relaxed. After tightening the band holding his hair off his face, Aaron started the bike.

"Are you sure you don't need the helmet?"

"You promise not to dump us and we'll be fine," Aaron yelled back. "Besides, if my brains go splat the kids get lots of insurance money."

"Kids?"

Aaron laughed at the shock in Joey's voice as they roared away from the curb. He was cautious on the first corner, but Joey leaned with him and the bike, not fighting it at all. He took the next one faster. Smooth sway, Joey following the lean like he was part of the bike. They stopped at a light. Four minutes, and they'd be on his bed and fucking, but he wanted to keep sharing this with Joey. The kids hadn't liked to ride, even Dylan at his most rebellious never tried to steal the old bike Aaron'd had then. Tonight he might eat some bugs without the face shield, but... He cranked his head around. "Want to ride some more?"

"Yeah."

The bed would be there when they got there. Reaching back for Joey's hand, Aaron slid it around his waist. "Hold on."

Joey wrapped both his arms around Aaron, under his jacket, a band of hard heat against the thin cotton of his T-shirt. The bike flew up the ramp, and Aaron took them over the river, Joey's *wow* just audible over the wind in his ears. Jax was pretty at night, the bridges that crisscrossed the St. John's lit up with yellow, blue and purple lights. Dark hid the poor parts, the rundown industrial sections, the graffitied, trashed parks.

Aaron zipped up Route 17, gunning the bike through the curves along the inlet, Joey pressed hot and tight to his back. It might as well have been public sex, the buzz of the bike on his balls, five feet seven inches of hot man draped over his back, teasing fingers stroking from his nipples to his navel on the straightaways. Aaron wasn't the only one hard when he turned off down a side road into the state park. The dick poking his back was substantial enough to be out of proportion on Joey's frame. Sue him, Aaron had been more interested in the heat of that ass and mouth last night.

After Aaron kicked the stand down, Joey swung off, stepping away into the dunes. With cloud cover, it was dark enough out here that after a few seconds Joey was almost invisible, even with his Tweety Bird hair.

Aaron followed. Joey stopped and flashed white teeth as he smiled. "Here?"

"I'm not too big on sand rash. I'll take you back to my bed."

Joey was smiling as if he knew something Aaron didn't. Snagging the belt loop of his jeans, Joey tugged him close again. "Really want to wait?"

Aaron did. He wanted Joey in his bed, stretched out so he could get at every bit of skin, drag those husky moans out of his throat, fall asleep to the smell of sex and sweat on Joey's warm skin, wake up and bury his morning hard-on back in Joey's tight ass.

But Joey's hand was already skimming the front of Aaron's jeans, stroking him through the denim, and there was no way he could make it back to South Jacksonville without getting off first. Especially not when Joey increased the pressure before popping open Aaron's fly. Despite the wind on the long ride, Joey's hand was hot when it latched onto Aaron's dick, milking a drop of precome from the tip to slick the way back down to his balls. Aaron tipped his head back and let Joey work him for a minute, anticipation tingling through every nerve. Joey's hand was hard-edged and rough, maybe from surfing since he sure as hell didn't get those calluses fucking up people's lives with social-service paperwork. The calloused thumb worked over the head before Joey jacked him, quick, strong tugs that had Aaron rocking his hips.

He wanted Joey's mouth again, but last night had been about taking. Tonight he wanted Joey to give it. He leaned in and kissed him, savoring the textures of Joey's mouth, the rasp on the top, the glide on the bottom and the flick of the metal bar. When Aaron lifted his head, Joey gave a half smile and dropped smoothly to his knees on the grassy sand.

As Joey took the tip of Aaron's dick between slick lips, Aaron met his dark gaze and whispered, "I'll do you so good when we get back, swear it. Eat you 'til you come."

Joey's groan rumbled down the length of Aaron's cock, and then he pulled the head, just the head, into such perfect wet heat Aaron felt it behind his eyelids, a flash of white. Quick light flicks of that tongue, ball catching on his rim, tugged the pleasure straight from his balls, loosening his knee joints until he was almost sinking down next to him. He'd have to remember that: need something to lean on when Joey sucked the balance right out of him.

Backing off for a second, Joey kept the night air off Aaron's dick with hot hands while licking and kissing down the shaft.

He bet his little Do-gooder could go all night, lick and tease him, bring him to the edge and then back off, bring him to the point where Aaron was on his knees, but all Aaron wanted was to get off. Now. But fuck if he would beg.

Joey must have heard him anyway, because he took Aaron to the back of his throat, rubbing him against the soft heat, before sliding up, lips tight, ball rolling up the underside, and then so sweet on the spot underneath that Aaron almost bent in half, hands sliding through the fluff of hair, grazing the patch with the stitches and jerking his hands free with a quick apology.

That mouth skimmed down again, soft palate pressing, spasming on him, holding him, before Joey started a fast bob, tongue swirling, hard suck. Aaron cradled Joey's head, thumbs rubbing along his hollowed cheeks, hips rocking in time with Joey's bobs.

Biting his lip to keep in his whines, Aaron tried to pull Joey back, but he dove forward, keeping Aaron tight against a hot throat with a still-busy tongue. A few seconds of heat building, riding that spark before it ignited and then he let it go, flooding Joey's mouth as the orgasm ripped through him. He swayed, Joey steadying him with a grip on his ass.

Jesus, dude could suck the orange off a carrot. A big, long carrot.

Joey climbed up, licking his lips. Aaron reached out to wipe a drop from the corner of that killer mouth.

"Come here." Aaron pulled Joey in with an arm around his shoulder, softly kissing away the last bit of his own come, lip sore from where he'd chewed it. Joey rubbed his hard dick up against Aaron's hip.

"Please," Joey whispered against Aaron's lips.

Aaron held him and reached down to free a surprisingly big cock, measuring it with his hand. "Wow, where'd you get all this?"

"Stole it from my last boyfriend."

"Knew you were trouble."

Aaron jacked him slowly, teasing under the thick head with a twist.

Joey climbed into him, mouth open and hungry on his.

"Don't, so fucking horny, please—"

Aaron sped up his hand, and Joey dropped his head on Aaron's shoulder as his hips bucked.

"Yeah," Aaron murmured in his ear, and Joey jerked, shooting up onto their bellies.

After Aaron petted him down, Joey turned around to lean back against Aaron's chest. Aaron wrapped his arms over Joey's biceps, relaxing into the heat of Joey's body. How the fuck did he stay so warm without a jacket?

They rocked for a minute, until Aaron's back was freezing from the wind off the ocean. Nudging his nose under Joey's ear, Aaron whispered, "Ready to go?"

"Gonna keep your promise?"

"Always do."

Using his own come-splattered shirt, Joey turned to wipe Aaron's stomach.

"You still warm enough?" Aaron looked at the thin shirt Joey was wearing.

"I'm fine." Joey followed him back to the bike. He slid his hand over the seat. "It's a gorgeous bike. Thanks."

Aaron nodded as he swung his leg over. Joey picked up the helmet and straddled the bike behind him.

"You can hang on again if you want," Aaron said over his shoulder.

Joey waited until they were back on 17 before he slipped his hands under the jacket and plastered himself to Aaron's back.

Chapter Five

Aaron watched Joey as he glanced around the bungalow. He seemed to be trying to see everything and anything on their trip through the rooms to the bedroom in the back, like he was planning on buying the place.

More looking around when they got into the bedroom. Aaron peeled off his shirt and dropped it in the laundry basket. "Do you need instructions or something?"

Joey looked at him then, a gaze that said he was prepared to take Aaron's sarcastic comment seriously. Aaron's dick said he wouldn't mind if Joey did, but they weren't going to get into some kind of formal game. No sirring, no safe words or Daddy-I'll-be-good whines. If Joey said no, it all stopped. Aaron hooked his fingers in his belt loops and widened his stance.

Joey nodded.

"Clothes off. On the bed."

Joey stripped, tossing his clothes in the direction of a chair, and climbed onto the bed. A dark blue bruise made a two-inch line over his left kidney.

"Where'd you get that?"

Joey craned his neck around like he could manage to see his lower back. Finally he brought his fingers to the spot. "Oh. The board hit me when I got buried this morning."

"Piss blood?"

"No."

"You think you could manage a day without damage?"

Joey shrugged. "I can try."

Aaron unzipped his jeans but left them on, feeling Joey watch him as he went around to the nightstand and dug until he found a big dildo. He tossed it on the bed next to Joey, following it with the bottle of lube. After using the remote to cue up the CD, Aaron put it back on the nightstand and watched Joey wait for him.

Joey didn't say anything, which was unusual enough to get Aaron thinking maybe Joey'd been a little more formally trained than Aaron was up for, but as soon as the music started, Joey sat up laughing.

"Marvin Gaye? Seriously? What's next? Barry White?"

It might be a little cheesy, but Aaron liked old-school soul. Points to Joey for ID'ing Marvin from three notes, but minus a hundred for being a shit about it.

"Do you want to make fun of my music or do you want me to eat your ass?"

Joey flopped back again. "Be my guest." Based on his snort, Joey thought he was pretty funny.

Aaron dove for the bed. Joey let his legs drop open as he bounced to the creak of the springs and then leaned up to meet Aaron's kiss. He could fall into that mouth again, forget about how he'd planned to get Joey so desperate for a fuck he'd be levitating off the mattress. Lifting his head, Aaron started on Joey's neck, quick nips, nothing hard enough to leave evidence if he had to work tomorrow. Joey threw his head back and rested his hands lightly on Aaron's shoulders.

Open wet kisses down Joey's pale chest, over flat abs, a nuzzle against the dark blond hair under his navel, and when Joey arched his dick toward Aaron's mouth, he started at the top again. Joey groaned and moved his hands off Aaron's shoulders, reaching up to grab at that fuzzy yellow hair. Aaron watched Joey for a moment, the wide brown eyes hidden by half-shut lids and sandy lashes, bottom lip disappearing under white teeth, hands pulling his hair so tightly his brow smoothed out.

Aaron made the next trip more slowly, pausing to lick and

nibble the dark rose nipples, to make hard stomach muscles jump under his tongue and lips, to suck a dark bruise onto the skin just above the cut of Joey's hip. His hips rolled, and Aaron licked the soft hair under Joey's navel, tasting the salt from his earlier orgasm, breathing the smell of his come. With one teasing kiss on the shaft of Joey's hard cock, Aaron ducked down to lick and kiss Joey's balls, using a hand to get them both in his mouth.

The sound from Joey's mouth was high and sharp, not anything like the husky whisper Aaron had heard before. He couldn't wait to hear what Joey sounded like with a tongue in his ass. He flicked the tight, silky skin underneath Joey's balls, and Joey lifted his hips, which didn't matter since Aaron scooped up that ass in both hands and leaned back on his knees so Joey's shoulders were all that was still on the mattress. The first flick of Aaron's tongue across that salty hole dropped Joey's voice down to rival Barry White's range, rumbling in his chest, sounding like it scraped his throat as he whispered, "Please, oh, God."

Joey's legs flopped over Aaron's shoulders, heavy and strong, but he didn't try to drag Aaron forward, just quivered and groaned as Aaron flicked again and again, teasing, tasting.

Using his thumbs to hold Joey open, Aaron lifted his head to stare down the length of Joey's body, watching his face while rubbing with his thumbs. Joey's hands stopped tormenting his poor hair and shifted to fists on the mattress, so tight his knuckles went white. His teeth sank deeper into his lip, but his eyes opened as if he could feel Aaron watching him.

No Bambi eyes now, they were dark, hot, intense. Aaron held that gaze until he dropped back down to tongue the rim, dip inside. When he lifted his head again, Joey's eyelids fluttered and then opened wide, as if he didn't want to stop watching either. Aaron stretched him and buried his face in Joey's ass, tongue in deep, lips sucking out a single harsh "Fuck" from Joey's throat.

Joey's thighs shook. Aaron knew Joey wanted to press his legs down, force Aaron closer, keep him there, tongue deep in his ass, but he didn't. Despite the tension in the muscles on Aaron's shoulders, Joey didn't move.

When Aaron lowered him to the mattress, Joey's breathing was as loud as a moan and as gravelly as someone with terminal pneumonia. Aaron nuzzled Joey's balls again before lubing up the dildo. Instead of the usual fake dick shape, the black silicone was smooth, curved and widest about a third of the way down. Just enough for a good stretch on the rim while the curve pressed the tip on the prostate.

Wiping his hand on his jeans, Aaron rubbed the tip around Joey's hole and along his crease. Joey rocked down to meet it when he lined it up. Aaron stopped him with a hand on his belly. "Don't move. Just open for me."

Joey froze, but Aaron could feel the muscles quivering under his palm as Joey fought to stay still while Aaron slowly opened Joey's ass with the thick silicone, gaze moving from Joey's face to his ass as Joey's body yielded under the pressure. Since Aaron couldn't exactly feel what he was doing, he wanted to make sure he didn't hurt Joey.

He hit resistance when they got to the thickest part. "Gimme your hands."

Joey reached down and Aaron guided them to the base of the dildo.

"Finish putting it in. Slowly." He pinned Joey's thighs wide.

Joey nodded, teeth chewing on his lip again.

Joey used his body more than his hands, pushing himself down as he held the base steady. Aaron watched the sweat roll along Joey's hairline as he worked through the thickest part, sliding all the way down. It didn't have a narrow neck like a plug, the width kept Joey stretched all the way. Aaron moved Joey's hands away and rocked the dildo inside him with a palm against the base.

Joey groaned and arched up so hard he practically did levitate. One long slow stroke with the dildo and then Aaron bent his head to swallow Joey's cock. The head was as thick as it looked, pressing against Aaron's tongue and palate as he slid his lips down.

61

More than shaking now, Joey vibrated as he controlled the urge to fuck up into Aaron's mouth. Aaron turned the dildo so the curve would press up right and then fucked it in time with the bob of his head.

With a sound like a sob, Joey punched the mattress hard enough to make them both bounce.

Aaron lifted his head. "Go ahead. Fuck my mouth. But tell me before you come."

Joey nodded. His hips stayed still through the next few strokes, but when Aaron drove the dildo hard against his prostate, Joey slammed up to the back of Aaron's throat. Mouth riding Joey's cock, Aaron paused only to lick the precome out of the slit and catch his breath before gulping Joey's dick in again.

"Shit. Now." Joey slapped at him, and Aaron pulled back with a long hard suck to flick his tongue around the head while Joey pumped thick cream over Aaron's lips. Joey shoved him away before even the last few spurts, pressing his cock flat against his stomach.

Aaron gripped the base of the dildo. "Ready?"

"No." Joey was still panting, rubbing his dick.

Aaron shrugged and reached down to shove away his jeans, intending to finish himself off.

"No," Joey said again.

Aaron lifted his head to look at him.

"Want you to fuck me. Just—gimme a few minutes."

Aaron groaned like that ass was already clamping down on his dick. A few minutes. Jesus. Okay. He could wait a few minutes. Maybe. If Joey would stop breathing like the air hurt him, a raspy hum as he kept pressing his cock flat against his belly.

Aaron rolled away and grabbed a condom, suiting and slicking up so he wouldn't be holding up the proceedings.

He leaned in to kiss Joey's neck, under his ear, down to his freckled shoulder, playing connect the dots with his tongue. Joey rolled his body in a long wave on the bed. "Now."

Aaron had to make himself pull the dildo out slowly, but

when his dick brushed the slick, twitching muscle, he lost control and slammed in all the way. Joey didn't seem to mind, reaching up to grab Aaron's hips and keep him deep.

Dragging down one of the pillows, Aaron lifted Joey's hips onto it, staring at the expressions crossing his face as the movements echoed inside him.

Peeling Joey's hands free, Aaron pinned them over Joey's head, leaning in until Joey's knees were up to his ears before starting to thrust deep and long. Joey's wrists jerked as his hands went to fists again, but he didn't try to push up, only tightened his ass around Aaron's dick, driving him just as crazy as the night before. Aaron swiveled his hips, and Joey's eyes fluttered closed. He stopped biting his lip, mouth open to let out husky moaned *yeahs*.

Sweat soaked Aaron's scalp, his hair sliding loose from the band to stick to his face. Drops of sweat tickled his spine, slipped in between their thighs. He released Joey's hands and planted them next to his head, driving forward and dragging a "Holy shit" from Joey's mouth. He left one hand where it was and brought his other hand down to his cock, knuckles scraping Aaron's belly with the quick jerk of a fist.

If Aaron believed in anything, he'd have been thanking God right then because he didn't know how much longer he could hold on. Even after the dildo, Joey's ass was tight, squeezing sweet friction around Aaron's cock until his eyes felt like they'd roll backward out of his skull. He couldn't let Joey wear him out, yank the orgasm out of him until Aaron had gotten Joey off first.

Joey's *yeahs* got louder, and with the first spurt of warmth against his belly, Aaron felt the bomb go off in the base of his spine, sending him pounding hard into Joey's spasming ass until he was drained and sore.

Joey was already relaxing around Aaron's dick, enough that he could ease out and pull off the rubber. He forced himself up enough to make sure it made it into the trash and then flopped onto his back, wiping the sweaty hair from his eyes with the sheet that had ended up on the floor.

"I like your hair down. It's sexy."

All that and Joey could still talk? Jesus. At least his voice was raspy.

After forcing himself up to turn off the lights, Aaron dropped back onto the bed and reached out for the alarm clock. "You have to work tomorrow?"

"Nope. You?"

"Gotta be in at three." He set the alarm for ten. That would give him plenty of time to start the day off right in Joey's ass.

Aaron's pulse was finally under a hundred, and he'd cooled enough to stand it when Joey rolled into his side. "Aaron?"

Where the fuck did Joey think he had gone? "Yeah."

"Do you have kids?"

Aaron swallowed the smile he felt twitching on his lips. "None that I know of."

"Have you ever had sex with a woman?"

"Couple times when I was sixteen. Just making sure. You?"

"I've always been sure." In the dark, Aaron could hear the smile in Joey's voice. "So?"

Aaron knew what the *so* meant. He was still asking about the kids. And for a second, Aaron was fucked out enough that he might have explained about Savannah and Dylan and Darryl and Sheree and Mom and Rafe. Then he shook his head and pulled Joey closer with an arm around his shoulder. "Joey?"

"Yeah?"

"Go to sleep."

Joey woke up thirsty, hungry, horny and sticky to the point of grossness. Lifting his head, he peered at the clock. Seven thirty. He dropped his head back onto the pillow, which was half soft micro-fiber-whatevers and half Aaron's rigid shoulder. During the four hours they'd been asleep, Aaron had draped himself around Joey from behind, arm heavy on his hips. He snugged his ass back against Aaron's groin.

No response but a deep sigh. Since Joey wasn't getting laid anytime soon, he was going to have to take care of the sticky, thirsty and hungry complaints from his body. He never could fall back asleep if he woke up on his own.

He wiggled under Aaron's arm to face him. The sharp lines of his face were softened by sleep, the long black hair tangled on forehead and neck.

"Aaron?" Joey whispered.

He got a grunt.

"Mind if I shower?"

A muffled "Mhmm."

That sounded close enough to "Go ahead" so Joey scooted out from under Aaron's arm. Starting for the bathroom he'd scoped out last night, Joey took a long look back. Except for the accident when he'd been a little preoccupied, he hadn't seen Aaron except in the dark. The ER didn't count since Joey had been totally obsessed with the whole shots and stitches thing and couldn't really check him out. He did now.

Aaron had shifted onto his belly when Joey crawled out and was now sprawled diagonally across the bed. The sheet Aaron had dragged over them last night was twisted around one leg, leaving one corner over his left shoulder and the rest of his long bronze body to stare at.

Noah and Mark had been big. Aaron was long. Lean stretched muscles on his back, the sexy curve of his hip into his ass, and then long thighs with muscled calves. Even his feet were long. Joey's body knew perfectly well how that length translated into dick size. And he didn't need to see Aaron's shoulders or arms to remember their strength when they'd lifted him.

Aaron's skin was a deep golden brown all over with a hint of chestnut. The kind of bronze Joey associated with an every-day-at-the-beach tan. But unless Aaron visited a nude beach, he'd always been that color because Joey couldn't find a tan line on him, and no one could get that color from a booth.

Joey's body felt the effects of their hard, acrobatic fuck when he swung his leg up into the high tub. He squirmed around to see if he had fingerprints on the backs of his thighs where Aaron had been holding on when he came, but Joey's flexibility didn't extend to an owl-like spin on his neck. He stood under the spray until the aches disappeared under the rush of hot water and sampled some of Aaron's shampoo. After scrubbing away the dried come and using a finger to brush his teeth, he made his way back into the bedroom.

Aaron hadn't moved. If Joey knew the guy better, he might have tried to wake Aaron with a blowjob, but as incomprehensible as Joey thought it was, there were some people who just didn't appreciate being woken up—even for sex.

Joey pulled on his briefs and jeans and made his way into the frighteningly immaculate kitchen. After downing two glasses of water, he started looking for breakfast. The cold cereal he found was tastelessly healthy and needed a generous application of sugar. He considered cooking something for Aaron, but didn't know what he'd like—and besides, he was afraid to mess up the surgically clean stove. Remembering the three coffee cups he'd seen on the floor of the ambulance, he decided he couldn't go wrong with coffee, especially since it came in premeasured packs. He washed out his bowl and glass, but couldn't remember which cabinet had held the sugar, so he left it on the counter.

The smell of brewing coffee hadn't summoned Aaron into the kitchen. Joey peeked into the bedroom and found him in exactly the same spot. Everything about Aaron's pose echoed the satisfaction Joey could still feel in his own body. The Smashing Pumpkins' "Cherub Rock" started playing in his head, which had been playing in Eduardo's bedroom when Joey lost his virginity. At the time, he'd wished it had been something a little less grunge, but now it always made him smile. Having that song pop up on his random mental playlist while he stared at Aaron, ass and cock still pulsing from last night, was either a really good or a really bad sign. Since Aaron wasn't going to wake up just from Joey aiming a fuck-me stare between his shoulder blades, Joey went back through the kitchen to the living room. He'd claim it looked like a museum diorama of a nineties American living room but even museum dioramas usually had clutter. He'd never seen a completely empty coffee table before.

Close examination of the entertainment center revealed a Xbox 360, a boxed set of all the *Die Hard* movies and three framed photos. The one on the top shelf showed a tall, blonde woman standing next to a burly guy with an infant in her arms. In the next, the same blonde woman was bracketed by two boys in graduation gowns, identical grins on their light brown faces. The third was a teenaged girl, also in her graduation cap and gown, curly black hair perfectly arranged under her cap, a proud laugh spilling from her lips. The girl and the boys were clearly siblings, but neither they nor the blonde seemed to share any resemblance to Aaron, except the blonde's height. Despite their disparate appearances, Joey knew he was looking at Aaron's family.

A toy guitar hung from a hook on the side of the cabinet and a quick search revealed a Guitar Hero disk for the Xbox. Joey grinned.

Since playing it at a friend's party, he'd been wishing he could get one. Of course, he'd have to unpack more than his bed and computer to hook one up. He gauged the distance between the TV speakers here at the front of the house and Aaron's bedroom at the back. If he kept it on low...

Aaron slapped off the alarm and swung his hand around on the cold mattress, looking for Joey. No warmth. No rolling over and fucking away his morning wood in that tight ass. The parts of the sheets that weren't under him were cold, so Joey had been out of bed for awhile. Aaron rubbed the hair out of his eyes and staggered into the bathroom. As he pissed, his sleep fuzzy brain told him two things. Coffee and music. The house wasn't empty.

When he dried his hands, the towel was still damp. So Joey'd found his way into Aaron's shower and kitchen. No Joey in the kitchen, but he'd left the sugar on the counter like he was hanging out a welcome sign to every roach in north Florida.

He poured himself a mug of coffee and went into the living room. Joey was swaying his ass in front of the TV, the Xbox guitar in his hands, bright-colored notes flashing by as he nailed chord after chord. Do-gooder had been left alone for awhile and fuck if he hadn't moved in.

The song ended in a flourish of notes and the game informed Joey that he did, in fact, rock. Joey raised his hands in triumph. When the main screen came up, Aaron saw that the son-of-a-bitch was almost done with the hard level. Aaron had just managed to knock Darryl off the high score on medium. As he waited for the next song to load, Joey went up to the cabinet and stared at the picture of the twins. Did Joey seriously think he got to dig around in Aaron's life because Aaron had had his dick up that ass twice? Cold and all-too-familiar anger burned in his gut.

"Having fun?" he asked with a sneer that should have told Joey he was in trouble.

Joey jumped and spun around. "Crap."

"Crap? What are you, twelve?"

"Thirty-one." Joey seemed to finally get a handle on Aaron's mood. The grin on his face disappeared. "Um, I made coffee."

Aaron held up his mug. "I noticed. You also left the sugar out."

"Sorry. I couldn't remember where I found it."

"Done playing house?"

"What?"

Aaron would have just told him to get out but then he remembered he'd brought Joey here on his bike. "Grab your shirt. I'll take you home."

Joey looked at his watch, like that had something to do with it. "I thought you didn't have to work until three."

"I don't. C'mon. Get dressed." Aaron went back into the kitchen and put away the sugar before wiping down the counter. Joey passed him silently on his way into the bedroom.

Aaron gulped down his coffee. As the burn hit, he slammed his mug on the counter. "Fuck."

"Guess you wake up cranky." Joey had pulled on his stained, wrinkled wreck of a T-shirt and now leaned on the fridge.

Aaron had woken up cold and horny, while Joey had been making himself at home.

"You ready?"

Joey shrugged. "I guess I am."

Of course it was pissing rain, so he had to take the beat-up truck. Its gas-guzzling, exhaust-spewing, rusted-out muffler probably would offend Joey's Yaris-driving sensibilities. Not that Aaron gave a shit.

He backed out of the garage.

"Noah and Cameron drove me to the bar. You can take me to my apartment. It's just off San Marco, on—"

"I remember."

Joey stared out the side window as Aaron drove through the Sunday-morning quiet streets. The God-fearing were all in church and the sensible were all in bed. By the time he'd turned down San Marco, he was willing to admit he might have overreacted. Joey didn't know how much Aaron hated roaches— not that he was going to explain sleeping with his hands over his ears, waking up to try to brush them off his sister over and over—and yeah, he didn't like it when something fucked up his plans, like the one he'd had about staying in bed until noon figuring out how much more bendable Joey was. But they were in front of Joey's apartment building.

Joey got out, digging his keys from his pocket, but turned back and leaned in the open door. "You know, you're a hell of a fuck, but a total asshole." Then he grinned. "Have a nice day." After slamming the door shut so hard Aaron was afraid the force would shake loose the rust holding the frame together, Joey jogged away.

Chapter Six

When Noah knocked on Joey's door at six twenty-two, Joey was hanging upside down on the sole piece of furniture in his living room. He'd managed to drag up the futon-couch thing he'd found at Target and take care of the "some assembly required", but when he tried to enjoy the fruits of his labors, he found them pretty hard and unripe. The couch wasn't any more comfortable to sit on with his legs over the back, but the blood rushing to his head was an interesting sensation.

Noah knocked again, deep voice rumbling through the thin door. "C'mon, dude. You're the one who sent me seventeen texts."

Joey swung off the couch and stalked over to open the door. "Five."

"Eight," Noah countered with a grin to show off his dimples and began ticking them off on his fingers. "One at eight a.m. Thank you so much for that." Noah stepped into the tiny hall.

"I wanted to tell you I was okay. If you didn't want to wake up, you should have had it on silent."

"One at ten thirty asking what I was doing."

"Fucking your boyfriend good-bye, I'd guess."

"Round one, anyway." Noah arched his brows. "At twelve fifty-eight a thoughtful reminder that I should drive Cam to the airport."

"Those security lines are long."

Noah cleared his throat. "Four, five and six I received while

I was still at the airport. Cam was amused."

"Really? I thought he didn't like me."

"He thinks you're fucking adorable."

"Then why does he always seem to avoid me?"

"I think he's afraid you're irresistible."

"Bullshit."

"Seriously. The last thing he said to me was 'If you fuck him wear a rubber.'"

"So I'm an irresistible slut?" Joey stuck out his chin.

"You know that's not what he meant."

"Holy shit, are you guys doing it raw?"

"So not the topic. And sorry, but I got seven while I was driving. And eight—what the hell did you want me to help you carry?"

Joey waved him into the living room. "I got it."

"What's that thing supposed to be?"

"Oh, don't give me that shit, Mr. Still Using His Mom's Cast-Off Couch. Besides, you're sleeping on it tonight."

"Joey—"

"We can surf before I go to work."

"In the morning?" Noah sounded horrified, but he sat on the futon-thing. "On second thought, I don't think I'll have any trouble getting off this thing." Picking up the headphones, he put them to his ear. "Godsmack? You only listen to Godsmack when you're pissed off. Oh, Joey, we tried to tell you that guy— Fine. I won't say it. Don't give me the eyes."

Joey switched off his music. "I know. I could tell he had asshole written all over him, but I swear, it wasn't the whole just-a-fuck thing." It wasn't. He could feel it. Aaron hadn't been treating him the way you treat a guy you're going to do once and then forget, not with taking him out on his Ducati and not with sitting with him in the ER. "Something happened but I can't figure out what."

"Well, if you can't, I don't know what you expect me to do."

"Listen to Sully Erna growl with me?" Joey hooked up the

player to his stereo.

Noah looked around. "Wow, did you actually unpack?"

"Mostly I moved some boxes around. But physical activity is highly effective for dealing with frustration."

"You got any other things you need carried in, because with Cam out of town—"

Joey punched Noah's shoulder. "Not that kind of frustration, idiot."

The waves were mushy, and Noah moped about Cameron's absence. When Joey got home from work on Tuesday and dropped his MP3 into the stereo attachment to pump Johnny Cash's tales of misery through the apartment, Noah snapped.

"That's it. I've been through snarling with Godsmack and whining with My Chemical Romance but if you're going as far as the Man in Black, we have got to get out of this apartment. What happened to you keeping me company as opposed to, you know, feeling better off dead?"

"Don't blame me because you can't live without your true love for a week."

"He's been gone a lot longer than a week before, and I didn't want to start smashing things. The misery is all you, man. So why the fuck don't you just call him?"

"I don't have his number. And there aren't any A. Chases listed for Jacksonville."

"Right. 'Cause that could stop you. Why don't you use your contacts? I'm sure you've already got someone wrapped around your finger you can get to track him down."

Joey did. He could call a couple of people—hell, he could just claim it was official business and go through work and get it—but if he did, he might as well move Aaron's name onto the list of almosts. Aaron wasn't the kind of guy you went around. Joey knew that already. So if he wanted sex with a guy who could work his body like it came with a pop-up help menu, wanted another chance to see the guy who showed him city lights and pitch-black beaches on the back of a gorgeous bike, Joey was going to have to go get him.

"Let's go out," he agreed.

"But we're taking your car. If you're getting some again, you at least have to drop me off."

"Whatever. Like you'll fit in my car."

Somehow Noah folded himself into the front seat of the Yaris, and Joey took him over to the part of Neptune Beach he'd explored.

"How's the conch soup?"

Noah scooped up another spoonful. "Good. But I had better in Hawaii."

"Because Cameron was there." Joey gave a half smile.

"Yeah, he made it just for me."

"You know what I mean." Trying to glare down at Noah never worked, and not just because of almost a foot difference in height.

"Unfortunately, I do." Noah laughed. "Joey..." Noah looked like he'd swallowed his tongue. Joey couldn't figure out what Noah had just stopped himself from saying. Noah would get to it if he wanted to.

"So—what's it like, fucking raw?"

Noah choked on his soup. "Jesus, Joey."

It wasn't like they hadn't had their tongues in each other's ass; what the hell would Noah be embarrassed about? Besides, Joey wanted to know.

"Tell me why you broke up with Mark, and don't do that 'he dumped me' shit."

"It doesn't matter."

Noah shrugged.

"You go first." Joey finished his soup.

Noah grabbed a roll as the waiter brought Noah another beer and took away their bowls.

K.A. Mitchell

Joey tried withholding the butter, but with Noah's reach, he simply snatched the bowl from his hands.

"Damn it. Okay." Joey tried to remember exactly when he'd known. Because he'd been able to fool himself with Mark for longer than anyone. Mark just seemed to get him. But Joey had realized the reason Mark got him was because Joey was doing all the work, that as toppy and sexy as Mark was in bed, out of it he was as easy to push around as a self-propelled lawnmower. And as much as that sounded like the perfect man—what complaint could there be when Mark did everything Joey wanted?—Joey needed—had to have—something worth fighting for. "It wasn't right."

"That's very illuminating."

Joey grabbed a roll and started shredding it. It was too stupid to admit. For everything he'd learned about other people, he couldn't figure out what the fuck would make him happy. And damn Aaron for starting the whole this-time-was-going-to-be-different feeling.

"It was too easy."

"You're crazy. You do know that, right? And me?"

"You weren't easy, but you were already taken. We don't have to go back further, do we? Because then I'll start ranking sex skills."

"Bastard."

"Actually, yes."

"Fuck, Joey, I forgot."

"I know, hon. It's not like I remember it. Starting life in a toilet only means it has to get better."

"Do I have tell you how fucking annoying your optimism is?"

"No, but you have to tell me what it's like to fuck raw."

Noah was so cute when he blushed. His eyes scanned the room like he thought a waiter would save him and then stammered out, "Good—great—awesome. Am I done?"

"Nope. That's cheating. I want details." Joey leaned forward, part of his eager attentiveness intended to make Noah

74

turn redder, and partly because he really did want to know.

Noah looked around them, took a deep breath and ran his words together. "When he starts, that's when it's really different because you can feel how hot he is, and every bump and— God, Joey do I have to?"

"I still have the dolls." Joey wiggled his hands as if he held the dolls he used when counseling kids who couldn't talk about their sexual abuse.

"Okay." Noah's voice lowered to a whisper and Joey leaned in farther. "The head feels so good if he slides it around and if he rocks the crown right under the rim, God, and even when he's fucking you, you just know there's nothing between you. And when you're inside—not that you care—"

"Hey, I've topped." To the arch of Noah's brow, he added, "No, and I don't mean just from the bottom, you smug prick."

"It's so hot and wet and you can feel everything. And I really can't— Thank God." The waiter brought over their dinners, and Noah looked like he'd had a death-row reprieve.

It wasn't like Joey hadn't brought the monogamy-tests-bare route up with Mark, but he'd always said there would be time to decide later. Maybe Mark had seen it coming just like Joey did. With ex-boyfriends spread out between here and San Diego it was pathetic to whine about his lack of a love life, but damn it, he wanted that. He wanted just once for that feeling to be right. To have something to hold onto. To finally get it.

Noah said good-bye the next morning and went to spend the last few days of his break playing uncle at his brother's house before he had to go back to Tallahassee. His last suggestion was "Call him or get over it." Like Noah had listened to Joey's advice when he was acting like an idiot over Cameron.

By one o'clock that afternoon, Joey had a screeching, squirming ten-month-old over his shoulder and two wasted meth-heads screaming at him and the cop who'd been sent with

Joey on the call to investigate the allegations of abuse. After finding the front door broken and boarded up, they'd gone around to the back. The door and a couple of the windows were open. One look in showed an apartment empty of adults and full of garbage, bottles, crystal pipes and even some waste— animal or human Joey didn't want to know—complete with a squalling baby in the middle of it. Before he and the officer could get the notice posted and themselves off the back porch the putative parents showed up.

Officer Preston, who had come along on the call, was about the size and shape of a barn door so he had no difficulty moving the hollow-eyed adults out of their way. But then something happened. That shouldn't have come as a shock after thirty years, since something always happened. Only mild surprise washed through Joey as it all unfolded.

The mother made a lunge for the baby. Joey moved back, Officer Preston moved forward, and the rickety back porch railing moved to another location entirely. Joey went with it, turning as he fell so he landed on his right shoulder, holding the baby safely up on his left.

The wet popping sound meant a dislocation, like the one he'd suffered to his left in a high school wrestling match. He knew what kind of pain he was in for, but even as the breath tried to get back into his lungs all he could think about was that baby. It was silent for a second, warm and solid against him, and terror kept Joey suspended from all sensation for five loud thuds of his heart. Then the baby started screeching again, the mother screaming and Officer Preston radioing for an ambulance.

When the pain hit, Joey managed not to puke on the baby and kept his sterling record of never fainting no matter what, though at the time passing into oblivion would have been welcome. The cop got the baby from him and blocked the kick the male parent aimed at Joey's ribs and then the sirens came.

Even biting a lip against nausea Joey could calculate the odds of Aaron being on the ambulance team, given that a city this size probably had at least a thousand paramedics, so he didn't know why he was disappointed when the guy bending over him wasn't Aaron. The guy was sexy though, Cuban from his accent and unfortunately, according to Joey's gaydar, completely straight.

After a friendly crouch and exchange of names calculated to put Joey at ease, Hector said, "We can do the reduction—put it back in—here, rather than waiting for the hospital."

Joey tried to concentrate on the crinkles around Hector's dark eyes to keep from biting all the way through his lip. Sweat ran down his back from his neck, and yeah, he should be used to stuff like this, but a dislocated shoulder was in the top five on the holy-fuck-that-hurts list.

Hector went on. "They'll give you a shot before they do it at the hospital, but trust me, it's going to—"

"Do it now." Joey remembered that getting the so-mildly-named reduction—like it was a sauce in a French restaurant—easily made number one on his list, but once the bones were back where they were meant to be, it was a lot more bearable.

Hector nodded at him. "You've done it before?"

"Other shoulder." And Joey wished they'd get to it before he had time to start shaking.

The other tech braced Joey from behind and Hector said, "On three," with a quick wink.

Joey closed his eyes on *one*, but that was all he heard over the disgusting sound and the dizzying wrench as Hector ripped off Joey's arm and pasted it back on.

Joey let out a couple of long breaths while they helped him with a sling, but the pain had subsided to something he thought might be equivalent to having been beaten on the shoulder with heated irons.

Joey winced as Officer Preston hauled up the man by his cuffed arms. "On the way to the station, we'll have a chat about kicking people when they're down, sir." He grinned at Joey. The mother's stringy blonde hair hung in her face as she was tucked into a different squad car, and Joey and the baby were packed into the ambulance.

Hector checked the baby over while they headed for the hospital, finding no obvious signs of physical abuse. The neglect was all too apparent though from the filth on him and his pale shrunken skin. Joey wondered when the kid had last been given anything to drink.

"Can we get some fluids in him?" he asked.

"Only if I hook him up to an IV. They'll have to check his lungs for damage from the meth fumes and if they decide he needs surgery..."

Joey nodded. They wouldn't want him to have anything in his stomach.

The baby had given up screaming awhile ago, preferring instead to shove a fist in his mouth, and just lie with tears still spilling from his blue eyes. Joey stared at him from his own stretcher. "Trust me, kid. It's going to get better."

The baby blinked.

Aaron was in the back of the ambulance when he heard about the call. Stephanie, the EMT who rode with Hector, was telling Elaine the PA about a "majorly adorable social worker" who'd been "attacked by some meth-heads who were abusing a baby." It didn't take any more than that. He knew.

He jumped down from the truck. "What happened?"

Elaine stubbed out her cigarette on the sole of her clog. "Dislocated shoulder."

Definitely Joey. How many adorable klutzy social workers could there be in Jax? "He okay?"

"I guess. He's down in the ER."

As Aaron went through the building, Kim came up alongside him. "Your sweet piece of ass is back, I see. He always get in this much trouble?"

Aaron stopped and changed his direction. Maybe he'd just get a cup of coffee. "He's not my anything."

"He's going to be fine, in case you care," Kim said to Aaron's back.

But it must have been a slow day at Shands, because Joey was the subject of three conversations Aaron overheard in the cafeteria. By the time he was at the cash register, he'd heard that Joey had fought off the crystal freaks and been pushed from the second-story window.

Some unsupervised, screaming eight-year-olds were playing tag around the tables so Aaron took the coffee to go, swirling the cup to cool it.

He met Kim going from the pharmacy back into ER. "I'm doing his discharge right now."

Why Kim thought Aaron would give a shit he didn't know. He also didn't know why he followed Kim into the exam room, except it was as good a place as any to drink his coffee.

Two nurses and another resident crowded around the table. Joey was propped up, sling on and wrapped tightly to his torso. Despite the laughter, despite the grin on Joey's face, Aaron's fingers itched to touch him, to cup the back of his neck and know the skin was warm, not cold and clammy with shock and pain.

When Joey looked up, Aaron realized the grin on that too-pale face was for Kim.

"Jae Sun, you're back. Aren't you sick of me yet?"

Kim let Joey call him Jae Sun? He hated that name. Kim laughed, and again the sound was so alien Aaron turned to stare at him.

"I'm so sick of you I'm discharging you. Did you find someone to pick you up?" Kim's eyes lasered the side of Aaron's face.

Aaron was about to explain that his shift had started when he clamped his teeth shut. What the fuck? Why did everyone think he was responsible for a guy he'd fucked twice? Joey was old enough—older than Aaron—he could damned well take care of himself. Aaron gulped down some coffee and bit off a curse when he burned his mouth.

"I did," Joey said. "They'll be here soon. I can just wait for them out front."

The ex and his new boyfriend must still be around, Aaron decided.

The nurses petted Joey's hair on the way out, and the other resident left as soon as Kim started running through the discharge notes. A nurse could have done it. Why was Kim bothering? Maybe he was planning on getting a piece of Joey's ass himself, though Aaron would have sworn Joey wasn't his type. If Kim wanted Aaron's leavings, he could help himself.

Aaron looked over Kim's shoulder at the records as he recommended an orthopedic who wasn't a total dick or a complete fuck-up for Joey's follow-up care and reminded him he couldn't drive while taking the codeine and Flexeril.

"Yeah, it'll be awhile," Joey said, glancing down at his arm. "My car's a manual."

Before Kim could volunteer to be Joey's personal chauffeur, Aaron started to leave. But Tall Dude blocked the door. The guy with him wasn't the stud boyfriend Aaron had scoped at the bar. This guy was a slightly shorter and straighter version of Tall Dude. Aaron wasn't a little guy, but Joey's ex wasn't just tall. He could give an NBA center a height complex.

"Can't I leave you alone for a day?" Tall Dude went to Joey's side, but didn't touch him.

"Apparently not." The guy who must have been Tall Dude's brother shouldered past Aaron and put his hand on Joey's good arm, which hello, the pain was probably all the way through his collarbone.

Aaron stepped forward but the asshole lifted his hand.

"Joey, I can't believe you've been in Jacksonville for a month and you didn't call us. Maria's pissed."

"Uh-oh." But Joey only grinned up at his ex's brother. Weren't they a cozy family? "But, you know—" Joey's gaze flicked briefly to Tall Dude.

The brother snorted. "I'll kick his ass if he's got a problem with it. You've got to see the kids. Robbie's almost four."

"Wow. I remember us driving over the night he was born."

Tall Dude crossed in front of the table and stuck out his hand to Aaron. "Noah Winthrop."

Aaron shook it, and offered his own name and hand, but there was a warning in Noah's eyes that made it more of a challenge than a friendly gesture. Aaron fought the urge to see what expression was on Joey's face as he met the pressure of Noah's grip.

"My brother Adam." Noah nodded at the guy who was showing pictures on his cell phone to Joey.

Joey made polite sounds of interest, more than Aaron could have managed if he were the one forced to look at pictures of someone else's rugrats after his shoulder had been recently reduced. Aaron would have crawled inside a bottle of scotch by now.

"I can't believe Jake's already in first grade."

Aaron had about all the reunion he could handle. The Winthrops would take care of Joey. He looked around for Kim to see if he wanted to go get some more coffee and realized the son-of-a-bitch had disappeared while Aaron was distracted by the brothers.

They bracketed Joey now, and despite the cell phone in front of his face, Joey raised his soft brown eyes to Aaron. And damn if he didn't want to walk over there and kiss the fuck out of him, then lock Joey up somewhere so he could go a week without another disaster—maybe heal up enough so Aaron could finally get that morning in bed.

A nurse came in with a wheelchair. Joey didn't even bother to protest. Given what Aaron had seen the past week, Joey had to be pretty familiar with hospital routine.

"You're coming over to our house," Adam said as Joey settled into the chair.

"Thanks, Adam, but really all I want is to be in my own bed." His bright grin flashed. "That pull-out thing I remember in your cellar is not what I want to put my shoulder on tonight."

Noah started to speak, but Joey interrupted him. "Go and

play with your nephews. I'm sorry I had to call you."

Fuck the stupid conditioning of guilt and responsibility. Aaron didn't owe Joey anything. And the guy would be fine.

"And how are you going to get around?" Noah asked.

"I'm off work for at least a week, and there's a bus line right next to my apartment." He looked up at Adam. "I swear I'll call you guys if I need anything." Joey looked from one to the other with the Bambi eyes. "Please. I just want to go home."

"Jesus. Stop with the eyes. Okay," Noah said.

Adam hadn't paid any attention to Aaron, but now Noah's brother leveled an assessing stare Aaron's way and nodded. "C'mon, Noah, we'll get the car."

Noah had been about to take the wheelchair's handles. "Why does it take two of us to get the car?"

Adam looked over at Aaron again. "Because I need you to move all the kids' shit off the seat so your gigantic carcass has a place to sit."

Noah smacked the back of his brother's head as they cleared the door, the standard sibling answer Aaron had seen a million times between Darryl and Dylan.

The nurse moved toward the chair, but Aaron said, "I've got it."

Joey was silent as they rolled down the hall. Aaron knew exactly what happened when a shoulder dislocated, had studied that the extreme pain alone was a reliable diagnosis of the injury. He'd seen plenty of people pass out or throw up from the reduction.

Maybe whatever drugs they'd given Joey were wearing off. All that laughing and talking in the exam room, and now Joey sat with his neck stiff. Aaron was sure if he leaned over he'd see Joey biting his thick bottom lip.

"You know, if you wanted to see me again, you could have just come by. You didn't have to fling yourself off a building to come to Shands."

"Didn't think I had a reason." Joey's voice was hard.

Aaron swung over to the triage desk and grabbed a pen,

scribbled his cell number on Joey's discharge instructions and put it back in his hand.

Joey turned his head, winced and faced front again. "I'm not sure I'll need it."

The doors whooshed open for them, and they went out of the stink disinfectant could never chase out of a hospital and into the warm sunshine.

Aaron came around to the front of the chair and leaned on the armrests. Joey looked up. In the light, his eyes were a clear warm brown, darker lines spinning off his pupils like sunbursts. Aaron wanted to kiss him, watch those eyes darken in arousal, soften as Joey begged to come. But none of that explained why he wanted to hand Joey his own key and have the Winthrops drop Joey off at his house on Mayfair Road.

"You gonna be okay?"

Joey started to shrug and then hissed in pain. "I know it doesn't look that way, but I usually am."

"I knew it was you," Aaron said. "When I heard some do-gooder had gotten hurt trying to get some kid, I knew."

Joey smiled. His lips curled up slowly, until it turned into a big grin.

Aaron reached out to brush a thumb against that smile, but a minivan pulled up and Joey's mountain of an ex climbed out.

Joey hopped from the chair without any trouble, no longer holding his head stiffly, like he was trying to hide all the pain in his arm from everyone—except Aaron.

"I've got him," Noah said as Aaron stood close when Joey was getting into the front seat.

No, you had *him.*

Chapter Seven

Aaron got Joey's apartment number off the hospital records, and Shands privacy policy could go fuck itself. He knocked on 3R—softly, since it was almost midnight, but louder when he didn't get an answer. Patience wasn't exactly part of his skill set.

After a minute of Aaron's steady knocking, Joey opened the door. He didn't look happy to see Aaron. Joey didn't look happy at all. He stepped aside, and Aaron shut the door before following him into the room which opened off the tiny hall.

Boxes surrounded a pathetic excuse for a sofa. No TV, just a stereo playing something that sounded like whining cats—at least the vocals did. Joey sat on the dark brown cushion covering a slightly tilted frame.

"What happened to your couch?" Aaron eased down next to him.

"Nothing."

"Why does it lean?"

"I didn't notice." A louder whine from the stereo followed by long twangs of bass, and Joey shifted carefully on the couch, until he faced Aaron. His face wasn't pale anymore, but his lips were grey instead of their usual pink. "Why are you here?"

Aaron wasn't sure he knew the answer. He'd just found himself taking the San Marco exit as soon as he'd crossed the bridge. "I thought you might need some help."

Joey's mouth pressed into a thin line, and he pushed off the couch. He came back with two bottles of iced tea and a bag of chips. He sat on the couch and tucked each bottle between his knees to open it, handing the first one off to Aaron, and then tore open the bag of chips with his teeth.

"See, eating and drinking. Wanna see me piss?"

"What the fuck is your problem?"

"Why are you here?" Joey said again, looking directly at him until Aaron had to take a gulp of tea to cover the fact that he couldn't hold that steady brown gaze anymore.

Fucker was direct. And as much as Aaron appreciated a no-bullshit style, he wasn't exactly thrilled with the challenge in that stare. "Because I want to be."

Joey nodded. "Okay." He stood again. "Coming to bed?"

Aaron knew there was no way Joey would be up for anything but sleep, but yeah. He wanted to follow him to bed. It was just—he looked at the box where the bottles and chips sat. "In a minute."

After putting the stuff away, he found Joey in the bathroom, offering up a box of toothbrushes still in the blister pack. That was a level of high-traffic readiness Aaron had never seen. He grabbed one off the top and lifted one corner of his mouth in question.

Joey shrugged, winced and said, "My mom's a dentist."

"No shit." That might explain where he got the toothbrushes, but not why he kept a huge supply handy. "You should probably cut back on the shrugging."

"I'm working on it." Joey handed off a tube of toothpaste and left Aaron in the bathroom.

It wasn't as chaotic as the living room. Shaving stuff, shampoo, basic equipment where it belonged. When Aaron went into the bedroom, he found that Joey had managed to get out of his khakis but was still in the dirt-streaked dress shirt he'd had on in the ER.

Without asking, Aaron stepped over and unwound the binding, then unbuttoned the shirt. "Do you want to try to get the sleeve off or should I just cut it?"

"The nurse about killed me putting it back on. Cut it,

85

please."

"Scissors?"

Aaron could see Joey stop the shrug before it happened.

"There should be a knife in the kitchen."

All Aaron found was a steak knife and the shirt didn't give up easily. Though when he finally hacked it to pieces, he could slide it off without even taking Joey's arm from the sling. The shoulder was already turning purple, the freckles Aaron's tongue had traced were faded against the darkened skin. "I'll get you some ice." As he reached the door he turned back. "Do you have ice?"

"I think so." Joey didn't attempt the shrug this time.

Aaron found half a bag of ice in the freezer and after digging through a box on the counter came up with a sealable plastic bag. He wrapped it in the remnants of Joey's shirt and carried it back in.

Joey was lying on his left side, facing away from the door. He'd gotten rid of his briefs and Aaron had to remind his dick that no matter how sweet that ass looked, how much he wanted to dip his tongue in the curve of spine, feel the soft hair there as he licked, it wasn't happening tonight.

He kept on his own shorts when he stripped. He climbed in and immediately pitched into Joey.

"Shit. I'm— What the fuck?" It was a waterbed. A fucking waterbed?

"Sorry. Forgot to warn you."

Aaron had dropped the ice pack in the sudden surge of motion, and of course it landed right on his crotch. The shock and stab of pain made his voice break into a range he hadn't hit since puberty.

Joey shifted around and started laughing.

"Want to feel how funny it is?"

Aaron grabbed the ice pack and hesitated. He couldn't wrestle Joey, couldn't fuck him, even kissing him to stop his laughing might hurt him. What the fuck was Aaron doing here?

Joey winced again, and Aaron put the ice pack against his

shoulder. Joey's lips parted and Aaron said, "Do not tell me it's cold, dumbass."

Every single movement sent the bed into rolling waves, and there was a hell of a lot of shifting as Joey tried to find a position that didn't put pressure on his shoulder.

"Jesus, how do you ever sleep on this thing?"

"I love it. It's the closest thing to sleeping on the ocean. You just have to let it move around you."

Aaron pushed up and the bed rolled him against Joey's shoulder. "Fuck." He'd known when he took the exit off the bridge Joey was too hurt to fuck. Why else would Aaron want to spend the night in this disaster of an apartment?

"Don't fight it." Joey tried lying on his back, but sat back up and rolled to his side.

Finally Aaron got the idea to use a pillow—which was, thank you, just the regular kind—to prop Joey up. With the pillow wedged below Joey's shoulder and along his spine, he could lean back while keeping his shoulder off the mattress and the pressure off his collarbone.

With Joey still on his side, his ass pressed right against Aaron's dick. That part of Aaron's body didn't know or care that Joey was hurt, and Aaron considered dragging the ice pack down to force a little self-discipline. At the very least he was going to have to move back some, but then Joey tangled his legs with Aaron's, blowing out a satisfied sigh, like Aaron had just swallowed him to the back of his throat.

"Perfect. Thank you. You're a genius."

Aaron hadn't solved global warming, but you wouldn't know it from the gratitude in Joey's voice. Now Aaron was trapped. If he moved, tried to tip his hips back so his dick wasn't focused on the temptation rubbing warm and firm against it, they'd probably be in for another half an hour of flopping around like landed fish.

The icepack had been on at least fifteen minutes, so he tossed it on the floor and put an arm around Joey's waist just below the sling, fingers gliding across the ripples in his abs. The touch tingled his own skin, like he'd finally scratched an itch he'd been trying to reach all day. Joey's skin heated his hand as if Aaron had wrapped it around a fresh mug of coffee. Warmth flowed up his arm until it pooled at the back of his skull then pumped a peaceful lethargy through his nervous system so that he dropped off without another thought.

Aaron could sleep. Anytime. Anywhere. And wake up fast when he had to. He couldn't have taken care of the kids while working and going to school if he couldn't. So Joey didn't have to make a sound for Aaron to know he was awake. His body became aware of the tension in the muscles under his palm, in the legs between his. The pain must have woken Joey up.

Aaron worked the graveyard shift when the kids were growing up, but he never got used to the way that the dark made even whispers seem loud. "Where are the pills Kim gave you?"

"I don't want them."

"Yes, you do. Don't be stupid." Why did Joey think he suddenly had to fake some tough front?

"I don't like the way they make me feel."

"You don't like pain-free?"

"The codeine makes me feel disconnected and the Flexeril makes me feel like I've just been wiped out by a killer wave."

"So you'd rather suffer."

"It's not so bad."

"Then why are you rocking?"

Joey stopped but the bed kept moving, the contrast making Aaron's stomach lurch. After a moment, a soft hum rose up under his hand.

"Are you singing?"

"Yes?"

Joey didn't have a bad voice—definitely not like the whining cats he'd had playing on his stereo. Light and clear. The melody dragged Aaron back toward sleep until Joey stopped singing. The muscles under Aaron's palm were still tense.

"What about something else? Motrin?"

"Well, there's one thing that helps me sleep, and I don't like to do it with my left hand."

And that was something Aaron could do. "Yeah?" He moved his hand lower, stroking the short hair trailing beneath Joey's navel before rubbing a thumb along the cut over his hip.

Joey jerked forward, setting off the bed. Aaron pressed him back. Motion sickness wasn't sexy. "Don't move."

Joey made a soft sound, like one of the notes he'd been singing, a sound that made Aaron's dick twitch. Since said dick was plastered against Joey's ass, and Aaron had forbidden said ass to move away, not putting said body parts together was going to be torture.

If he got Joey off quickly, Aaron could take care of himself and get back to sleep, but the sounds Joey made were so sweet, Aaron didn't want to rush. He wanted to give Joey as much distraction from the pain as they could handle, bring him to the edge and keep him there, back off then wind him up again.

But Joey had other plans.

As soon as Aaron wrapped his hand around the silky shaft of Joey's dick, he begged, "Fuck me."

Aaron kept stroking, pulling Joey's cock down to give him pressure inside.

"Not enough." Joey sounded as desperate as if they'd been going all night and he still hadn't come.

"I don't want to hurt you."

"Please."

Aaron was starting to realize Joey was damned used to getting whatever he wanted. Something inside said giving in was dangerous, the kind of mistake Aaron would regret, but his dick wasn't listening. It rode the crease of Joey's ass, gliding on sweat and precome, and when Joey tightened around it, that was more than a guy could take.

Aaron lifted his head. Now that he'd been awake for awhile he could see enough to make out the shapes around the room, the glitter of Joey's eyes. "Lube?"

"Next to the alarm clock."

"Condoms?"

"Um. I'm not sure."

That didn't match up with the guy who kept a whole box of new toothbrushes in his bathroom. That kind of readiness should be matched with a condom/lube dispenser fixed over the bed.

"Maybe in the box in the kitchen," Joey suggested.

"Fuck it." Aaron sat up, trying to hook his wallet out from his pants without the bed pitching him onto the floor. Joey following him up didn't help at all. Aaron grabbed Joey's hip and pressed him down again.

He rolled away and snagged his pants. If Joey would stay still, Aaron could definitely get the hang of this bed. What kind of rhythm could they get going if they fucked, if he got Joey on his back, legs around Aaron's hips, the motion slamming them together? He looked down at the sling. Slamming wasn't happening tonight.

He fished a condom out and picked up the lube before sinking back into the swamp mattress.

Joey was a lot less pliant and needy than he'd been with Aaron's hand on his dick. "The bed's tricky to fuck on. Takes skill. Or practice."

"Yeah?" Aaron responded to the challenge before he could stop himself. Manipulative little shit. He pumped some lube over his fingers and rubbed them down Joey's crack.

Joey jumped. "Cold."

"Uh-huh."

Back on solid ground, Aaron smiled as he dipped a finger inside, light and quick, but Joey gasped.

Aaron made sure Joey's body was supported by the pillow between them and then raised himself up so he could watch Joey's face. Though it must have hurt, Joey tipped his head back and winked. Aaron drove in one finger, then two, twisting, pressing with his knuckles, thumb rubbing the skin under Joey's balls, until the grin turned to open-mouthed gasps and there weren't any more winks because Joey couldn't control the lids fluttering over his wide brown eyes. Aaron wasn't pumping his wrist hard, just pressing the gland between his fingers and thumb.

Watching Joey's face, the way he'd bite his lip between gasps, Aaron realized Joey was as helpless as if Aaron had tied him up. With one arm stretched out along the mattress for balance and the other pinned by the sling, Joey couldn't even jerk himself off, couldn't do anything but ride Aaron's fingers, feel what Aaron wanted him to.

"Gonna come if you keep that up." Joey's whisper was hoarse.

"Go ahead."

Joey's eyes screwed shut, ass clamping so hard on Aaron's fingers he couldn't move them.

"Not enough. Want to come with your cock in me."

Aaron didn't appreciate being topped from the bottom, but Joey's voice was so rough Aaron didn't care who was running the show. He rolled the condom on and guided himself in. So hot. So tight. Always that sweet rush of sensation when he got inside, as new and surprising as the first time, and he hoped he never got used to it.

And an ass was an ass, but Joey...Joey milked Aaron's cock all the way, made him want to stay hard inside him all night so he could listen to those sounds in Joey's throat, taste his skin.

Aaron leaned forward to mouth the soft flesh behind Joey's ear, breathing in the sleep-sweat smell, still full of sun and sand despite the trip to the hospital.

Trailing his tongue along Joey's neck and ear, Aaron nudged his way in deeper. With Joey on his side, legs together, it took a couple of thrusts, and Aaron couldn't get all the way in until he grabbed Joey's hips and dragged him back.

Joey let out a sound Aaron could feel, deep in his gut, like when he fired up his bike. Then Joey tried to get the bed rocking, and Aaron had to hold him still because Joey's ass was pulsing around Aaron's cock, and Joey was letting out that deep rough sound again, and Aaron was a crack addict's heartbeat away from losing control.

"Stop," he said as Joey's muscles tightened again.

"Or what?"

Joey wanted to play some more and normally Aaron would be ready for it, but there wasn't a threat he could follow through on with Joey recovering from a dislocated shoulder.

He lifted Joey's leg so he could thrust and bit the top of his ear. "When you're out of that sling, I'll show you *or what* until you can't walk."

Joey's hips rolled against Aaron's, or maybe that was the bed moving with them and against them as Aaron started to stroke. Joey purred, and Aaron would have sworn that wasn't a sound he wanted to hear in bed with him until Joey did it, until it vibrated between them, until it meant Joey needed this as much as Aaron did.

Aaron grabbed Joey's hip again, holding him steady while rolling in circles inside him. They were both sweating now, and every second he stayed like this his dick screamed louder at him to move, to drive into that tight heat until he came. But the bed wasn't sloshing around, and Joey was just silent, breath slowing to match Aaron's, as if Joey could feel what Aaron was waiting for. As if Joey knew the longer they stayed like this, lungs and hearts and bodies working together, the better it would be when they fucked their way to the finish. Aaron bent his head and kissed from freckled shoulder to soft ear, back and forth while he kept up the slow swivel.

Joey's breath sped up along with Aaron's until they were both panting. He didn't have to tell him; Joey hooked his leg up over Aaron's and Aaron finally gave into his dick's demands, moving with short quick thrusts. He reached for Joey's cock, jacking him in the same rhythm, and everything tightened at the same time, the skin under his hand, the ass around his cock, his balls, his teeth on the skin of Joey's neck, everything unbearably tight before it blasted free in long hard shocks.

When Aaron could remember how the muscles in his legs worked, he untangled them and cursed at the bed while struggling up to ditch the rubber and wipe off his hand, Joey's belly and the sling. As the waves died down, he murmured, "Think you can sleep now?"

"Yeah."

Aaron was almost asleep when Joey shifted around so that he looked at Aaron's face.

"I really like your dick in my ass, but that doesn't mean you get to treat me like shit afterwards, okay?"

It was because Aaron was almost asleep, stupid from coming so hard, that he agreed almost instantly. "Okay." But then he thought of the cozy scene with the brothers in the hospital. "But don't get the idea that because I like putting my dick in your ass that this is going to be a meet-the-family and play-house kind of thing."

Joey looked at him steadily. "Okay." He shifted back onto the pillow. In less than a minute, his breath was slow and even with sleep.

Aaron rolled on his back and stared at the ceiling.

The clock said nine thirty when Joey rolled out of his empty bed accompanied by tolerable stabs of pain from his shoulder and followed the sound of Aaron's voice into the living room. The futon-couch was upside down and partially dismembered. Aaron knelt next to it with his bare back to Joey, a screwdriver in one hand and a cell phone pressed to his ear with his chin. Aaron's wet hair was slicked back in its usual ponytail, the ends falling just below the top knob of his spine.

"How many times do I have to tell you? Miss some safety shots too, or they'll know you're hustling."

Joey retreated into the bathroom, but Aaron's voice

followed him.

"You dragged your brother into this? Christ, Dylan. Put him on."

It's not like Joey was trying to eavesdrop, since he was starting to think this conversation might violate the whole meet-the-family prohibition Aaron had made last night. Though taking Joey's couch apart seemed a bit like playing house to him.

"Bullshit." There was a bang which made Joey wonder if his couch would ever stand on its stubby legs again. "Put him on now." Aaron's forceful growl. The commanding voice that made Joey's dick hard and leaking when Aaron used it in bed—or even out of it. Thank God, Joey'd already pissed.

"Darryl. Do not help your brother hustle pool. Do not stake him when he's hustling pool. Do not shill for him if he's hustling pool. Are we clear?"

Joey brushed his teeth, but Aaron's voice was audible even over the water.

"Good. Because I will so come to Texas and kick both your asses. Put your brother back on."

There was only so much stalling Joey could do in the bathroom, but at least the toothbrush in his mouth had kept him from asking where in Texas. It was only the biggest state Joey'd lived in. Assuming he had a connection was ridiculous. He shut off the water and dried his hands. He went back into the living room. Aaron was tossing the screwdriver into the air, spinning it and catching the handle each time. The couch appeared to be roughly in the same shape as it had been before.

"I don't care what I did. You need money ask me for it... Dylan. Your brother is not you. He doesn't know how to fight. You're going to get him killed. You want to see that?"

Joey remembered the picture of the smiling twins in graduation gowns on Aaron's entertainment center. His brothers.

"Good." Aaron slapped the phone shut.

Joey moved to stand in front of him. "What happened?"

Aaron's eyes narrowed. "I thought I said—"

Joey pointed at the wreckage of his couch. "Did it need emergency surgery?"

"You put the legs on backward."

"What do you mean? There were four legs, four spots."

"But they were supposed to be angled like this." Aaron screwed in the last of the legs and lifted the couch upright.

"Maybe I liked the way it leaned." Joey went into the kitchen and started looking for his cereal. He could have sworn he left it on the counter.

"What are you looking for?" Aaron leaned in the doorway in nothing but unbuttoned jeans, long flat muscles on display, right down to the cuts over his hips. Joey's stomach forgot about breakfast as it did a round-trip bounce to his feet.

"Um, breakfast."

"Yeah, well, you don't have any food."

Joey located the box in one of the cabinets. "I have Cocoa Puffs."

"That's not food."

"It is with sugar and milk on it."

"You don't have any milk."

Joey opened the fridge. "Shit." But there had been milk left in the carton yesterday when he went to work. He looked at the carton in the garbage and back at Aaron.

"I could only find instant coffee. It was disgusting."

Joey shook out a handful of Cocoa Puffs and stuffed them in his mouth.

Aaron shut his eyes. "Take a shower and put on some clothes. I'll get you some breakfast."

Joey could be mouthing his way down that flat chest before Aaron opened his eyes again. But Joey was hungry and his mouth was full of Cocoa Puffs.

When they went out into the parking lot, Joey headed for Aaron's bike, but Aaron pulled him back, gently. "Not with that sling on. Where's your puke green car?"

95

"It's seafoam pearl." Joey pointed. His attempt at a superior tone was ruined when a laugh snuck out. It was a strange color and a stupid name, but he'd liked it when he'd seen it in the catalog. Tossing Aaron the keys, Joey asked, "You don't trust my balance?"

Aaron made a sound somewhere between a cough and a laugh but it was too short to tell the difference. As Aaron popped the locks, Joey waited at the passenger door for his answer.

Aaron put a hand flat on the roof of the car. "Would you trust our lives on your balance with that sling on?"

Joey blinked. His life, yeah, but someone else's?

Aaron nodded, and they climbed into the car.

"Sure you can drive stick?" Joey fumbled as he tried to lock in his seatbelt one-handed.

Aaron looked over at him with half-lidded eyes and a smile tickling his lips. "Yeah. I can handle it." He covered Joey's hand with his own and clicked the belt into place.

Joey's gut clenched tight on the handful of Cocoa Puffs, and his dick pressed against the buttons of his jeans, blood rushing down so fast he got dizzy. Shit. Joey should have blown Aaron in the kitchen this morning.

The smile spread to half Aaron's mouth and he rubbed his thumb across Joey's lips as if he knew Joey was thinking about wrapping his lips around Aaron's cock.

"Later," Aaron said as he started the car.

Joey expected that breakfast would be in some diner full of bikers and waitresses with big hair, but Aaron drove across the river and pulled into an International House of Pancakes parking lot.

Joey looked at the familiar blue-peaked roof. "IHOP?"

"Someplace you like more?"

There wasn't. Joey could always eat at IHOP. It was after the breakfast rush of a weekday morning, so they were seated immediately. Aaron offered the biggest smile Joey had seen so far to the waitress who filled his coffee cup.

Wait, no.

She poured a cup for Joey and took his order for juice and sweet tea with a wide smile of her own.

"Planning to float on all that?"

Just in time, Joey remembered not to shrug. "The Cocoa Puffs were dry."

Aaron made another cough/laugh and opened his menu. Joey didn't bother; he always got the same thing. Chocolate chip pancakes with whipped cream and a side of bacon. Aaron made a face when he placed his own order for a Spanish omelet.

As the waitress walked away, Aaron started drumming his fingers on the table. He'd been the one to suggest breakfast, to drive them here, and now that he'd had his first cup of coffee he seemed ready to leave.

"What's the weirdest rescue you ever had?" Joey asked, hoping he could start a conversation that would forestall a reversion to ass-hatted behavior.

"My first decapitation is a pretty vivid memory."

"I'll bet."

"But as far as someone living, one time we got called down to the pier to pick up a woman who'd been out at sea and rescued by a yacht."

Joey watched Aaron's face as he told his story. His eyes got a little unfocused as if he were still seeing the whole thing, long-fingered hands only moving when he needed emphasis.

"No one knew she was missing. She'd been out alone, in a sailboat. Overturned. She had an air pocket in the cabin, but she was pinned by the way the boat had rolled. Survived for over a week on some fruit floating around. So dehydrated, stuck in all that water she couldn't drink. I'd have gone nuts."

"Wow." Joey wanted to know what Aaron had survived to put that admiration in his voice. Because Joey got it. Shit happened, even if you were too young to remember it. You either fought and won or you died.

The waitress was back with bigger smiles for both of them as she put down the plates. She didn't look old enough to be

K.A. Mitchell

out of high school. Joey wondered if she had a scary survival story, a kid at home, family to support. He'd leave her a big tip.

Joey grabbed the butter pecan syrup and started pouring.

"You all right with your left?"

Joey could even manage legible if over-large writing with his left hand. Eating wouldn't be an issue. "Why?"

"I wasn't sure if you normally used a whole bottle of syrup on your pancakes."

Joey put the bottle back. "Normally, I do."

Ignoring the disgust on Aaron's face, Joey dipped a strip of bacon in the syrup puddle on his plate. "The toughest thing at my job is surviving the patchouli all the wannabe hippies wear. They leave it in a trail, and the smell lasts for hours."

A palpable freeze put a layer of ice on Joey's coffee. Well, that was a conversational bomb. He wondered what part had triggered the chill. Patchouli? Hippies? He hacked at the pancakes with his fork and dragged a chunk to his mouth. Washing it down with some tea, he licked the syrup off his chin.

The action started a thaw. Aaron's eyes warmed as they tracked the motion of Joey's tongue. On the next forkful, he made sure to get syrup all over his lips.

Aaron took a long drink of coffee as Joey cleaned away the syrup, slowly. "Your ass gonna cash that check?"

"Or my mouth." Joey drank some juice.

"Works for me."

As it turned out, Joey didn't have to worry about leaving a big tip for the waitress. The looks passing between them meant breakfast was going down fast. Joey sealed the deal by keeping a nice shine on his lips. When he licked some of the syrup off his wrist, Aaron grabbed the check the waitress had dropped off and threw a ten on the table for the tip.

"Now."

Joey scrambled out of the booth and followed. He tried to blow Aaron in the car, but the sling got in the way, and Aaron took up too much space in the front seat of the Yaris. When they crossed the river and missed the turn to Joey's apartment,

98

Aaron cut short Joey's question.

"If we go there, we're doing it in the elevator."

Joey wondered if anything in his six-month lease covered that.

They were in Aaron's garage a few steps from the door when Aaron hauled Joey close and licked the sweet taste still on his lips and the inside of his mouth and possibly his throat. Joey tried to smile, but then the syrup flavor in his mouth got darker and richer sharing it with Aaron. When they both groaned, Joey dropped to his knees on the cement.

Aaron fell back against the wall, tools clanging to the floor as he hit them with his shoulder. Damn, Joey wanted to do this in a bed, somewhere he could get a better angle, but everything was moving too fast for finesse. He barely had time to tease with the ball on his tongue, to flick and press it against Aaron's slit before Aaron started jerking, desperate noises coming from between his clenched teeth. Joey opened his jaw and let Aaron fuck his way inside, trying to relax enough to let him pop the head past the muscle of Joey's throat. With his tongue running along the vein on the underside of the thick cock in his mouth, Joey felt the pulse that meant Aaron was coming. Joey could have pulled off, but he wanted it. Wanted everything. Every salty bitter drop.

He wiped his chin with his hand, and Aaron reached down to help him up.

"Jesus Christ." Aaron let his head fall back against the pegboard.

Leaning in, Joey licked along the sweaty skin of Aaron's neck to his ear, rolling the ball over the curves. Aaron's wet dick kissed Joey's belly under his shirt, and Joey rocked his own cock against Aaron's thigh.

Spinning Joey around, Aaron pinned Joey to his chest with an arm around his waist. "If I'm going to be doing this for awhile, I'd better learn how to get it right." He yanked open Joey's jeans and tugged his cock free of his briefs. "Tell me."

"Under my balls first. Rub."

Aaron found the right spot immediately, dragging out shudders until he had to steady Joey with a free hand.

"And I like it wet."

Aaron brought his palm up to Joey's mouth, and he licked it, soaked it, tonguing between the fingers.

"Long strokes. Slow, but hard."

Aaron's hand was bigger than Joey's, calloused in different spots, but the stroke had him sliding into the rhythm. He glanced down to watch and covered Aaron's hand with his left.

"Rougher. Drag it tight on the head."

The build was sweet. Joey's lids got heavier but he didn't want to stop watching the red head of his cock in the tight circle of Aaron's brown fingers.

Aaron's deep voice in Joey's ear tickled like a tongue on his skin. "Do you fuck yourself?"

"Sometimes."

"Fingers? Dildo?"

"Yes." Joey's ass clenched around the imagined pressure, but it only made him want to be fucked more.

Aaron behind him, hand gripping his hip, rough dirty whispers and his hand pulling harder, faster, until Joey wanted to beg for a dick in his ass.

"How big?" Aaron's hand slid back, inside the loosened waist of Joey's jeans, and gripped one cheek in a hot hand, squeezing hard enough to bruise.

His balls drew up, tingling right on the edge. Aaron's thumb dipped into the crease.

"Fuck." Joey wanted to wait, wanted Aaron's thumb in him, dry or not, but the wet friction on his dick was too much to ignore. Aaron jacked him with the tight strokes Joey loved, and when Aaron twisted his wrist on the head, Joey couldn't fight it anymore. It started with a wrench that was almost painful and then it was sweet and thick as syrup, pumping pleasure through his dick, his thighs, his ass.

"Fuck," he panted again as he looked at the rope of come he'd shot across his shirt.

Aaron slowed until he was thumbing the head, wringing out the last little jerks of so-good, stopping just when Joey would have shoved him away.

The low rumble in his ear startled Joey until he realized it was the first time he'd heard Aaron laugh.

"I think I've got something else you can wear. It'd be hard to pass that off as a syrup stain from breakfast."

Aaron found him a shirt that wasn't too big on him, and Joey bit his lip rather than ask whose it was. Darryl's? Dylan's? It had come from behind one of the closed doors in the hall. As Aaron made himself some fresh coffee, Joey rummaged in the fridge for something cold. His fingers finally tightened on a bottle in the back, behind two different kinds of energy drinks, canned espresso and a half-empty six pack of Sam Adams. Guy liked his caffeine.

Joey had pulled the bottle out enough to see he'd found some iced tea when Aaron said, "If you make your orthopedic appointment in the morning, I'll drive you. But I have to be in at three. Every day but Monday."

Joey's mind went a little blank, and he tried not to drop the bottle. And he'd thought the sound of Aaron laughing was a shock. Last night he'd made it pretty clear what he wanted from Joey, and it didn't extend to wanting to drive him to doctors' appointments. Despite the fact that Joey still felt that perfect wave of *him* every time they were close enough to share breath, he'd been willing to accept Aaron's ultimatum, as long as he accepted Joey's. Providing taxi service went beyond not treating Joey like shit. It was nice. But he didn't want Aaron to think he couldn't handle things on his own.

"I can take a cab. Or get someone from work to drive me." Joey straightened up.

"Well, if the appointment's in the afternoon you'll have to. But if I come with you, I can tell you if the doctor's feeding you a line of bullshit."

"Social work gives me a pretty fine bullshit detector." Joey poured some of the iced tea down his bruised throat.

"I'd have thought that was the basis of your education."

Joey swallowed quickly enough to cough. "What?"

"Bullshit." Aaron leaned against the counter, eyes narrowed in a challenging stare.

So that was what had provoked the chill at breakfast. Aaron didn't like social workers. Wouldn't be the first time Joey'd met someone with that opinion. Sometimes Joey didn't like them much either.

He downed more tea. "Which part is bullshit? Psychology or sociology?"

"You could have just rubbed your chin and said, 'Now what makes you feel that way?'" Aaron finished in an exaggerated German accent. "It's all bullshit, so keep it to yourself."

Someone in the social sciences had seriously fucked up at some point in Aaron's life, but it wasn't Joey and he wasn't going to take shit for it. The counselor in him wanted to dig deeper, but the part of him that wanted Aaron's cock in his ass again was smarter than that. And damn if that part wasn't going to get what it wanted. He finished the iced tea, put the bottle on the counter and started for the living room.

"Where are you going?"

Joey turned back and leaned across the counter separating them. "I'm going to go sit down while I wait for you to get over your hissy fit and drive me home."

Joey didn't know exactly what reaction to expect, which was unusual for him. But despite a glimpse here and there, Aaron was hard to figure out.

What he got was another of those one-syllable laughs that sounded like it was forced from Aaron's diaphragm with a punch and a sneer. "Fuck you. I am not having a hissy fit. You can't handle criticism about your job. What are you all—saints, sacrificing yourselves for the greater good?"

"Don't you think that's what you are? Self-sacrificing to save people?"

"I save lives."

"That baby could have died in that meth house."

"And what, he's better off now? Half a dozen placements,

ten foster homes and then maybe if he's lucky he can end up in jail getting three squares and a bed courtesy of the taxpayer." Aaron leaned forward over the counter.

Joey was starting to piece it together. The pictures of Aaron's family—all step or half siblings—probably meant some kind of social service intervention.

"So I should have left him there? Is that the adrenaline-junkie's paramedical decision?"

"Because you do-gooders and your system knows what's best for everyone. No matter how much it fucks up someone's life."

Aaron was so close to him now, close enough for Joey to smell him—sweat and come and coffee—and Joey's dick was done with risking a chance to get Aaron in bed again. No more digging.

"Look, I don't know what social worker pissed in your cornflakes, but it wasn't me. So." Joey grinned. "Is this where we have angry sex?"

Aaron's face was expressionless for an instant and then he started laughing. Not the soft murmur from the garage or the bitter cough. Deep genuine laughter. His face going from hard-edged sexy to beautiful as the laugh lit his eyes, arched his cheeks, reddened his lips.

He folded his arms on the counter and leaned in until his lips were an inch from Joey's. "Is that what you do when you're losing an argument? Shake your ass at it?"

"It's worked so far." Joey's grin widened, the ball on his tongue flicking against his teeth.

"It's a good thing you didn't try to be a lawyer. Wouldn't be as effective in court."

"My parents wanted me to be. I started talking when I was one."

"Imagine my surprise." Aaron leaned the extra inch and kissed him.

Chapter Eight

They didn't have angry sex.

Aaron shouldn't have been surprised at how quickly things heated up between them, either. By the time Aaron remembered the sling and stopped trying to drag the guy over the counter, Joey was already groaning into his mouth. Aaron went around to kiss him without cabinets and Formica in the way, and Joey rocked his already-hard dick into Aaron's groin. If it weren't for the sling, Aaron would have fucked Joey right over the counter. But not because Aaron was angry.

The sight of Joey, all five and a half feet of him, glaring him down and calling him an adrenaline junkie still made him smile. The little shit wasn't afraid of anyone, but he wasn't mean or obnoxious, like a yippy miniature Doberman. Joey simply believed what he said, believed all the bullshit, that the system worked, that people wanted to be happy, kind of like Sheree—except for the fact that Joey had a seriously hot ass that Aaron was two minutes from plowing and Sheree was his sister so...no. And he needed her out of his head right the hell now.

Spreading his legs so their cocks rubbed together took care of that. Aaron wasn't thinking about anything but his dick and the ass under his hands. Of course, that was all fine until he lifted his head for air. Which Joey didn't need since he started talking right away.

"So if this is angry sex, do you think I could throw you on the bed and make you fuck me?"

"You could try, but I think with the sling, I'll handle throwing myself. You can watch."

Aaron led the way into his bedroom and stripped before flinging himself into the center of the bed.

Joey unfastened his jeans and moved close enough for Aaron to push them off. When Joey got Darryl's T-shirt tangled around his sling, Aaron started laughing again. He stood and unhooked the sling long enough to get him free. Maybe while Joey was around neither of them should bother with clothes.

Aaron rolled over to grab the lube and a condom, and when he came back, Joey got his hand on Aaron's dick, working it in awkward strokes.

"Dude, you do suck with your left hand."

"No, I suck like this." Joey smiled as he lowered his head to wrap his lips around the head of Aaron's cock.

The steel ball flicked under the head, over and over, until Aaron was aching with the need to thrust. It would take an hour to come like this with that too-quick, too-light pressure but damn, it would be a hell of an hour. Joey lifted his head and licked his lips.

Aaron slicked his fingers with lube. "Get up here."

Straddling Aaron's body, Joey knee-walked up until his dick was touching Aaron's lips, that fucking grin still in place.

One hand holding Joey's hips to keep him from moving closer, Aaron kissed the tip and slid his other hand beneath Joey's balls. Aaron stroked the smooth skin with slippery fingers, rolled the balls across his palm. Joey could have pulled free, pushed his cock past Aaron's lips, but that wasn't part of the game. And Aaron wondered how far Joey wanted to play.

Parting his lips enough to take the tip into his mouth, Aaron sucked under the crown while running a thumb down Joey's crease to his hole. Steady pressure on his hip warned Joey to stay still as Aaron popped his thumb past the tight muscle. He felt Joey's body react, felt the contractions on his hip as he tried not to move, tasted the need in the precome leaking from his slit. Aaron took Joey's cock deeper, tongue sweeping over the weight, the silky-tight skin, before pressing it up against the roof of his mouth. The muscles squeezed Aaron's thumb as he sucked harder, worked the thick cock to the back of his throat.

When he pumped with his thumb, Joey's hand slapped down on Aaron's chest. "Stop."

He pulled his head back, letting Joey's dick slide across his cheek.

"Show some fucking self-control," he growled, but his lips curved as he twisted his thumb and started a long tight bob on Joey's cock, mouth mimicking the way Joey'd said he liked being jacked.

Joey frowned for a second, brow wrinkled in concentration. Aaron wanted to put his other thumb inside, rub them against each other, thick and rough in Joey's ass, pull him apart, while Joey fought the orgasm building in his balls. But with Joey's arm in a sling, Aaron wasn't sure Joey could keep his balance if Aaron moved his hand off Joey's hip.

From the way Joey was biting into his lip, one thumb and Aaron's mouth were enough to make Joey work hard to hold back. Aaron drew it out as long as he could stand it, watching the sweat break out along Joey's hairline, the way his mouth went slack before he regained his concentration, the way his chin kept dropping to his chest as his eyes squeezed shut. When the pressure of smooth, wet walls on his thumb made his dick too jealous to wait, Aaron pulled his hand away and let Joey slide from his mouth again.

A nudge on his hip and Joey was sliding back. He worked the condom down Aaron's dick and lifted himself on one foot and one knee. Slicking the latex, Aaron guided his dick in as Joey lowered himself, stopping with the head halfway.

Christ, tight pressure right on the head, squeezing him. From the way Joey licked his lips he was enjoying the stretch, so why had he stopped? Aaron tipped his head to see Joey's eyes. He was plotting something with his I'm-gonna-get-what-I-want look, chin stuck out.

Aaron raised the hand holding Joey's hip and brought it

down with a stinging slap against Joey's ass. "Take it."

A hard clench on Aaron's dick as Joey's body reacted to the spank. Oh, he definitely liked to play.

Aaron laid another sharp smack right over the last one. Joey groaned and took him in all the way. Every time they did it, Aaron swore the little blond couldn't work his cock tighter or better, but Joey did, not even moving but pulsing his muscles all around him, the soft walls closing in hot sweet pressure.

Joey looked at him with a challenge in his stubborn jaw, and Aaron spanked him again. "Move."

The slaps and the way he took Aaron deep and fast didn't have any effect on Joey's erection but to make it leak and twitch.

"Now." The word snapped and timed with his hand on Joey's ass.

Joey got up on his knees and rocked, sliding up and down on Aaron's dick, muscles flexing. Balancing himself with a hand on Aaron's shoulder, Joey rode him, slamming down so his ass slapped against Aaron's thighs with every stroke. Aaron put another handprint on him, listening to the husky groan Joey made as the heat hit him.

Aaron grabbed the hot skin in his hands. "Faster."

Joey moved, fast enough that the sweat started to drip onto Aaron's chest. Each time he squeezed Joey's ass, he let out a deeper moan and slammed down harder.

"So." Joey's voice was rough with exertion, the words broken into the rhythm of their bodies. "Is. This. Angry. Sex?"

"Not even close."

The way Joey tightened around him made the last vowel drag out into a moan.

Aaron worked his hips to meet Joey, to meet the hot skin as it slapped back down. Joey's hair stuck to his forehead now, the front strands long enough to get in his eyes. Aaron reached up and pushed it back, and Joey smiled down, the look in his eyes making heat spread out from Aaron's gut.

He grabbed Joey harder and brought his still-stinging palm

down in a loud smack.

Joey's eyes opened wide with surprise but he kept rocking, fingers squeezing Aaron's shoulder.

"Need," Joey panted.

Aaron rubbed his hand over the burning skin of Joey's ass.

"Need what?"

"Jerk me off."

Aaron brought his knees up to give Joey some support, and Joey leaned back, teeth almost tearing through his lips as the shift pushed Aaron's cock forward inside. Joey's eyes stayed squeezed shut.

Aaron fisted Joey's dick, jacking him fast and tight and hard. Joey's hips moved in quick jerks as he worked himself on Aaron's cock, worked it against the gland inside him, worked it until they were both right up under the edge.

Joey's dick pulsed against Aaron's palm, skin tensing, and he let his own body run right up the ramp with Joey's. The first splash of warmth up on his pec sent Aaron over, shooting into the rubber inside Joey, long shivering pulses of pleasure that forced deep groans from his chest. Joey collapsed on top of him and Aaron reached down to grab the end of the rubber before he slipped out.

As Joey slid off onto his side, Aaron saw Joey'd managed to get more come on his sling. He'd have to snag another one for him off the truck tonight.

They argued again when Aaron made Joey wait while Aaron checked the traffic alerts on the computer. Joey tried not to roll his eyes in impatience. They weren't going to be late for anything, what did it matter if there was traffic?

And then Aaron pissed him off again when he pulled Joey toward the pickup instead of Joey's Yaris to take him back home.

"This way I can put my bike in the back. It's not like you can drive it anyway."

Joey couldn't, but it was his car. And given Aaron's tendency to disappear for more than a week, Joey'd rather his car sat in his parking lot than Aaron's driveway.

"Unless you want to stay here."

Joey thought maybe he'd made that up in his head. But Aaron was waiting for an answer, standing next to him, drumming his fingers on the doorframe.

What happened to not playing house? The words caught in Joey's throat as he thought of Aaron's expression shutting back down, no laughing, no quick smiles. Joey could call him on his bullshit or he could see how it played out. "I'd rather go home. Thanks." He smiled. "I think I'll make it into the truck by myself."

"Try not to break something else."

Aaron pulled into a convenience store a minute later.

"Do you want me to pay for the gas?" Joey asked.

"No, I'm just going to grab you some food."

Joey liked being taken care of from time to time, but this didn't feel like consideration, it felt like his life being rearranged to suit Aaron. "I'll be fine."

"All right, then I'm going to get some stuff for me."

Joey wasn't pouting exactly, but he stayed in the truck while Aaron went in. Joey didn't know why his mood had gone sour. But when Aaron backed out of his driveway leaving Joey's car behind—even though he knew he couldn't drive it—he felt like Aaron was treating him like an accident about to happen, something he could patch up in his ambulance and send on to the ER.

Aaron came out with a full bag and another cup of coffee.

"So do you ever let the blood level rise in your caffeine-stream?" Joey shifted his legs to make room for the bag on the floor.

"Not if I can help it." Tossing the empty cup from the holder out the window, Aaron put his fresh coffee in its place.

Joey pushed open the door.

"Where are you going?"

"To pick that up."

"Are you fucking serious?"

"Uh-huh." Joey stepped down and went around the front of the truck to grab the cup. He walked over and tossed it in the dumpster, feeling Aaron's stare all the way.

When Joey climbed back in the truck, Aaron turned to give Joey the full effect of that icy-blue glare. "What the hell was that about?"

"Why can't you just put it in the trash?"

"What the fuck difference does it make?"

"What the fuck difference does it make to you that I did?"

"Fine." Aaron dropped the truck into reverse and backed out of the lot.

As soon as Aaron pulled up next to his bike in the parking lot of Joey's apartment building, Joey jumped down from the truck. Though being in a hurry to get back to his still-in-boxes apartment seemed stupid.

"Hey," Aaron called. "I replaced your milk." He dug a carton from the bag on the floor and handed it to Joey. "Don't forget to recycle." Aaron's lips twitched.

"Thanks, but I think I'm becoming lactose intolerant." Joey put the milk back on the seat and slammed the door. Paying Aaron back for that smirk was completely worth dry Cocoa Puffs.

Joey was able to get an orthopedic appointment for ten thirty the day after tomorrow. When he called the doctor Kim had recommended, the receptionist told him Doctor Kim had called to make sure Joey got in quickly.

He poked at a couple of boxes until he found the one that had his TV. The apartment came with cable, but he hadn't bothered to hook it up. He hadn't planned on spending a lot of time in these three little rooms. If he hooked up his MP3, he'd end up playing music that aggravated his mood, which right now was a combination of boredom, anger and disappointment.

And he had a playlist for all three. Maybe he could go back to work after his appointment.

Despite his shoulder, he managed to get the TV free of its box and set it up on top of a box of books. The freshly arranged bones and muscles in his shoulder didn't cause a tenth as much pain as they did yesterday, just a deep-down ache and a sharper reminder each time he thought about shrugging or snagging something with his right hand.

His ass didn't hurt either, just a tingling warmth when he'd pulled his jeans on after they fucked. It hadn't taken Aaron long to figure that kink out, and give it to Joey as perfectly as he did everything else to Joey's body, the arrogant fucking asshole.

After Giles, he'd been afraid to ask any of his lovers for it. Giles had always taken it a little far, like he wanted to make Joey feel wrong for liking the rough stuff so much. Noah wouldn't. Mark would, but it was so safe, perfect trust protected by rules. It was like riding a man-made wave, everything controlled and predictable. No risk, no hanging on the edge wondering how far you could go, how far he would push. Nothing like fucking Aaron.

Joey picked up his phone and considered whether he could get away with just sending Noah a text to let him know how he was doing. Knowing how pissed he'd be if Noah did that to him, Joey opened the phonebook and called Adam.

He accepted the scolding from Noah's sister-in-law about not telling them he was in Jacksonville, and then waited while she went to find Noah. It wasn't just Maria and Adam, Noah's parents, too, had made Joey feel part of the family. Sometimes he thought losing them was a part of what had made leaving Noah so hard, so that it took him months to finally make the break after realizing Noah wasn't ever going to get over Cameron Lewis.

"How's your shoulder?"

For the first time, Noah's deep resonant voice didn't make Joey wistful. "Fine. It's a lot better. I'm going to the doctor in a couple days, and he'll probably send me back to work."

"And how's what's-his-name?"

"Huh?"

"Your voice is fucked out, like you've had a dick down your throat."

"It is not," Joey protested.

"I notice you don't deny the dick part. Hey, listen, the ER doctor talked to Adam. Says what's-his-name—"

"Aaron."

"Aaron's an all-right guy. But. Joey...just don't expect too much."

"What if I'd said that to you about Cameron two years ago?"

"I'd have told you to fuck off. And fuck your Masters in Counseling, turning that back on me. Did you hear what I said?"

"Don't expect too much. Right." Joey should have just sent a text. Why didn't he get to expect it all? Why was he supposed to settle for something, not try to get what other people had?

"Joey, I'm sorry. I just—I want—fuck it. Maybe I'm a little bit jealous."

"Of me or Aaron?"

"Fuck you. Sometimes it's a little hard seeing you use those eyes on someone else."

"You just miss Cameron. When's he coming back?"

"Not for another fucking week. But it's his longest trip this year. Do you want company?"

"No." But Joey answered too quickly.

"Aaron's there?"

He might be later. Or not. He hadn't said a word when Joey slammed the car door. Not that Joey had left room for mature conversation. He couldn't remember when he'd ever gotten pissed off so fast by a guy, although a poll of his exes would probably reveal that Joey did a good job of pissing them off.

He was designing the statistical analysis in his head when he realized he hadn't answered Noah—mostly because Noah was calling his name.

"No, he's at work."

"Call after you talk to the doctor, okay? I'll be back at work by then."

"Okay."

Joey struggled with a couple more boxes, but trying to put things away with one hand was too frustrating. He managed to excavate a box of condoms though, and throw them on the box he was using as a nightstand. If Aaron did show up, at least he wouldn't know Joey hadn't unpacked them because he hadn't had sex with anyone since he moved to Jacksonville.

A heavy rain storm approached, and all the local news stations had blinking emergency boxes showing the radar going from dark green to yellow and red as it hit the city at sunset. Joey dozed off to the sound of rain pounding the windows.

Aaron rubbed himself raw with the thin towel, but the shower wasn't enough. Ten wouldn't be enough. An accident like that and all the gloves and raingear in the world couldn't keep the blood off you. Even in a downpour.

Hennie met him outside of the locker room, her chin tilted in question. Usually after a night like this they hit the bar a block from her apartment and Aaron crashed on her couch. Exactly how many drinks would it take to forget how the little girl had looked as she bled out even as he was trying to get a bag in her? At least a fifth to not see her eyes pop open that last second when they lost her.

Aaron shook his head.

Hennie shrugged and knocked out a cigarette as they hit the parking lot together. It was still raining, though not the blinding torrents that had put Mandy Howard in a drawer with a toe tag instead of safely on her way to Disney World when her dad missed the sign showing the twenty-mile-an-hour turn on the fucking interstate. Her mom was in a drawer next to her, Dad in a coma upstairs.

Aaron slid into his pickup and didn't even try to justify

taking the first exit off the bridge. The route was the same one that led to the bars, but that wasn't where he was heading and he knew it. What he wanted tonight was to bury all that blood and death inside Joey. Pour it down his throat, fuck it into his ass until Aaron was clean again.

When he knocked at 3R of the Parkview Apartments, he realized it was two thirty, but Joey answered. And when Aaron saw that smile, he couldn't. Didn't want to give any of the black despair inside him to a guy who smiled like that when Aaron dragged himself to his door in the middle of the night, to a guy who smelled like sunshine and the ocean.

To Joey.

From the looks of the lighted living room, Joey hadn't even been to bed yet. The TV was on and an empty chip bag sat next to a glass of water.

"Hungry?" Joey asked.

Aaron dragged his gaze from the chip bag. "No." Not hungry. Not with Mandy's wide-open, terrified eyes still there every time he blinked. Joey sat on the couch.

"I have to admit, it's more comfortable since you fixed it."

"You think?" Aaron sat next to him. But he didn't know why. If he wasn't going to fuck Joey what the hell was Aaron doing here?

Joey leaned in and Aaron met him halfway, lifting his arm to stretch out over the top of the lumpy cushion instead of putting weight on Joey's shoulders.

"It doesn't hurt."

Aaron turned to look at him.

"Much," Joey amended. He shifted closer, hair smelling like coconuts. The conditioner Aaron had found in the bathroom this morning explained that, but not the rest of the beach smell. And Jesus, Joey was warm. Aaron didn't know how cold he was from the rain until Joey pressed against him.

"What are you watching?"

"Mostly insomnia commercials."

"For sleeping pills?"

"No, the kind of commercials that are on in the middle of the night. Miracle diets, make your dick bigger, God's Greatest Hits. Guilt-reducing, life-altering, soul-saving solutions for only nineteen ninety-five plus shipping and handling."

Joey's words were so bitter, Aaron moved away to look down at him.

"What?" Joey asked.

"Sounds like something I would say."

"What, I don't get to be cynical?"

"I thought you believed in making things better."

"I do. But nineteen ninety-five isn't going to make anything better."

"And picking up a coffee cup will?"

"Yes."

Aaron let his head drop back against the cushion. What the hell did a coffee cup matter with the smell of blood and bowels still burning inside his sinuses?

"What happened?" Joey asked.

"Nothing I need counseling for, Do-gooder. Just a shit day at work."

"Want to go to bed?"

There was another offer tucked in there. It wouldn't have to be about burying the image of Mandy's eyes, frightened, pleading. It could be nothing more than fucking, two bodies pumping toward release. But Aaron didn't even want that. He just wanted to smell and touch, feel Joey's live skin next to his own.

The bed rolled them together.

"I can lie on my back now."

Aaron put his head over Joey's heart.

"We should go to Disney World."

"Fuck that." Aaron lifted his head and rolled away, the bed tossing him to the rail.

"It's only a couple hours away, and it's the happiest place on earth, right?"

"Fuck prepackaged happiness. The only happy people in this world are the ones who don't know what the fuck is going on."

Joey shifted onto his left side and ran a hand down Aaron's face, over his arm with warm, solid fingers. "What do you want?"

"Sleep." Aaron turned facedown into the sweet-smelling pillow.

Joey's hand stroked along Aaron's back, kneaded the muscles around his spine.

"But that's nice too," Aaron admitted.

Joey was a lot better at left-handed massage than left-handed jacking. The warmth left by his hand stayed on the skin, spreading deep into the muscles, down to chilled bones. Fingers drifted over Aaron's ass.

"Do you ever?"

"Sometimes."

"Do you want it now?"

"I just want to go to sleep."

Joey started back at Aaron's neck, knuckles working the knots before shifting to his shoulders. That would have been fine, but then Joey said, "I saw it. The accident. On the news. You were there."

Fucking cameras were everywhere. Aaron jerked away. "What part of 'I want to sleep' is so confusing for you?"

Joey didn't reach for him again, but after he fell asleep, Aaron turned back to face Joey, threading his fingers through his hair. The roots growing in were much softer than the fuzzy yellow ends, especially over the shaved part. The new hair tickled Aaron's palm as he moved his hand. When Joey curled into him, Aaron didn't roll away.

The first time he woke up, Joey was behind him, head on Aaron's shoulder, sling poking his back, pubes tickling his ass. And hot like a wool blanket. Aaron peeled him off and rolled onto his stomach. When he woke again, closer to dawn, somehow Joey had ended up on the other side of him, ass pressed into Aaron's groin, shoulder under Aaron's chin. Aaron took a deep breath of sweet coconuts and slipped right back under.

Joey woke up with a dick in his ass. Well, not completely in his ass—like he would have minded. A slow fuck was a hell of a way to wake up, though getting a cock in his ass wasn't something he could sleep through unless he was majorly drunk. Right now, Aaron's morning wood was riding the crease of Joey's ass, tip in the small of his back. He started to move and the heavy weight of Aaron's arm across his stomach pulled him back.

"Not today." Aaron's voice was even sexier in the morning, sleep blurring the consonants more than his usual soft accent, the tone deep and rough.

"What?"

"You're not sneaking out of bed this morning."

Joey didn't bother to point out that Aaron was the one who'd given up on morning sex yesterday by leaving Joey in bed and going off to yell on the phone and dismantle the couch. Reminding him of that would be counterproductive since it didn't take a degree in psychology to know Aaron was enough of a control freak to interpret Joey reasonably stating his case as a challenge worthy of an argument, and that would be the end of morning sex.

And Aaron whispering, "You said you can lie on your back? Want it on your back?" with his consonants still soft and blurry was way sexier than anything Rene had ever muttered in his broken French.

"Yeah."

Aaron lifted his arm, and Joey rolled onto his back. The waterbed cradled his shoulder without pressure, even when Aaron lifted Joey's hips onto a pillow. After Joey nodded okay to the question in Aaron's eyes, he began to kiss and tongue his way down Joey's chest, a hard suck on a nipple, a quick bite over his hip. When Aaron moved lower, Joey spread his legs. He hadn't exactly woken up uninterested, and by the time Aaron was licking the inside of Joey's thighs, his dick was leaking against his belly.

Aaron looked up at him, and Joey could see how much Aaron needed this. Not the way he had needed him last night, when he didn't seem to want what Joey expected. What Aaron needed now was to put things back on familiar ground. Fucking. Not comfort. Not holding someone so you didn't have to think about how life sometimes sucked. Just having fun. Getting off.

The realization that Aaron had felt the shift in the way things were between them and was now working to get things back to what was comfortable for him made Joey smile. Okay. This side of Aaron he got.

"What?" Aaron's expression was wary.

Reassuring him was easy too. "Fuck me."

Aaron's teeth flashed in a quick smile before he lowered his head again and licked a wet stripe from under Joey's balls to the root of his cock. Kissing his way up, Aaron gave the head a tight, noisy suck that made Joey gasp.

"Tell me if your shoulder hurts."

"What if the problem's with my ass?" Joey grinned.

"Then it sucks to be you." Aaron grabbed a condom and the lube from the box holding the alarm clock. But he only circled the hole with a slippery finger, dipping the tip inside, teasing until Joey was trying to squirm down onto Aaron's hand.

Joey looked up from squirming in time to see Aaron's smile. It was beautiful, though Joey'd never say that out loud. But it was, like the way sunsets and oceans and Christmas trees were, when you just stared and the sight hit you inside your ribs. Right now Aaron's smile was a sensation more intense than even the fact that finally he'd pushed two fingers deep enough.

And giving this to Aaron, letting him take control, begging

him with wide eyes, chasing away the last of the cold misery the
gruesome accident had put in his eyes, knowing that smile was
because of him made Joey feel like he'd swallowed one of those
sunsets.

"Yeah." Joey bent his knees to open himself more. He felt
sorry for guys who never understood how powerful surrender
was.

Aaron's gaze stayed locked with Joey's as he picked up the
condom.

"I got it, Lefty." Aaron took it from him. "Don't want any
damage." But with the smile still reaching those light blue eyes,
Joey knew that what might have sounded like derision was
Aaron's attempt at affection.

Joey was ready and he wanted it, but even with Aaron
hooking his shoulders under Joey's knees, his body wouldn't let
Aaron in. The pressure pinched and then it hurt and Aaron
eased back. Maybe the muscles weren't awake yet. It didn't
matter because Joey wanted that cock inside him *now* and he
knew how the hell to relax and he used his heels to drag Aaron
back to him.

"Okay," Aaron whispered, eyes focused on Joey's face. He
pressed forward, shallow thrusts rocking the bed, working side
to side. Joey's heartbeat centered right there, every nerve, every
pulse echoing that deep sharp ache. Just when he thought he'd
have to tell him to stop, the pain spiking sweat on his scalp, the
pressure turned sweet, his body giving in like a sigh.

Aaron held himself still once his balls rested against Joey's
ass. Long black hair fell forward over Aaron's face, and Joey
reached up to touch it. With a smile, he said, "So, you just
going to fall asleep there?"

"Oh, you're in for it now."

Joey couldn't catch his breath while Aaron fucked him fast
and hard.

Couldn't catch his breath from the pleasure pounding
through him every time Aaron thrust so deep inside, Joey could
feel him in his throat.

Couldn't catch his breath when every trace of careless arrogance disappeared from Aaron's face, when the expression in his pale eyes was raw and open, when Joey's name slipped from his lips on a whispered groan.

Aaron leaned in to kiss him, soft and wet, nothing more than lips and shared breath.

"Fuck." Aaron jerked his head up, eyes squeezed shut. "I can't get any traction on this fucking bed."

Aaron pulled out, so roughly it hurt a lot more than it had going in. Especially since Joey knew the bed had nothing to do with the interruption.

"Think you could hold on with one hand if I fucked you over the couch?" The smirk was back in place.

Emotions moved so swiftly across Aaron's face that Joey might have thought he imagined the look, but he didn't imagine Aaron whispering his name. He was back in control now. Joey could go along for the ride or get buried in the sand. So far, he'd liked taking risks.

"Sure." Even if it was impossible to control the wave, there were ways to control the ride. "Since you're not up to the challenge."

Aaron just laughed. One of those quick coughed ones that sounded like it hurt. "Yeah. So you want to finish this or not?"

Joey held out his hand, and Aaron took it in his sweaty, lube-sticky one, pulling Joey up and off the bed. Fortunately for their aching cocks, the back of the couch was only six hobbling steps away.

It was a lot harder than Joey thought it would be. Not the fucking. Aaron was good at that no matter where they were. With this new angle Joey knew he'd be coming just from the fucking, from the way Aaron hammered into his prostate, then rubbed sweet and slow, before moving to long deep thrusts, sending the smack of skin on skin echoing through the tiny apartment.

It wasn't hard at all to let Aaron hold him, help Joey balance with an arm around his waist, hand pressed to his chest under his sling. Aaron dropped wet kisses against the top of Joey's spine, groaning each time Joey met a thrust by tightening his ass. And once Aaron put a hand on Joey's dick, matched the deep strokes in his ass, it wasn't hard at all to shoot all over the back of his new couch.

What was hard was what came after. When Aaron went to get rid of the condom, leaving Joey panting and hanging on to the frame of the couch, eyeing the pattern of come drying on the dark cushion. Now without the distraction of sex, his mind had time to replay that look on Aaron's face.

No matter what crazy song Joey's head might have started singing about finding that forever boyfriend, until now it had been a one-sided dream, nobody involved but Joey—and whatever he chose to tell Noah. And it could have been just one of those sweet fantasies, where he imagined what their house would look like, what their dogs—or maybe kids—would look like. He was fine with just fucking, as long as Aaron didn't act like an asshole the second he got off.

But seeing that look, knowing just for an instant there might be something to it, that Aaron wasn't only here for sex, an instant where affection and need spilled over, scared the crap out of Joey.

Aaron needed Joey. Aaron'd needed him last night and he'd needed him this morning. Not a *need to fuck you 'cause you're hot*. Not a *need you to pick up some stuff at the grocery store*. Not a *need you to help me figure out what to do*. But just needing Joey. No one had ever needed him like that.

It was too much to think about at eight o'clock in the morning.

He heard the shower come on. Was it an invitation? Because he wasn't sure how to RSVP. If they'd finished this up in bed, and Aaron had dropped on him sweaty and fucked out, Joey would have run a hand in silky hair, relaxed in the post-come high, enjoyed a few soft kisses as they came down. He'd know what to do.

Or was the fact that Aaron hadn't come back more of a stop sign? Joey usually rolled through those. In life and on quiet streets.

He rolled through another one and went into his bathroom.

"Hey."

Aaron tugged the curtain back a little. "What?"

"What was that about?"

"What?" Aaron said again. But he was no longer visible.

"Pulling out of my ass so fast you left a burn." Joey climbed in the tub.

"Thought you liked it rough." Aaron swallowed. "Sorry if I hurt you. Won't do it again."

Joey just looked at him.

"I told you I didn't like the bed." Aaron handed over the soap.

"Yeah, you did."

Aaron ducked his head under the spray, knees bent to fit, and then turned around the other way. Wet, his hair went almost to the middle of his back. "The look might have worked on Tall Dude, but it's not working on me."

"Who, Noah?" That was a perfect way to describe him. Joey couldn't wait to tell Noah he'd made an impression. "If that look doesn't work on you, why did you turn around?"

Aaron turned back and met his gaze. "So playing Bambi usually gets you what you want?"

Joey blinked and kept pleading. "Usually."

"All it does is get me hard. That what you want?"

"Sometimes."

By the time Joey managed to scrape off some stubble left handed, Aaron was dressed, hair combed and leaving wet streaks on his shirt.

He leaned in the bathroom doorway. "Gonna cut your throat."

"I'm done." Joey rinsed off the razor and the rest of the lather on his face.

"Did you call the ortho?"

"Tomorrow, ten thirty."

"I'll drive you." Aaron didn't wait for an answer. He was already on his way to the apartment door. He opened it, but turned back for a second. "You need anything?"

I need to figure out what the fuck is going on. Joey stopped the shrug just before the muscles screamed. "Nothing I can think of."

"See ya."

See him when? Tomorrow when he picked him up? Tonight? In an hour when he decided he needed something else disguised as a fuck?

"Yeah."

Three rooms. No food. Too early to order a pizza.

Joey ate some chips and a couple spoonfuls of peanut butter and hooked his keyboard up to the computer. But his head couldn't make any music.

A long nap left Joey wide awake, so he was still up when Aaron knocked on the apartment door after midnight. Not only wide-awake but frustrated, since the song that had been so perfect in Joey's head while he was asleep wouldn't make the transfer from his head to his keyboard, and it wasn't only because his right hand was out of commission.

He might have yanked open the door with a bit more force than necessary.

"What the fuck's the matter with you?" Aaron asked.

"Nothing."

"Y'look like someone told you they'd stopped making lube."

That dragged out a laugh. "Shut up."

Aaron stepped through the door, crowding Joey against the wall. "And then how would you get those nice fat cocks you love up that tight little hole of yours?"

Between the rush of arousal and the laughter, Joey's bad mood dissolved in a grin. "I'd find a way."

"C'mon." Aaron jerked a thumb at the door. "Grab some stuff."

"What?"

"Grab whatever you need for a couple of days."

"To go where?"

"My house."

Joey stared, but Aaron's pale eyes didn't give him any clues.

Aaron folded his arms across his chest. "I'm tired of tripping over boxes. I hate your bed. And you don't have any coffee."

"And what does any of that have to do with me?"

"You can't drive, and I don't want to have to come over here to fuck you."

Slow down. It wasn't as if Joey hadn't moved in even faster with some of his other boyfriends. Even though he'd kept an apartment for another six months, he'd basically been living with Mark from the first time they fucked.

But those other guys, he was able to figure them out. He still couldn't predict much about Aaron, except that asking questions instead of following orders pissed him off.

"Need help?" Aaron said.

Sex. Food. Guitar Hero—when his arm healed a bit more. Aaron. Not necessarily in that order. But Joey should hang out a stop sign.

Aaron grabbed Joey's chin and kissed him. Slowly. Thoroughly. Until the only reason he could think of for staying was the same reason he could think of for going.

God, he hoped he didn't screw this up.

Chapter Nine

At four in the morning, Joey was in Aaron's bed with Aaron's tongue in his ass. Aaron held Joey off the mattress and rimmed him for what felt like an hour, until Joey was almost crying with the need for harder, deeper, God-please-fuck-me-now. The only relief he got was when Aaron stopped to lick at Joey's balls, to suck them into his mouth. And that wasn't much relief because if Joey didn't get something besides the silky rub of Aaron's hair on his dick, Joey was going to die.

When Aaron finally lowered Joey back down onto the mattress, the look in those pale blue eyes wasn't the need Joey had seen last night. They just held the happy shine of knowing Aaron had Joey ten miles past desperate. Joey wondered if he was ever going to get a chance to try to read this complex man's expressions in daylight.

Aaron smirked. "Ready?"

"Aaron fucking Chase, I swear to God if you don't fuck me right the hell now I will put pink fucking ribbons all over the Ducati."

"Benjamin."

"What?" Joey's balls were turning blue and Aaron was muttering names?

"My middle name." Aaron was grinning now. "Not fucking, Benjamin." He lifted Joey into his lap, turned him around and fucked him with them both on their knees. And this time Joey could see the numbers on the clock, see that this time it was almost an hour, an hour of building up and dropping back, until nothing but need filled up all the spaces in Joey's head.

No words, no music, no wondering where this was going or whether he was going to like the destination. No fantasies of the future, nothing but the reality of this man holding him, the smell of their bodies together thick enough to taste, the rhythm of their breathing. Aaron's cock lifted him, grounded him. By the end they were so in synch that Joey knew when he reached for his cock to bring himself off, Aaron would be right there with him—even without a word or a change in their rhythm.

When Joey woke up again, hours later, it was to Aaron smacking him in the head with a pillow and yelling about the doctor's appointment.

"Should'na fucked me unconscious then," Joey muttered as he rolled out of bed.

"Didn't hear you complaining." Aaron sounded extremely pleased with himself.

It wasn't as if Aaron didn't know he was an amazing lover, but Joey supposed Aaron still liked to hear it. Joey filed that away.

When Joey stumbled back into the bedroom after his shower, he realized the ache in his thigh muscles shouldn't have been the only aftereffect from last night. He tried to look at his ass in the mirror on the closet door.

Aaron made one of his coughed laughs at the bedroom door. "Sore?"

"No." And that was the weird part. "Not even beard burn."

"Don't really grow one." Aaron went back to the kitchen.

If Joey's only functioning arm weren't busy dragging on his clothes, he would have done the classic V-8 smack on his head. Once again, his IQ was good for shit when it came to noticing things. Aaron's bronze skin, the long silky hair—Joey had just thought Aaron kept his pubes well trimmed. Of course, the pale eyes had thrown him off. Given the pictures Joey'd seen, he'd bet Aaron's dad had given him the hair and the skin.

He went into the kitchen where Aaron was scrambling eggs.

"What nation?" Just in time he remembered Aaron's

reluctance to discuss his family and didn't add *is your father.* Most people Joey met were proud of a Native American heritage.

"What?"

"No beard," Joey explained as he poured himself some orange juice. "What Native American nation are you?"

Aaron slammed the pan against the burner. "Fuck do I know or care. My mother said she thought my father might have been some carny she fucked."

"Oh." Joey stuffed that in the file too. "I don't know who my dad is either."

"The dentist like to get drilled by random dudes?"

Aaron turned to face him, back against the stove, wide stance like he was daring Joey to take a swing at him for the crack about his mother. But if those insults could make Joey lose his temper, he'd have had to switch professions a long time ago.

"I don't know my birth mother either," Joey said. "The dentist and the movie producer adopted me when I was a baby. My birth mother walked into a free clinic, squirted me into the toilet and left. A nurse found me and got me breathing."

Aaron picked up his coffee. "Jesus," he said into the mouth of the mug.

"It's not like I remember it or anything." Joey shrugged. "Ow. Shit. I keep forgetting."

Aaron pulled in his lips as he turned back to the stove. Joey thought Aaron was fighting a smile.

Aaron didn't particularly care if Joey wanted him in the exam room. Doctors were often full of shit, and Aaron wasn't sure he'd believe Joey's report if he was trying to avoid another shot.

The doctor seemed surprised by Joey's range of motion and the reduction in the swelling and bruising. Joey hadn't been kidding when he said he healed fast. The stitches in his head had already been pushed out, and the scrapes on his face were pink with new skin. With Joey's start in life, Aaron guessed it paid to be resilient. Even his own bitch of a mother hadn't dumped any of them in a toilet and left them to die.

The doctor cleared Joey for desk work on Monday, but not for the field, and said Joey could ditch the sling and drive his car as soon as he could raise his arm shoulder height without excessive pain.

Joey claimed playing Xbox would be excellent physical therapy, so after his appointment they played Halo until Aaron left for work, stopping at the door to issue an entirely non-playful threat of what would happen if Joey left any food out.

On Sunday, they played again for a blow job, and Aaron knew he'd been hustled because no way did Joey get that good in one day of practice.

"Sucker." Joey flopped back on the couch and unfastened his jeans. He still wore the sling, but used his hand more and more—like when he was kicking Aaron's ass at Halo.

"Fuck you."

"After." Joey grinned.

So Aaron did. Joey rode Aaron on the couch, head flung back so that he wanted to lick the tightly stretched tan skin, bite it, mark it so Joey could see it on Monday when he went to work and know that Aaron would fuck him that night.

Joey was asleep on the couch when Aaron got home on Sunday and woke him with a few kisses and a grope. As Joey rode him facing away, Aaron dug his fingers in tight on Joey's hipbones, and slammed him back on his dick.

"When you sit at that desk tomorrow, you're going to feel me."

"Good. Hate. Desk. Work. Might. As. Well. God." There was a pause of nothing but harsh breaths and groans as Joey adjusted to the new pressure on his prostate. "Get. Off. On. It." Joey's muscles pulsed, and he jammed himself down faster.

Jesus, how many times had Aaron been in this sweet, tight

ass, in that hot, fucking mouth? And all he wanted was to do it again. And to listen to Joey laugh. To come home from work and bury his face in Joey's neck, breathe in that smell.

Now he leaned in to lick the sweat off Joey's shoulder. His spine rolled, ass tightening again. The tension built in Aaron's balls. "Go ahead," he urged. "Got a working right hand now."

Joey shook his head, rocking back and forth.

Aaron brought a hand to Joey's back, sliding a finger down his spine to the crack of his ass, lower, to the spot where Joey's body stretched to take in Aaron's cock. He rubbed and Joey whimpered, pressed down and Joey moaned.

"You can...put it...inside...if you want." Joey's husky whisper almost set Aaron off.

"Fuck." He clenched his muscles to keep from coming. Pulling Joey off, Aaron shoved Joey on his back on the couch before kneeling between his legs. With Joey on his lap, Aaron couldn't turn his wrist and he wanted to be able to watch, even if it was only from the light of the TV.

He held the base of his dick as he slipped back inside, keeping his hand between them.

On the next slow stroke, he laid a finger alongside his dick and pressed forward. Joey bucked and groaned but he didn't try to jerk away.

"Wait," he whispered.

Aaron wasn't sure he could. Jesus, so so fucking tight. And feeling the wet soft wall on his finger seemed to translate right to his dick like they were fucking raw. He wanted to rip off the rubber and feel it. Slick tight muscles grabbing the naked skin of his cock. His balls were filling, climbing.

He looked down. Joey's eyes were wide open, black against skin made blue in the light of the TV.

"Joey. Fuck."

"Okay, you can move now." But each word shuddered out of him.

Aaron watched as his finger and dick started a different rhythm, sliding his finger a little side to side, until Joey's mouth opened on one long sound without a breath, and he grabbed for his cock, wincing. Aaron hoped it was that he grabbed with his right and not because he needed Aaron to back off because Christ, he couldn't. Couldn't stop watching the way Joey's body took him in, hot and slippery, stretched so tight around his finger and dick. Couldn't stop the climb, the rush loading his balls, his cock, until his whole body seemed to turn itself inside out as he emptied himself into Joey.

He held the condom and eased his dick out, driving three fingers back inside to zero in on the swollen gland, rubbing, tapping, until Joey pumped rope after creamy rope across his chest—and another fucking sling.

Aaron came back from dumping the condom to find Joey in the same position he'd left him.

Joey's head hung off the arm of the couch, warm brown eyes pleading like he was still grinding down on Aaron's cock.

"If it's all right with you, I'm just gonna stay here."

Joey's leg trembled as Aaron lifted it off the back of the couch.

"Let's get you into the shower." He pulled Joey up by the good arm and stripped off his sling. Guilt sent ice water pumping through Aaron's stomach. He had to make sure he hadn't made Joey bleed.

Aaron helped Joey down the hall to the back bathroom, but after a few steps he was almost carrying him.

"Sorry," Joey said as Aaron took more of his weight.

"I'm not."

"Not about the sex, asshole."

Aaron sighed and picked Joey up, lifting legs around hips, Joey's arms around his neck.

"Put me down."

"So you can make me crash into a wall too? I'm not sorry about the sex and I'm not sorry you're so fucked out I have to carry you." Aaron lowered Joey to his feet in the shower and climbed in after him. As soon as the water ran warm, Aaron pulled the shower tab and soaped Joey up.

"I can wash myself."

"But that's not as much fun."

"I seriously don't know if I can go again. And believe me, I never say that."

"I believe you, and I'm done for awhile too." Aaron turned Joey to rinse the come off his chest and then spun him back around to check his ass.

"I'm fine." Joey tried to pull away.

"Because you have eyes in the back of your head?"

Joey was almost squirming. "I don't need you to take care of me."

"Not from what I've seen, so stop being a baby and let me check. I promise not to stick you with anything."

Joey didn't laugh, but he stopped trying to make them both fall. Finally, he let Aaron check.

"Swollen, but not bleeding."

"I told you that."

From behind, Aaron couldn't be sure, but he thought Joey's chin was sticking out. "Is this some kind of need to be the do-gooder thing?"

"Like you would want someone taking care of you, I-know-everything-because-I'm-an-EMT."

"Paramedic."

"Whatever."

"Not whatever. Those extra course hours were a lot of fucking work." Trying to stay awake long enough to get the kids off to school after Savannah moved out. The texts blurring as he tried to force them into his head, the times he had to leave class because Dylan had screwed up again. Jesus, Aaron'd been lucky not to lose him.

When he looked, Joey was rinsing the bubbles out of his hair.

"Smooth," Aaron said.

"What?" Joey tried to fill his soft eyes with innocence, but Aaron had his number.

"Making it about me instead of you. They teach you that in Therapy 101, right?"

Joey fought a smile.

"So what the fuck is the big deal about me looking at your asshole? Not like I haven't seen it. And you sure as shit aren't shy."

Joey took a deep breath. "You've been taking care of me one way or another since you met me. Thought you might be sick of it."

Fuck knew Aaron ought to be. And as soon as Joey could drive, yeah, he'd dump him back in his own apartment so he'd have the place to himself again. But he wasn't sick enough of Joey to want that to be the end of it. They could still fuck. Hang out even. Maybe he'd drag Joey out with Hennie. It'd be funny to see what came out of Do-gooder's mouth when he was smashed.

"You'll be the first to know, trust me. What time do you have to be up tomorrow? I'll drive you in." Going to the parking lot of the DFC wouldn't kill Aaron, even if he'd rather cut off an arm than walk in the building.

"Oh, Vivian from the office is picking me up." Joey stepped out of the shower.

"Here?"

"That okay?"

"Yeah." But it itched his brain like it wasn't. The kids weren't underage anymore. It didn't matter if the Florida Department of Families and Children knew he was a big old queer. They wouldn't be trying to take the kids away. For fuck's sake Joey worked there, and they hadn't bounced him out.

"Aaron?"

"I said it was fine." He toweled off and wiped down the inside of the shower and tub before whipping the towel into the hamper.

Monday was his day off, but Aaron woke up Monday morning when Joey rolled out of bed, even though he managed to slap the alarm before it started beeping. Joey turned back. "Want coffee?"

"I'll get some later."

He started to flop back onto his stomach, but he had to piss. When he got into the bathroom, he could hear Joey singing softly. The guy had a nice voice, and Aaron didn't want him to stop. He leaned against the door as the coconut-scented steam floated out.

"'Romance is mush,'" Joey sang.

He had that right. The song sounded like some kind of jazz or blues. Which, added to the whining cats, the Disney tune he'd been singing with that kid in the car, and that he seemed to know the words to every Guitar Hero song, meant Joey had some pretty varied taste in music. But he still didn't get to make fun of Marvin Gaye.

"'And there I'll be while I rot, with the rest of those whose lives are lonely too.'"

It was a fucking depressing song. Accurate, but depressing. Totally not Joey. Aaron shuffled in.

Joey's head popped around the curtain. "Sorry I woke you up."

"You didn't. My bladder did. What was that song?"

"'Lush Life' by Billy Strayhorn. Gay African-American composer in the forties."

Shit. Black and gay in the forties? No wonder dude was depressed. But what was Joey's reason?

"Hate your job that much?"

"No, though I'm not thrilled to be typing up case reports one-handed all day. Why?" Joey smiled. "Oh. I just love the song. It's pretty."

But the line about rotting away reminded Aaron he hadn't been over to Baker to see Rafe in a couple weeks. Maybe Rafe could tell him what the hell to do about Dylan the next time he tried to get Darryl killed. Aaron was running out of threats. They were Rafe's kids anyway.

Even though Mom had made sure he never got to raise them.

Aaron flinched when Joey touched his arm.

"Damn." Joey's hand was rubbing over the locked tight muscles in Aaron's biceps.

"What?"

"So that's what you look like when you're really mad. It's kind of scary."

"So why aren't you scared?"

Joey smiled and stretched up to kiss Aaron's jaw. "Because you're not mad at me."

Aaron's hand hovered over the chessboard, looking for a way to block Rafe's move. Aaron could see the attack coming, but he couldn't seem to find a way to stop it. The noise level in the canteen at Baker's Correctional Facility wasn't conducive to concentration on chess, especially not if he was going to try to give Rafe a decent game.

At last, Aaron slid his white bishop to the board's edge and took Rafe's rook.

Rafe grunted and stared down at the board. His hair wasn't even grey anymore, the tight curls were going silver white, though he couldn't be more than fifty. Aaron supposed fourteen years in prison would do that to anybody. Even someone as even-tempered as Rafe Williams.

Rafe didn't look up from the little board as he said, "So what did you want to ask me, kid?"

"Huh?"

"Third game. We talked about Sheree making the Dean's list again and the boys getting up to the same old shit and you're still here getting your ass kicked. You didn't come over here for chess."

"You're just trying to distract me."

Rafe shrugged with only his lips.

Which could mean Aaron was right and he was finally going to beat Rafe at chess, or that Rafe just wanted Aaron to think that so he got careless. Rafe always got Aaron thinking in circles.

He swallowed. "Mom."

Rafe hardly ever wasted motion, but now he was still as a statue. "You hear from her?"

Aaron knew Rafe was hoping for a yes. That the closest thing Aaron had ever had to a father could even think the bitch would ever bother to show up again, that Rafe would even want her to come waltzing back into their lives when she was half the reason he was stuck in prison made Aaron want to whip the chessboard across the room. He thought the guards watching from the walls might consider that a problem.

"No. I haven't. And I hope to fucking hell I never do."

"Ought to let it go, kid."

"Like she did us? What the hell for?"

"Being pissed off all the time is no way to live your life."

"I'm not." He wasn't pissed off all the time. Hadn't really been pissed off much lately. All the sex took the edge off, he guessed.

"What did you want to ask about your mother?"

"Why do you think she was an addict? Why couldn't she stop?"

Rafe flattened the pieces on the board with one big brown hand. "If you're trying to tell me—"

"No." Aaron shook his head. And he could have been ten again, the first time his mom had brought Rafe home. Aaron had been scared shitless. Most of the guys his mom brought home would smack him just for fun, and Rafe had looked like he could put Aaron through a wall with a flick of one of his solid wrists. But Rafe had never hit him. Or Savannah. Or the twins and Sheree who popped up a year later. For five years no one got smacked, and Aaron and Savannah had enough to eat and stuff to wear and even stuff for school. "No," Aaron repeated. Because the one person he had ever cared about disappointing—and one of two he'd ever let down—was sitting across from him in an orange jumpsuit.

"Guess maybe some people are born that way," Rafe said at last.

"So I could be like that?" Aaron had always worried he'd inherited a tendency toward addiction from his mom. He'd never even smoked a joint after sixteen. As long as his only drug was caffeine he figured he was safe.

"It ain't cut and dried like that, kid. You think you like dick because of DNA or because you never knew your daddy?"

"I don't know." It was too fucking lame now. To wonder if the reason why he couldn't seem to stop thinking about Joey— and not only about fucking him, but the smell of his skin and that big grin and the way he was sneaky enough to hustle Aaron at Halo—was because his mother's addictive personality was somehow manifesting in Aaron's obsession with a blond piece of ass.

"What's up?" Rafe laughed. "Boy trouble?"

Much too lame to bring up. Aaron looked down at the chessmen rolling on the little piece of cardboard.

"I had 'mate in five moves," Rafe said.

"Bullshit. I was gonna win." Aaron folded the game up. "You need any more money for the commissary here?"

"There's enough. Don't worry about it. The kids probably call you for cash every other week."

"More like every week."

"Aaron, kid, you really okay?" Rafe had reached out, but the no-touching rule kept his hand from landing on Aaron's arm.

"I'm fine."

"Hey, I've been taking plumbing courses. When I get out next year, I'll make more money than God. Pay you back."

"Sure, Rafe."

Chapter Ten

Despite being bored out of his mind, typing with one hand and having to use the mouse left-handed, by lunchtime Joey had finished entering in the data from the pile of files the head of his department had dumped on his desk before disappearing in a cloud of patchouli. Even though she fortunately was gone, the patchouli lingered. It had saturated the files so that every breath had Joey wishing people still smoked in offices. At least then he wouldn't be breathing this sickening smell.

He sent emails to almost everyone he knew, looked at a few new music sites, poked around on YouTube, and it was still only twelve thirty. If he went down to lunch, he'd probably get another pile of folders.

There was something else he could do. A couple of keystrokes and he'd know exactly why Aaron hated social workers. Know what had made him look ready to kill something this morning. It wouldn't be unethical, much.

It wasn't as if Joey planned to share the info with anyone ever, and maybe he could help. Maybe with the information he'd know if he could ever be the answer to what Aaron needed. Joey typed in the name, adding B as the middle initial—ABC, that was cute—added the address, the license on Aaron's truck and then put his hand over the mouse.

After Joey clicked, he couldn't undo it. Couldn't unknow it. Even if Aaron never knew.

What if this time it was different? What if Aaron really was it? What Joey had always wanted? The perfect wave without the wipeout, the Baby Ruth *and* the Snickers bar, the soul-deep connection that wouldn't fade or break.

His finger tapped the mouse lightly. Like it almost wouldn't be his fault if the screen came up. It would just be a fluke, right?

If this was going to be the one that was different, then Aaron would tell Joey everything waiting behind that click when he was ready. Joey moved the mouse, exited the screen and went down to the cafeteria.

There was a fresh stack of patchouli-steeped files waiting for him when he got back. He'd done just enough work that he'd stopped gagging every time he opened a folder when a *search completed* message flashed at the bottom of the screen. He clicked on it without thinking.

Holy shit. Aaron. The hair on the back of Joey's neck prickled like it did before a thunderstorm.

Joey didn't get any history. Only the header with the address and other basic information. But Joey had seen fewer case notation links for kids who'd spent their whole lives in one placement after another.

He couldn't believe he'd done this. Knowing that if Aaron found out he'd hate him, actually hate him, made Joey want to puke into the wastebasket.

That was something Joey couldn't face. If it didn't work out, if he ended up walking away—or pushing Aaron away—Joey'd live. It had hurt to walk away from Noah, but Joey'd done it. For both of them. But Aaron would hate him. That face would go hard and flat and cold. Blue eyes icy. Joey would rather cut off a body part than have Aaron hate him.

He eyed his index finger as if he were about to sacrifice it and then used it to hit the reset button on the computer. Redoing the last hour of work was worth removing the temptation. Though one thing he couldn't reset was knowing that Saturday was Aaron Benjamin Chase's thirtieth birthday. That was fine. Aaron was going to celebrate it whether he knew it or not.

◇

Their opposing schedules meant the only time Aaron saw Joey was when he crawled into bed next to him at around twelve thirty. One night Joey had texted him with an offer to stop by with pizza on his dinner break, but Aaron said he'd already eaten. Things were good the way they were. Aaron got an armful—or anything else he had in mind—of Joey at night, and that was all he needed.

They didn't fuck every night, only because on Wednesday Aaron was an extra couple hours at work, and even the heat of Joey's body and the smell of his sweat as he rubbed up against Aaron couldn't keep him awake long enough to do anything but tuck Joey in against his side before sleep hit Aaron like a brick to the back of the head.

On Friday, Joey was waiting on the couch with Rafe's old chess clock in his hands. He'd ditched the sling the night before.

"What's this?" Joey held up the clock.

"It's for chess. For timed play. You get so much time for your moves during the game and if your flag drops, you lose." Aaron took it from him and wound it up, setting it for five minutes. "Here, I move and then hit this button and then your time starts to tick away."

Joey watched before licking his lips in a way that Aaron had learned meant really good things for his dick. And tonight, he wasn't tired. Even if he was eighteen minutes away from turning thirty. Which he devoutly hoped no one on the planet knew or remembered.

He'd already had his birthday gift. Somehow he and Hennie had managed to get out on time. Tucker Harrison earned his ticket to the ER by skateboarding stoned, in the dark, without a helmet. With any luck, the head injury scrambling his brains would improve his common sense. They handed Tucker over at 23:05 and didn't get sent back out.

But if Joey and his tongue wanted to give Aaron another

present, he was pretty sure he wouldn't mind.

Joey took the clock back. "I thought it was like a riding time clock for wrestling."

"How'd I miss that? Riding people is a sport?"

"Sort of." Joey smirked. "But it'll work almost the same."

"For what?"

Joey ignored his question. "So if we set this for say, twenty minutes and took turns—"

"At what?"

"Making each other come," Joey said as if it were the only possible answer.

"You think I can't make you come in twenty minutes? I can make you come in ten."

"Wanna bet?"

That fucking manipulative little genius. He'd maneuvered Aaron into this whole thing. And Aaron hadn't even seen it coming. But he'd still win. This wasn't Halo, where Joey had skills Aaron hadn't seen. He was positive they were both bringing their A-game to bed. Joey being out of the sling wouldn't change a thing except that Aaron could fuck him harder.

"What's the bet?"

"Thirty minutes. Whoever comes first loses. Or whoever doesn't make three moves before time runs out."

"And the winner gets?" Aaron asked.

"Loser does whatever the winner wants tomorrow."

"You know I have to be at work by three, right?"

"Yup."

What was the worst that could happen? Joey demanding a dozen blow jobs? Joey wanting to top? Aaron could handle that, unlikely as it sounded. It wouldn't matter anyway because it would be Joey's jaw aching tomorrow. A dozen blow jobs sounded like a great way to spend his birthday.

"You're on." Aaron set the clock and placed it on his nightstand.

Joey peeled off his clothes and sat in the center of the bed. "You can even go first."

His smug smile wouldn't last for long. Aaron wouldn't need three moves, or thirty minutes. Joey was already getting hard. And fuck, so was Aaron.

He stripped and started the clock.

But he knew he still had time, Joey couldn't—wouldn't last. Aaron would even give Joey a chance—not out of a sense of fair play when it was clear Joey had set all this up—but because Aaron wanted to see what Joey would try when it was his turn.

So all Aaron did on his first turn was kiss him. Hard, deep and wet, pinning Joey's hands over his head and grinding their cocks together, but still just kissing. Joey was groaning and panting when Aaron reached over and slapped the clock, leaving himself twenty-three minutes for his next move. Because that would be all it would take. One more move.

As soon as Aaron dropped onto his back, Joey was on him, but not moving with the kind of speed Aaron would have thought. Joey licked and sucked on Aaron's nipples before tonguing down past his navel. Aaron felt a weird disappointment that didn't belong with the expectation of an imminent blow job, especially one from Joey's hot mouth, but Aaron had expected something a little inventive. And then Joey bypassed Aaron's dick, licking down his groin and lifting him to get at his ass.

"Roll," Joey whispered, breath tickling the wet skin under Aaron's balls.

Aaron flipped onto his stomach and spread his legs, forgetting all about taking his time. Joey and his tongue ring playing in Aaron's ass was too good to wait for.

He wasn't wrong. He almost completely forgot about the bet as Joey started licking. When he drove in with his tongue, the ball flicked over the rim and Aaron ground his dick against the sheets.

For a second, when Joey stopped to breathe, Aaron got enough neurons firing to remember there was a reason he wasn't supposed to be getting off like this, with a tongue in his ass and his dick on rough cotton, even if his balls were pretty sure getting off right the hell now was the only reason for Aaron to keep breathing.

He squinted over at the clock. *Fuck*. It had only been ten minutes?

Joey leaned over, and Aaron heard him digging in his nightstand drawer. If Joey thought he was just going to shove the big dildo, or his own dick up Aaron's ass without a little more prep and some serious negotiation, the bet was off.

But whatever Joey came up with was small enough to hide in his hand.

And then Joey let Aaron feel it, let the string of beads slide over his spine and down to his crack. Those small balls were something Aaron played with on his own.

The tightness in Aaron's chest eased until Joey pressed the first slick round bead against the tight ring of muscle. As long as Joey didn't get all smugly cocky and start whispering "Relax" in Aaron's ear, they'd be fine.

Joey pressed and the ball popped through the pressure, the sting of the stretch over before it even started. The beads themselves weren't big enough to make getting them in difficult. It was when a couple of them were in, that full sensation, the shift and press against Aaron's prostate that would make it that much harder to stay in charge of exactly when his body hit the point of no return.

The fourth bead went in with a shove from Joey's finger and then the finger followed inside, finding a ball and rolling it across Aaron's prostate in a steady rhythm that made heat flash through him in time with the press. When Joey used a hand on Aaron's hip to roll him onto his back again, bent down and started licking and sucking on Aaron's balls, he knew he was so very screwed by seriously underestimating one short, blond surfer boy.

Joey lifted his head and sucked hard on the crown of Aaron's dick as one hand tugged a ball down far enough to put pressure on the inner muscle.

And then Joey slapped the clock. "Your turn."

As soon as Aaron's arms and legs remembered how to work, Joey was going to regret giving up his turn. Aaron sucked in a deep shaky breath and reached down to pull out the beads.

Joey's fingers locked around Aaron's wrist. "If you don't like someone's move in chess do you get to undo it?"

The little shit. "No." He was so going down now.

Aaron put Joey on his stomach with a pillow under his hips and rolled down a rubber. Slicking his dick with one hand, Aaron used his other thumb to stretch and lube Joey's ass, one eye on the clock. Even twenty minutes of hard fucking should be enough, and Joey only had twelve minutes left on his time.

He lifted Joey's hips and pressed in slowly, smoothly, Joey opening for Aaron like he'd prepped him for a lot longer than a minute. With the pressure inside his own ass, Aaron had to stop and fight for control when Joey's soft walls pulsed around Aaron's dick, heating the tight skin, even through the rubber.

Grabbing Joey's hips, Aaron started pumping fast, hard enough to make Joey jump forward a little every time their hips met, even with Aaron's grip. He reached up for Joey's left shoulder and hauled him back onto his dick, and Joey's groan promised victory—with fifteen minutes to spare.

Aaron pushed Joey face down into the mattress again and reached around his hips to grab his cock. Joey's ass clamped hard around him. Every thrust Aaron made tightened his own ass around those balls, fucking and getting fucked, Joey clenched around him, both of them groaning loud enough to vibrate the mattress.

Looking for any advantage, a way to slam Joey's prostate harder, strip his dick faster, anything to get Joey over the edge before Aaron fell first, he pressed down over him, skin to sweaty, scalding skin, Joey's sand and surf smell breaking through the thick cloud of sex in the bed. Aaron's stomach got tight and hot, not only because he was close—too fucking close—but the hot flashes of pleasure were swirling with something else in his gut. Pride and admiration, tinged with an almost rough anger. Joey might not be able to walk and chew gum at the same time but fuck if he wasn't going to win. Again.

The tension in Aaron's stomach spread into his balls and dick. Before it could hit critical mass, he reached over to slap the clock. He still had eight minutes.

Joey looked over at the clock and then at Aaron who had rolled onto his back and was panting like he'd finished a triathlon. He looked pissed and pleased at the same time, and Joey wondered if there could have been another way to force some fun on Aaron for his birthday. Since he hadn't been able to think of one, he'd jerked off three times waiting for Aaron to get home so that he'd be able to last long enough to win the bet. Which he now had eleven minutes to do.

He stripped off the condom.

"What happened to the whole not undoing the other player's move?"

"The condom isn't a move, it's a—" Shit, what was it called in baseball? He'd seen enough games with Noah. "—a field condition. If you were playing outside and it started raining, you'd come inside, and wipe off the board, right? But it wouldn't undo a move."

"My dick is part of the field?"

"It's part of the playing surface."

"Your parents were right. You should have been a lawyer."

Ten minutes. It had to work, because there was no way he could hold out again if Aaron started fucking him. Joey hated the residual taste of latex, but they were going to have fun on Aaron's birthday tomorrow. Even if getting there made Joey gag a little.

He pushed in the last two beads and kept two fingers inside to get at least one of the balls right on Aaron's prostate. The taste of success was a splash of bitter precome, much better than the latex. Joey pressed again until the slit was spilling steadily, slicking it down the shaft with his spit. The harder he pressed, the more fluid he got so he drove his fingers up while swallowing Aaron to the back of his throat, tongue and ball rolling down the vein on the underside. One, two gulps and the first spurt of come hit the back of Joey's throat, but Aaron jerked free before Joey could lick him clean.

"Bastard," Aaron panted.

Joey grinned and wiped his face on Aaron's stomach. A reach for the end of the beads was interrupted by Aaron rolling out of bed. "I'll do it."

Joey's flag on the clock dropped before Aaron came back from the bathroom, kicking off Queen's "We Will Rock You" in Joey's head and putting a grin on his face. He could put up with the guy being a sore loser, could even handle finishing himself off though he was heartily sick of his own hand today— and his right hand was sick of him. Because tomorrow was going to be fun.

Joey was jacking his dick slowly when Aaron came back and stood staring at him, the pale blue gaze seeming to go through Joey's head, and thank God he hadn't looked at Aaron's case file because Joey would never have been able to keep the knowledge secret. Just one of those searching stares and Joey would have spilled his guts. The birthday plans, though, those he could keep quiet.

Aaron stopped staring and dropped to his knees. After dragging Joey to the edge of the bed, Aaron sucked in the tip of Joey's dick, big hand working the shaft. The steady flick of Aaron's tongue should have taken a lot longer to drag Joey's orgasm out of him, but he'd been fighting it so hard, been so focused on holding it in that all it took was the pressure of Aaron's thumb stroking the ridge along Joey's balls and down to his ass before Joey shuddered and came.

Aaron woke up to find Joey staring at him. Fuck. Fuck Joey and that stupid bet and fuck himself for being so goddamned sure he'd win it. And fuck himself for even remembering it was his birthday. He'd always let the kids play Boss of the Day on their birthdays. Fate had a fucked up sense of humor.

He sighed. "What?"

"What do you mean?"

"What do you want?"

Joey grinned. "Everything."

Neither the grin nor the answer was reassuring. But instead of demanding Aaron roll over, because after last night he was pretty sure Joey's first command while playing Boss of the Day would be climbing on top and fucking away, Joey simply said, "For now, shower. Then breakfast."

Aaron was still eyeing him warily when he slid the plate of eggs across the counter, waiting for the other shoe to drop. "Now what?"

"After breakfast, I want to ride over to Neptune Beach on the Ducati."

When Aaron just drank his coffee, Joey raised his right arm over his head, slowly, but over his head. "See, all better for riding."

"All right." Maybe it would rain. But even the fucking forecast was falling in with Joey's plans.

What Joey wanted turned out to be some kind of street fair next to the beach on Atlantic Boulevard. Booths selling crap to illegally wasted teenagers on spring break. It was going to be a shitload of non-fun. If Joey noticed Aaron's lack of enthusiasm as they made their way down a side street to the middle of the crowded fair, the manipulative bastard apparently didn't care. He didn't exactly drag Aaron into the party, but Joey took off and Aaron could pussy out or man up and pay the bet, so he followed the fluffy blond head.

Now that some of the harsher yellow tones had faded and the new growth made the hair lay more softly on Joey's head, the hair wasn't so bad anymore. Or maybe Aaron was used to it.

Joey looked back to give a *c'mon* wave, tripped over a stroller and landed in the muscular arms of an older, balding guy who was too well-maintained to be straight. The guy took a long time getting Joey back on his feet, and even longer to let go completely.

By the time Aaron was standing close enough to put a hand on Joey's back—not that Aaron would since Joey didn't have "Property of A. Chase" tattooed on his hot ass—the older guy was handing Joey a card with a number inked on the back. Joey stuffed it in the back pocket of his jeans and grinned. "Thanks again, Chris." Joey started walking away.

Aaron looked down at him. "Damsel-in-distress routine get you a lot of dick?"

Joey stared back at him for a moment before he answered, and he didn't trip over anything. "Sometimes," he said at last with a wince-free shrug.

Then he stepped around so Aaron crashed into him and had to grab on to keep them both from falling. Joey rubbed a thigh between Aaron's legs, the grin on Joey's face completely different from the one he'd given his other rescuer. "But I'm keeping pretty busy with this one at the moment." Joey shifted his hip right onto Aaron's cock and then stepped away.

"I'm not jealous."

"Didn't say you were." Joey's nonchalance about the whole fucking thing was more annoying than him getting cruised right in front of Aaron. "Hey, look."

Did Joey have some kind of built-in detector that knew when Aaron was about to get pissed enough to tell Joey to get the fuck out of his hair? Because the distraction worked. The booth Joey was pointing to was handing out free samples of some new energy drink, and Aaron never turned down free caffeine. He forgot what he was going to say, which was good, since whatever it was would definitely have been in violation of the you-don't-get-to-treat-me-like-shit-after-you-get-off agreement. Not that Aaron *had* gotten off this morning. Even though it was his birthday and he'd woken up with a hot guy in bed next to him.

He actually felt better after a can—okay, maybe he'd smiled and winked at the girl handing them out and gotten two, but hey the cans were small. He didn't even give a shit when Joey stopped at a table covered with leather and beads and shells and started poking at the jewelry. Aaron wasn't into much decoration on a guy, but a couple of the pieces were nice. Joey was checking out a leather necklace with a quarter-sized piece of sea glass the same shade of warm brown as Joey's eyes in bright sunlight. Joey picked it up and poked at the knots and the clasp like he knew what cheap leather surfer jewelry was supposed to have, so Aaron tuned out when Joey started to talk to the guy across the table.

The fair had attracted a mixed crowd, not so heavy on drunken frat boys that they'd be in a fight if Joey got a little up close and personal again, but not quite as public-grope friendly as the area outside the San Marco bars. Joey moved away from the table, shoving the necklace with the soft-edged translucent amber pendant in Aaron's hand.

"What?"

"Hold it for a second." Joey tucked his wallet back in his pocket and then grabbed the necklace, fastening it around his neck. "I got something for you too." He stepped into a space between two booths.

"Oh Christ, what?" If this was going to be one of those turquoise-and-silver-look-so-natural-on-you-what's-your-nation-Indian things, Joey'd be getting a whole different kind of bead shoved up his ass.

"Hold out your arm and close your eyes."

"Seriously?"

"Who won the bet?"

"Who set me the fuck up?" Aaron stuck his fist out away from his body, but fuck if he was closing his eyes.

Joey kept the piece hidden by his own hand as he wrapped the leather around Aaron's wrist and tied it off.

He looked down when Joey let go. If he had to put up with wearing it today because the little shit had hustled him—again—at least it wasn't too bad. A few strips of black leather knotted together with a single oval bead of dark polished steel on the top of his wrist.

"Hematite," Joey said, tapping the bead.

"Sounds like a kind of tick."

"They're supposed to be good for circulation or something." Joey moved back into traffic. "I had a boyfriend who made jewelry. Mostly wire and crystal and shells and stuff like that. He's got a pretty good online business."

"Tall Dude?" Aaron couldn't picture Joey's ex bent over a pile of tiny beads.

Joey laughed. "Noah? No. Not him." He looked like he was counting off in his head. "Two before him. Rene. In New Orleans."

California, Louisiana, Tallahassee and now Jacksonville. The guy got around.

"Exactly how many ex-boyfriends do you have?"

Joey made the same face he'd made when he'd reached for something with his right hand after he'd hurt his shoulder. "Ten?"

"You're asking me? What exactly do you consider a boyfriend?"

"I don't know—more than a fuck buddy. Like knowing some of his friends. Doing things other than just fucking."

"*Just* fucking?"

"Well, a lot of that too." Joey grinned, tipping his head up.

The necklace looked hot on him, made his tan throat even more lickable. Aaron thought about Joey riding him, watching the glass circle slam into the notch of his collarbone as Aaron fucked up into him. Did Joey consider Aaron a boyfriend? They were doing things other than fucking right now. Oh shit. Joey had dragged him on a date. Aaron was on a fucking date.

He didn't know whether to laugh or walk away. He stared at the barricades at the end of the block. He didn't exactly have anything against dates—as long as Sheree's dates happened so far away he didn't have to think about them. He just hadn't been on one, hadn't exactly planned to ever go on one. What was the point? You either fucked the guy when you met or you didn't.

The crowd was thinner down here, and a guy came up behind them on skates, eyes so fixed on Joey's ass that even Aaron could feel the stare. The guy turned and skated backward after he passed them, reached the barricades and circled back around, tucking a card in Joey's front pocket before skating through the barricades again.

Jesus Christ. Aaron had no idea a street fair in Neptune Beach was such prime cruising ground. "That happen often?"

"Even without the damsel-in-distress routine. Don't tell me you don't get hit on." Joey's gaze raked the length of Aaron's body, lingering like a touch on his crotch and at his shoulders.

"Not—" *Not when I'm with someone?* Aaron had never been *with* someone. Never really looked for sex anywhere but a bar or a club. "Not like that. And I don't take guys' numbers if I don't plan to call them."

"Ouch. The poor broken hearts in Jacksonville. It doesn't cost anything to be polite." But Joey didn't say whether he planned to follow through on any of his invitations.

"It's like lying," Aaron said.

"How? It's not a promise or anything. It's just not hurting people's feelings. Not being a prick."

"So I'm a prick?" Exactly what kind of a prick would have raised three kids when their mom took off?

"You already know you are." Joey's voice was soft but warm, like he meant it as a compliment. "Just like you know you're good at your job and good in bed."

"What happened to great?"

"All right, great." Joey smiled. "But you're not a prick because you don't care about people. It's because you're strong enough to call them on their bullshit."

"But still a prick. Thanks."

"Aaron." Joey's warm hand landed on Aaron's forearm. "I like the way you are. You tell the truth no matter what. Yeah, it makes people think you're an arrogant son of a bitch, but I like knowing where I stand with you. I like knowing I can believe what you say."

Aaron tried to deny the warmth that hit his stomach—the same flood of pride he'd gotten when he'd looked at the papers outlining Sheree's full ride to Tulane, pride in her and pride in himself for getting her there against all the odds. Joey's words zeroed in on the spot inside Aaron that wanted, still wanted, no matter how many times the world shit on him and told him he couldn't have it. Almost against his will, he pulled Joey in tight against his side, running a hand through the soft hair.

One thing Aaron had always held onto was that he'd never lied to the kids. Never broken a promise. That Joey understood how much it mattered felt good even as it freaked Aaron the hell out.

He stopped himself before he ended up kissing the top of Joey's head, for fuck's sake. Aaron didn't shove Joey away, only dropped his arm and turned back toward the rest of the fair. "Well, you can believe me when I tell you not to add me to that list of boyfriends."

Because Aaron didn't have any room for a boyfriend in his life. Not one like Joey with all these ideas and insights. Not one who could manipulate him into losing a bet so sweetly Aaron felt like thanking him. And certainly not someone from the Florida Department of Fuckups and Cunts who believed picking up coffee cups and taking babies from meth houses could actually make the world a better place.

"I have no intention of adding you to the list," Joey said. But his smile made Aaron wonder if Joey was lying through his white, even, mommy-the-dentist-loving teeth.

If anyone asked, which anyone didn't because Joey evidently knew better, Aaron's sense of honesty would have forced him to admit that he started to have fun at the fair. He couldn't pinpoint the time, but it was a bit before Joey found a booth that made mouth-watering souvlaki and bought them both a stuffed gyro. Maybe about the time when the buzz from the energy drinks kicked in.

Aaron refrained from comments about how much meat Joey could stuff in his mouth and then made a production of finding an overflowing trashcan and putting their wrappers and napkins in it. When Aaron crossed back to Joey, the fucker was laughing at him. It wasn't as if Aaron wanted a round of applause, but hey, he tried.

He didn't need to ask. Joey started explaining, "I just think it's funny that a guy who wipes out the shower after every use and freaks out over a crumb on the counter has such an issue with getting garbage to a trashcan."

The words died in his head before he'd let them out of his mouth. *Have you ever had to worry about a DFC inspection that could put your siblings in foster care to be abused and raped? Have you ever had to fight roaches for something for you and your sister to eat?* "I don't have to live here," he said out loud.

Joey shook his head. "Everyone else does."

"Not my problem."

"What exactly is?"

"You."

Joey took such a sudden step back it was like he'd been shoved. He'd turned and was ten steps away when Aaron caught up to Joey and grabbed his shoulder. "Joey. No, not like that. I—I told you I didn't like all that social worker shit. The questions."

"Fine. Enjoy the peace and quiet. See you around."

"Will you stop that for a second? Fuck. No wonder you've got ten ex-boyfriends. Stop acting like some kind of fucking princess."

Joey sputtered and Aaron smiled. "Hey. You're the one who called me a prick." Aaron pulled and Joey followed. "Sit down for a second."

Joey let Aaron lead them back to the bench where they'd eaten their lunch. "Look, just don't go all therapist on me, okay? I keep the house clean and I freak out at crumbs on the counter because I lived in some pretty shit places growing up. Places so disgusting there wasn't a single spot you'd want to set foot on. Places with lots of roaches and rats."

Even when he stopped talking, Joey didn't say anything. He wasn't nodding or doing any of that other clichéd therapist crap. He looked horrified. What the hell kind of work did he do that he'd never seen anything like that? Aaron knew he wasn't the only kid to grow up like he had.

Aaron took a deep breath and looked away. "So yeah. I don't like to think of having to live like that again, and I get a little nuts at the idea of ever having to deal with cockroaches again. I—" He wasn't going to tell him about having to dig through the dumpsters behind Wal-Mart to find something for the kids to wear—even before Mom took off. "I don't like public trashcans, okay? And I really don't see what the fuck the point is because there's always going to be trash around, but I get that you do."

He turned back to face Joey. If he was giving Aaron the whole sympathy and patient understanding—fuck, if there was one bit of pity in Joey's big brown eyes—Aaron was going to walk off and leave him there.

But Joey looked anything but sorry. He looked like he wanted to punch something. "Fuck," was all he said before he bit his lip and looked down.

"Bet there're a million social workery questions in that head of yours."

"No bet." Joey glanced back up and smiled, but he still looked mad. Aaron realized he'd seen Joey annoyed, like when Aaron made fun of him with the milk, but he hadn't actually seen Joey angry.

"Save 'em, okay?"

"I'll try." Joey stared at the ground and then tipped his head sideways to look at Aaron. "Princess?"

"You do get this kind of bossy, don't-fuck-with-my-tiara attitude when you get pissed."

Joey's lips twisted, but it wasn't a smile. "Okay, but call me nellie and I'll punch you out—even if I break a nail."

"I'll try to avoid it. You got plans for dessert?"

"Ice cream."

Chapter Eleven

After watching Joey take two licks of an ice cream cone, Aaron decided the state criminal code on lewd and lascivious behavior intended to provoke or incite a disturbance should be amended to include something about Joey Miller eating ice cream in public. As soon as he caught Aaron watching, Joey turned finishing the cone into a pornographic display worthy of any of Aaron's favorite online sites. He considered running over the dunes and right on into the ocean to cool down enough to keep walking through the fair.

As carefully as he watched, Joey's behavior didn't change at all after Aaron's admission. No sympathetic looks, no suddenly acting like Aaron was a fragile creature in need of therapy to overcome his traumatic past. Joey smiled and flirted and Aaron used a glare to ward off another guy with his number ready to slip in Joey's pants.

Joey caught the exchange and popped the whole rest of the cone in his mouth. Aaron's dick twitched in response. He was about to suggest they head back to the house when they got to the other end of the barricades. This was where the beer tent was, and beyond the barricades, Aaron could see a large crowd gathered around a booth with big red letters heralding the Thrust-O-Meter. They both had to show ID to get behind the barricade and into the crowd. Below the giant lettering announcing the Thrust-O-Meter was information about it being a fundraiser for a local HIV-AIDS clinic. The booth was staffed by a hot guy and a pretty girl who went into some funny routines about why everyone should spend five bucks for a shot at winning a bottle of lube. Every time they got to the end of their patter praising the amazing qualities of the lube, they and the crowd chorused, "And it even comes for you."

Aaron looked over the crowd and saw a young guy, egged on by some friends, plop down five bucks for his chance. The Thrust-O-Meter was rigged like a typical Strong Man pole, where you tried to hit the base with a hammer hard enough to send a marker up the post to ring a bell. There were clichéd dirty phrases along the post, one side for thrusting into guys, one side for thrusting into girls. But instead of using a hammer, the guy who approached put his hips against a padded lever and with one thrust for practice tried to slam forward hard enough to ring the bell. The guy got two thirds of the way up to the marker that read "In His Throat" and "Beaver Blaster".

Aaron turned to say something to Joey and saw he had wriggled his way up to the front of the crowd. If Joey was signing Aaron up, Aaron was going to kill him. He tried to shove forward quickly enough to intercept him, but Joey's money was already on the counter.

"All right. Let's hear it for Joey."

Aaron stopped as he watched the guy help Joey lower the height of the padded lever.

"Oh, this should be good."

Aaron turned at the sound of a familiar voice and saw Kim and Elaine from the hospital standing by, beers in hand.

"Something we should know about your little blond?" Kim asked.

Elaine smiled over the top of her beer cup.

Aaron shrugged with his eyebrows and turned to watch Joey. He held the hand grips and the bubble-shaped ass tipped back. On the practice try he got the marker up halfway to "Kidney Punch".

Aaron felt Kim turn to look at him with his annoying superior expression. How Kim could manage to make Aaron feel like Kim was looking down at him when Aaron had seven inches on the guy he couldn't figure out.

Joey smiled and tipped his hips back farther.

"Shit," Kim murmured.

Maybe he'd missed seeing Joey's ass since he was always on an exam table when Kim saw him. Aaron had to bite his tongue to keep from snapping, "Finders keepers."

Joey slammed forward, driving the marker just shy of the bell, all the way up to "Rectum, Damn Near Killed 'em".

"Whoa. Surprised you've lived to tell the tale," Kim muttered.

When there were no other takers, Joey put another five on the counter.

Aaron only smiled. Joey got almost as high on his third and fourth tries.

Elaine finished her beer and stepped up. After a murmured conversation with the booth-runners, she was allowed to use her arm to thrust. "Hey, it's what I fuck with," she said over her shoulder to Kim and Aaron.

Elaine didn't need two tries. The bell rang and the woman presented her with the lube and a certificate. She waved and went back into the beer tent. A woman with tits even Aaron knew were impressive followed her in.

"Guess she's getting lucky," Kim sighed.

Joey started forward again.

Aaron pulled him back. "What the hell? Do you always have to win?"

Joey's face was red from his brief workout. His shoulder had to be hurting. "Maybe I really want the lube. It's 'the most sexually space-aged substance in the known universe'."

"So I'll buy you a bottle. They're selling it."

"I want to win it."

"Why, trying to collect more numbers?"

"Are you jealous?"

"Fuck no." And it wasn't a lie. He didn't care how many numbers got stuffed down Joey's pants. Joey hadn't shown any real interest in anyone.

Joey shrugged. "It's for a good cause."

"Is this some elaborate manipulation to get me to do it?" Aaron growled the words into Joey's ear.

"No." The tension went out of the arm Aaron was holding. "I don't even really want you to do it," Joey said on a sigh.

"Afraid I'll get a better offer if someone sees how good I am?"

"Prick." Joey punched him lightly.

"Princess."

"Just let me do it one more time."

"Jesus Christ." Aaron dug out his wallet, ignoring Kim snickering behind them. "I'll do it before you hurt yourself."

"There is a doctor present," Kim reminded Aaron.

"Fuck you."

"The only one fucked here is you, Chase."

Aaron almost turned around to ask Kim what the hell he meant but then he remembered the sudden need to pull Joey in tight, that he'd bothered to explain himself to Joey, and Aaron had the feeling he knew exactly what Kim meant. Stepping up to the padded boards, he saw exactly how Elaine had won. It wasn't so much strength as leverage and angle. Just like fucking for real. He didn't grip the handles, but held on lower, where he'd grip Joey's—or any guy's—hips and made one medium stroke to test his theory. The marker went halfway up. He kept his hips in position, cock and balls safe in the empty space between the padded boards, and went up and in. The marker flew up and banged against the bell.

Ignoring the catcalls and whistles, he tossed the certificate on the ground and handed the lube to Joey.

"My hero." Joey batted his eyes.

"That's all he gets?" Kim asked.

"He gets spectacularly blown," Joey said.

"Oh yes he does," Aaron agreed, leering at Kim.

Joey wrapped an arm around Aaron's neck and dragged him down so he could whisper in his ear. "I fucking hate you."

"No you don't."

"No. I don't."

Joey's quiet agreement left a queasy feeling in Aaron's stomach.

They decided to save the lube for later, so Aaron did get spectacularly blown.

Joey pushed Aaron down on the bed and took him at an angle, throat hot and tight with every swallow. Aaron wrapped his fingers in the softer new growth at the roots of Joey's hair and held on for the ride. The tight grip only made Joey groan and then he was humming, bobbing, holy shit, Aaron swore Joey was singing as he sucked. Just as Aaron felt the burn in his balls, Joey pulled off and fucked the slit with the ball on his tongue ring, fast and light, lips a vise around the crown.

The last thought Aaron had before his brain melted and shot out of his dick was that he owed a kidney to whoever had taught Joey how to suck cock.

Aaron lay there, trying to find enough breath, enough spit to reciprocate when Joey said, "You'd better get in the shower if you're going to make it to work."

Aaron rolled onto his side so he could look at him. "Exactly how is it that on a day when you get whatever you want you don't get off?"

Joey's slow smile, the heavy-lidded blink, gave Aaron's dick ideas it should have known it wasn't in any shape for.

"Because when you get home I want you to top the shit out of me."

Aaron's kitchen counter was gleaming under Joey's careful attention when he got the text message: *Lvg erly b rdy.* He had planned to be ready when Aaron came home, but now Joey would have to hurry. With the new bottle of lube in hand, he studied the label before squirting some on his fingers. It did feel different, not particularly more slippery, but a different texture. It truly was closer to actual come, except it didn't seem to get sticky. It even tasted pretty good.

At first he didn't know why he'd gotten so intense over winning that stupid contest. He always wanted to win, at anything. His psych classes said it was because of birth order, firstborns naturally being more competitive. But it was more than that. After he'd thought about it, he realized it wasn't about winning as much as it was winning in front of Aaron that was important. Especially after what Aaron had said about growing up.

Every time Joey thought about what Aaron had told him, Joey felt anger flash through him, like it always did when kids got betrayed by the people who were supposed to be looking after them. Knowing what it had done to Aaron frustrated Joey to the point where he needed to show his strength in a way Aaron could understand. So Aaron could see Joey could take care of himself—and Aaron if necessary—instead of thinking of Joey as the damsel in distress.

Maybe he shouldn't have made that request of Aaron before he went to work. Maybe it should have been just Joey taking Aaron in, wrapped around him, keeping him safe. But if Joey had changed the way he acted, especially the way he acted in bed, Aaron would know and it would piss him off.

With all that thinking, Joey barely got back out of the bedroom before Aaron was coming through the back door.

Joey tucked his hands in the pockets of his jeans and licked his lips as Aaron came toward him. "You are early."

"Got someone to cover the last hour of my shift." Aaron put a hand on Joey's neck and dragged him forward. "Fuck. I was hard the whole way home." His other hand fisted Joey's shirt, pulling until their hips met. Aaron's mouth came down until his breath was heating Joey's lips. "Call this ready?"

"Yup."

"I don't think you followed directions."

"So what are you going to do about it?"

Aaron's hand slipped down Joey's back, into the waistband of his jeans. "I'm gonna— Fuck."

Joey's knees got wobbly as the harsh groan in Aaron's throat made Joey's already-hard cock leak. Aaron's fingers found the base of the plug in Joey's ass. "Fuckfuckfuck," Aaron murmured in Joey's ear, voice sounding like it had been scraped raw by gravel.

He wiggled the plug, and Joey groaned into the sweat, humid-night smell of Aaron's neck.

"Didn't jerk off, did you?" Aaron released his shirt, and Joey swayed a little. Aaron's hand rubbed over Joey's cock.

Joey shook his head.

"Off." Aaron pulled on Joey's jeans.

Joey tipped his head up for a kiss, but Aaron stepped away and sat on the couch. Joey couldn't imagine how he'd ever thought Aaron's eyes were cold or hard. They were practically glowing now as he spread out in the center of the couch, watching. Joey unfastened the top button of his jeans and then rubbed his cock through the denim, the motion making his ass shift around the narrow neck of the plug.

Aaron's eyes darkened and Joey unzipped his jeans, reached inside and drew his cock through the opening. He licked his thumb and rubbed the head.

"If you come now, you'll be really sorry," Aaron growled.

"I know." Joey bit his lip and closed his eyes, because if he kept watching Aaron watch him, Joey was going to be sorry. Still stroking his cock, he used his free hand to slide the jeans off his hips.

He kicked them off his ankles and then turned around before he bent to pick them up, so Aaron could watch the skin stretched around the plug, and couldn't keep a moan from slipping out of his own mouth. Joey folded the jeans and put them on the chair, smiling as he reached for his shirt.

"Just the pants."

Oh shit. Joey's breath got sticky, trapped and thick in his throat. Aaron knew what he was doing. Half-naked always felt much sleazier than naked. Aaron peeled off his own shirt and jeans and sat in his briefs.

He crooked a finger, and Joey came close enough to touch. The crooked finger tangled in the hem of his shirt. Joey stared at the spot, the only spot where Aaron made contact. It wasn't skin, even with the jut of Joey's cock a whisper away from Aaron's wrist, and Joey still couldn't catch his breath.

"Hey." How could Aaron's voice be so steady?

Joey looked up and met his eyes.

"No more topping from the bottom, okay?"

Joey nodded and stopped himself before he grinned again. If Mark had ever caught him at it, the teasing, the trying to get what he wanted, he never called Joey on it. That Aaron did, and that he was telling Joey to stop, tightened something deep inside him. Like the moment when he got up on a big storm-driven wave, and he had no idea how it was going to break.

He waited, and fuck if Aaron didn't draw it out until Joey almost broke. At last, he shifted his grip on Joey's shirt and let his knuckles brush Joey's belly, just above where Joey's cock was trying to grow an extra inch to get some touch. Aaron pulled Joey off balance and onto the couch, then dragged him until he was lying face down across Aaron's lap.

Joey wanted to sigh in anticipation, even as his muscles tensed. A few slaps with the plug in would feel so good. Aaron's hand came down against Joey's ass and he arched into it, but it was only a light smack, just enough to tingle the skin. Aaron followed with a dozen more, barely slaps, just hard enough to wake up the nerves.

The realization hit him right as Aaron increased the intensity of the slaps. This wasn't a game. It wasn't a mock punishment or even a power play. This was all about sensation, give and take, going to the edge together. Aaron wasn't only going to spank him a couple of times and then fuck him, Aaron was warming his ass so every single stroke was a deliberate push higher, farther in and out of themselves. He hadn't given Joey a safe word, though Joey was pretty sure if he got vocal enough Aaron would stop, because this wasn't just a scene.

Aaron was making something with him, and while no one watching it would call it love, with Joey's heart slamming and his skin buzzing everywhere, not only from his hips to his thighs where the blows landed, it was pretty close to it.

The slaps had gone from tingling to stinging, leaving a rush behind as his ass got hotter and hotter. Even when Aaron's hand didn't touch the plug, the blows went into Joey's body, fucked him, pure pleasure inside.

Aaron stopped and rubbed the hot skin, soothing a little of the burn. Joey was kind of disappointed. He'd been sure it would last longer, and he didn't want to lose any of the sweet inch-deep ache. Aaron grabbed the base of the plug and started to pull it out, then fucked it back in a couple of times, until Joey moaned and clutched the couch arm over his head. He hadn't been forbidden to do anything—except trying to push not so subtly in the direction he wanted to go. He could move or talk. But he didn't want to do anything. Even the MP3 player in his head had stopped playing instrumental techno and gone silent, the only sound the echo of his quick hard breaths coming from Aaron.

As Aaron slipped the toy free, Joey tried to use his muscles to hold it in, but he couldn't. Empty, his ass stung more. But not enough that he didn't want Aaron to keep going. Joey dug his fingers harder into the rounded couch arm as Aaron started spanking him again, harder, slower, but with not quite enough time for Joey to catch his breath before the next crack of heat on his skin. Sometimes Aaron would hit him a couple times in the same space, and when Joey tried to shift, to move some different skin under that hard hand, Aaron just put his free hand on Joey's back and held him still. The slaps near the top of his ass hurt a little more, less meat under the skin, but the ones low, almost lifting his ass off his thighs, stung like an electric shock, and Aaron kept going back there again and again.

Joey knew he was sweating, and he was pretty sure the slickness of the arm over him and the legs under him wasn't just from him. His dick was a sixteen ton spike of iron, and his balls rocked with every slap. He'd never been pushed so far, never had it go to the point where he'd really want to safe-word out, but he was almost there. The lines of pleasure and pain were so blurred in his head that his entire body was nothing more than a giant nerve ending held too close to the fire.

Maybe his breathing changed, or maybe it was something in the way he held his body, but at the moment when it was almost too much, Aaron stopped again, rubbing, soothing, and this time Joey wanted it. He arched his scalded ass into Aaron's hand, sighed when Aaron's thumb sank into the crease and then inside.

"Six more." It had been so long since either of them spoke that Joey almost jumped at Aaron's words. "I'm going to give you six more."

Joey heard the question in that quiet statement. The thought of Aaron's hand coming down hard on skin already white-hot and balloon-tight was scary, but so was the idea of stopping. Joey had never gone far enough to get to the other side, never been forced to ride until it dumped him and if he was going to wipe out, melt down and start crying and begging, he'd rather do it here with Aaron than with anyone else.

Aaron hadn't asked, but Joey nodded anyway. He told himself to relax. It wasn't Aaron's hand Joey felt, but the cool nudge of the plug at his hole. He pushed back into it on a groan, the full sensation in his ass turning all that heat into want. God, he wanted to get fucked.

The first hard slap took his breath from his lungs and his thoughts right out of his head. Aaron's palm landed right over the base of the toy and drove it deep inside even as his fingers must have gone two inches into Joey's flesh. Okay. That hurt. But now with the silicone in his ass, the sudden pain turned into an adrenaline rush, and damn, he hadn't felt this high and confused since college.

The next blow came before he had time to sort it out and again, the initial blast of pain rolled into something good and completely unexplainable. And his heart was going to rip through his chest. It wasn't pleasure diffused and achy and almost a cramp like when he came from just getting fucked. The pain sensations were all right in his skin, but the powerful waves that followed came from deep inside.

Aaron pulled the toy out again. "Last three. Just you and me."

"Yeah." But it was lightning cracking across already-burnt flesh and nothing to spread it inside.

Aaron waited for Joey to catch his breath, but he didn't want to. Didn't want this.

"Please," Joey said.

Aaron's hand lifted off Joey's back, cold air rushing onto sweat-soaked skin. "Please what?"

It wasn't sarcastic. Quiet. Expectant.

Please fuck me. Please stop. Please don't. Please make me see if I can. But Joey only nodded and Aaron let his hand fly against Joey's skin again. He didn't have words for all the different feelings anymore, it hurt, it felt good, it burned, but when Aaron's hand came down over his back to hold him for the last one, Joey's whole body hummed with knowing that this was what he wanted, and even though he'd played in dungeons with rules and etiquette and tops who'd probably practiced for years, he'd never be safer, never feel more like every inch of him was protected, never know better what it was to be so close to someone, someone who knew what his body wanted more than he did.

The cry from his lips wasn't pain when the last blow landed. It was almost like coming, pushed past anything you could control so that your voice wasn't your own.

Aaron moved fast then, sliding out from under him, stretching Joey out on the cushions and crouching between his legs to kiss and lick the skin his hand had heated. His hair fell forward, a cool and silky contrast to the warmth of his mouth.

He kissed up along Joey's sweat-dotted spine to the nape of his neck before lying out on top of him, wrapping an arm around his hips to fist Joey's cock. "Come with me. C'mon."

Even the soft cotton of Aaron's briefs scraped against Joey's ass like sandpaper.

"Want you to fuck me."

"Later. Promise." He started with long strokes then slicked down the precome from Joey's slit and started jacking him fast.

"The couch."

"Fuck it. I'll clean it up."

Joey rocked his hips, and Aaron's cloth-covered dick slid against the crease of Joey's ass.

"Fuck, Joey. So fucking hot. Jesus."

Aaron had never said anything like that to Joey before. His balls hiked up.

"C'mon. Come for me, please. So good."

Even coming was going to hurt, and Joey knew it. His body could only handle so much sensation. It ripped through him fast, but still good, even if it felt like all the heat in his ass shot through his dick.

"Yeah." Aaron ground down harder, and Joey bit his lip.

But he met the friction on his ass by arching up into Aaron's downward push, kept moving while Aaron jerked and shuddered against him.

Joey had no intention of ever even trying to remember how to move. He was going to stay here for the rest of his life, Aaron's weight like the best down quilt, Aaron's heart slamming against Joey's shoulder, rough, hot breath on his neck. He didn't fall asleep, just drifted in and out. He probably would have fallen asleep if Aaron hadn't moved, taking all of Joey's warmth with him.

"C'mon, dude, not sleeping here." That was Aaron's matter-of-fact voice. The one he probably used on the job. The one that got you to calm down when some freak industrial accident had cut off your arm.

It was nothing like the rough whisper he'd been using, and Joey wanted to regress to petulant teenager dragged from bed by his mother, burrow under the covers and beg for five more minutes, but the covers were gone and now he could feel the cooling mess on his stomach and the ache in his hands from where he was still holding the sofa arm like a life raft.

He shifted and the last of the good floating feeling went away, leaving him sticky, cold and sore. He climbed onto his feet and made sure things were steady before he started for the bedroom. He wasn't going to give Aaron another reason to feel like he had to half-carry him. Joey barely remembered to strip off his shirt before sprawling onto the sheets.

Aaron didn't join him right away. Joey could hear him moving around, probably trying to get come off the couch.

With Joey stretched out on his belly, his arms were pushed out so that his shoulder ached in protest. He rolled onto his side, trying to find a way to placate the twinge in his shoulder and the deep swollen throb in his ass. He didn't regret anything, but he was going to be feeling Aaron's hard hand for days.

Joey hadn't even started to drift when he felt Aaron's weight hit the bed. He pulled a sheet over them both, and pressed up along Joey's back, dropping sharp quick kisses on his neck. The kisses were nice, much better than the impersonal "not sleeping here," but after what they'd just done together, and he knew it sounded like a ridiculous way to describe kinky sex, but after the intimacy, everything else felt cold and distant. Even the press of Aaron's soft cock against Joey's still-burning skin was less a reminder of where they'd gone than something that Joey wanted to complain about so he could get to sleep.

But Aaron's hand stroked along Joey's side, drifting gently over his hip as Aaron whispered, "Jesus, Joey," in his deep voice and Joey felt that connection, felt everything they'd done rush back into him, click into place, and he was asleep in seconds.

Aaron didn't think he'd been out for even an hour when he woke up with Joey sprawled on top, his body heat sinking right into Aaron's bones, a bit of drool on his shoulder. He ran a hand down Joey's back, stopping just at the dip in his spine above his ass. Fuck. Aaron had tried stuff before, played a little, knew some basic shit from porn, books and hanging around, but he'd never been part of anything like that. And he still didn't know how he'd become a part of it this time.

He'd planned to fuck Joey over the couch, the counter, on the floor, against a wall and then suck him hard and do it again. But when Joey showed Aaron exactly how ready he was, Aaron lost his mind for a bit. And then watching Joey told Aaron exactly what to do. Exactly what Joey needed. Every hitched breath, the stretch and tension of his muscles, the hard wet rub of his cock on Aaron's thigh let him know how much further they could go. Sex with nothing more than his hand on Joey's ass, and Aaron still felt like he'd been deeper than ever inside Joey's body.

Even now Aaron wanted to fuck him, yeah, but even more he didn't want to stop touching him. Like it'd almost hurt if he did.

Joey rubbed his head on Aaron's chest, a scrape of stubble.

"Don't wipe your drool and eye boogers on me, dude."

Joey laughed and lifted his head. "Aren't you tired?"

Aaron was. But his dick was pulsing, his hand itching to move lower and learn how hot Joey's ass still was. "I've been a parent and I work as a paramedic. I'm used to sleep deprivation."

The muscles under Aaron's hand went rigid, and Joey lifted his head. Aaron supposed he couldn't bitch about a question, since he'd been the one to bring it up.

"Parent," Joey said. The even inflection kept it from being a question. Barely.

Aaron let out a long breath. "My mom took off when I was a teenager so my sister and I kind of raised our younger brothers and sister."

Aaron turned to meet Joey's steady gaze. Even in the dark, Aaron could see his answer had sparked a million more questions. Joey's teeth flashed as he bit his lower lip, sucked it in. Aaron was pretty sure Joey was about to draw blood he was trying so hard not to ask them all right now.

The heroic effort deserved a reward. "One," Aaron said.

"How old?"

"Me or...?"

Joey considered that for a second. "Your youngest sibling. How old when your mom left?"

"Six."

"Wow." Joey's focus went inward. Like when he was trying to add up his list of ex-boyfriends. He was probably trying to extrapolate everything from that one answer, his head all busy with things that didn't involve how good it would feel to put their bodies together again.

"Oh." Joey's teeth flashed again, this time in a smile. He rubbed against Aaron's thickening cock. "That's why you woke up."

"Well. Yeah."

Joey blinked and then stretched his neck up to meet Aaron's kiss. It went from a whisper to a groan in an instant, Joey's tongue wet and slick, his breathing already getting ragged. Aaron's hand slipped down the last few inches and found skin that almost burned a layer off his palm.

"Shit." He groaned the word into Joey's mouth and rolled him under.

Aaron watched Joey's face as his ass made contact with the sheet under their combined weight. He winced, and then flicked his tongue across his lips and moaned, calves climbing up around Aaron's hips as their cocks rubbed together. Aaron slipped down and sucked Joey fully hard, working his balls, rubbing the ridge underneath.

Joey bucked up, pushing the head of his cock into Aaron's throat, but groaning, "No. Fuck me. C'mon. Stop."

Aaron pulled off and licked at Joey's balls, dragging his thumb lower to find him still slick and stretched.

Joey climbed up away from him and turned on the light. After digging in the nightstand, he tossed a condom and the new bottle of lube down.

Aaron rocked back on his knees, ripped open the condom

and held up the lube.

"It's really good. Put some under the condom."

Aaron tested it on his fingers, handing the rubber back to Joey. The stuff did feel nice. Felt even better on Aaron's dick as he spread a little over the head and some down the shaft. Not enough to risk the condom sliding off.

Joey sat up, groaning as his weight shifted, and slipped the condom over Aaron's cock. He stroked the rest of the lube on his fingers over the top of the rubber and Joey sank back down, ankles locking around Aaron's back. Sliding his sheathed dick around the outside of Joey's hole, Aaron looked down. Joey's new necklace moved with his quick hard breaths, shifted side to side as Joey tried to wiggle down onto Aaron's dick.

"Fuck me." Joey's voice was warm, husky, almost like he was singing that jazz song again. Aaron wondered if Joey could sing while getting fucked. Thought about being surrounded by his voice while inside his body.

Aaron pressed the tip in. Heat and pressure combined with the slippery lube under the latex—God. He moved forward until only the head was all the way in, feeling Joey's heartbeat around him, everything smooth, wet, hot. Fuck, Aaron swore they were sharing a pulse.

He pulled out again, and Joey's voice got huskier. "Fuck me. Don't—"

Aaron pushed the head in again. He wasn't teasing. It just felt so good. The muscles fluttering like a tongue on the head of his cock, clamping down to try to pull him in deeper.

Joey tried to push his way down, force Aaron all the way in. "Fuck me, fuck me, Aaron, fuck me. I'm going to kill you if you don't fuck me right now, I—"

Aaron dragged back, the sensitive rim on his dick rocking just under the tight ring of Joey's ass. Joey's voice lowered to a growl, and Aaron flexed his hips to drive all the way in, his whole cock squeezed in slippery heat.

Joey's hands turned to fists, first on the sheets, then in his own hair, and finally grinding into his eyes as Aaron started to thrust, Joey's heels grinding into Aaron's back, pulling him closer every time. He wasn't one to talk in bed beyond any necessary communication, but when he cupped Joey's ass and lifted him, Aaron could feel Joey's groan bone-deep and had to ask, "How's it feel?"

"Feel you inside and out." Joey's fists moved away from his eyes and he smiled. "Almost like I'm still over your lap."

Settling Joey's ass on his thighs, Aaron lifted Joey's legs over his shoulders. "Tomorrow, I'm gonna fuck you on your knees and my hips'll slap you like you're still getting spanked."

"Yeah?"

Aaron reached around to rub hard on the sore skin, and Joey's neck arched back. His dick never flagged, hard and leaking against his stomach. Heat built at the base of Aaron's spine, spreading into his balls. He held on long enough to grab Joey's cock, trying to jack him while dragging across his prostate with every thrust.

Joey put his hands under his own thighs to open up more, Aaron's cock sliding deeper, even as the walls of Joey's ass squeezed heat and friction on the skin of Aaron's cock.

Aaron stared down at Joey again. Not at the necklace, or the way Joey was chewing on his bottom lip as he groaned over and over, but down into the wide, dark eyes until instead of feeling like he was going to come, Aaron felt dizzy, like he was going to fall.

Joey's ass clamped down hard, a tight flutter as he shot onto Aaron's hand and wrist. Finally, Aaron let himself fall, head dropping onto Joey's until their foreheads were pressed together. Aaron shuddered out every last drop into Joey—into the rubber—but fuck, what it would feel like to actually empty himself inside Joey, to slide those last few strokes on come. Aaron jerked again, and Joey rested his hands on the back of Aaron's neck.

Aaron didn't want to move, didn't want his cock out of Joey, but everything was so slick he had to check that the condom was still doing what it was supposed to. Joey's fingers locked around his neck when he started to move, gold-brown lashes dropping to cover dark, sleepy eyes. So maybe he wasn't the only one high off the electric connection in the touch of their skin.

"Gotta ditch the rubber, Joey. Just a sec."

Joey released his neck and let his legs drop open. He made a face when Aaron pulled out, and Aaron figured sticky probably didn't feel that good on Joey's ass right now. Aaron wiped him off with the sheet, since with Joey's body heat they didn't need it anyway, even if the A/C kicked on.

Joey was still on his back, and Aaron dropped on top of him. Joey managed a half-hearted attempt to touch Aaron's head before he dropped back off to sleep. Aaron put his face in the pillow over Joey's left shoulder and sank into sleep thinking about sex on the beach.

A noise that didn't belong woke Aaron around three. Joey was a full-body heating pad plastered to Aaron's back, but he didn't wake when Aaron sat up. Someone—someones were in the house. He hadn't heard a window break, and he'd locked both doors before coming to bed.

"Be quiet."

"You be quiet, asshole."

Aaron relaxed back into the mattress. The slapstick duo of Darryl and Dylan were staggering down the hall from the kitchen.

"Christ, Darryl, Aaron'll probably shoot us on accident if we wake him up."

"Me on accident. You on purpose."

"Funny."

"Do you really think he has a gun?"

"Wanna find out?"

"No."

Aaron could imagine Darryl sliding his glasses back up his nose. Both the twins had needed glasses at fourteen, but Dylan had switched to contacts at sixteen.

They made their unstealthy way into their bedroom and shut the door.

When Aaron sat up, Joey had rolled onto his belly but movement didn't change the even rhythm of his breath, sleeping the sleep of the extremely well-fucked.

It's not like Aaron's brothers didn't know Aaron was gay, they'd just never been confronted with physical evidence of it before.

This should be interesting.

Chapter Twelve

Blaring music and screeching tires jarred Joey awake with a pounding heart. The explosive action movie Aaron felt the need to play at bed-shaking volume was punctuated with a clichéd trash-talking soundtrack. Joey crawled to the end of the bed, intending to stagger out and suggest more pleasant ways of shaking the bed and waking up the guy sleeping in it.

By the time Joey put his first foot on the floor, a few more details became part of his consciousness. His stomach muscles ached, his thighs ached, his shoulder ached, and his ass fucking hurt. The last in a good way though, a deep rush of sensation that got him thinking about Aaron fucking him, touching him, groaning his name in a way that made Joey's stomach drop like he'd caught the sharpest breaking wave in front of a hurricane. He also figured out it wasn't movie dialogue he was hearing.

His unusually slow-to-process morning brain could be blamed on being fucked senseless. It shouldn't have taken him this long to recognize the blasting hip-hop music and sound effects as Grand Theft Auto on Xbox. And the bad movie dialogue was actual conversation between two new voices. Male teen voices.

Aaron's brothers.

Walking out—even dressed—would be in clear violation of Aaron's no-meeting-the-family rule, but since Aaron had already tossed out the no-playing-house rule, Joey didn't think it was going to be a problem. He had no intention of hiding in

Aaron's bedroom until Aaron decided to smuggle Joey out the back door. And if Aaron did mind, that was his problem.

Joey had wanted Aaron when they met, felt that spark when they kissed, but now—especially after last night—Joey wanted the whole deal. The whole family, friends, talk-over-coffee, hang-out-and-play-Halo, *wanna-go-to-the-movies-before-or-after-we-fuck* deal. When Joey had said he had no intention of putting Aaron on the list of ex-boyfriends, Joey had meant it. Because he was more sure than ever that this was it. No more exes. No more next times. Just Aaron.

There was a pair of jeans loose enough to stand pulling over Joey's still radioactively warmed ass at the bottom of the duffle bag he'd been living out of. As he dug them out, he looked at his laptop and mini Casio keyboard in the case next to it. He hadn't taken them out once in the last week, hadn't felt like working on any of his songs. It wasn't as if he thought Aaron would laugh at him, since Aaron seemed to like Joey's singing, but the urge hadn't been there. He was however positive that if he checked his ass out in the mirror like he wanted to and Aaron caught him at it, he would crack up.

Joey stuffed his last pair of clean briefs back in the bag. The elastic would cut right into the edge of his thighs, but he wasn't sure he could handle the rub of denim if he went without. He found a pair of soft worn boxers in the bottom of Aaron's dresser and pulled them on. He debated between one of his work shirts and a T-shirt and went with the T-shirt. It was tight, but it wasn't like the twins wouldn't know why he was there—or would they? A blast of panic spit acid into his empty stomach. What if the kids—the kids Aaron had raised—didn't know he was gay?

He slipped down the hall, hoping he could catch Aaron's eye for a clue, but Aaron didn't look around until Joey was all the way in the kitchen. A steaming mug of coffee was in one hand while the other stirred what looked like a carton of scrambled eggs and turned a panful of bacon.

"Hey," Aaron said, as if his brothers were in the living room playing Grand Theft Auto every morning, "there's some juice left."

Joey felt a little like he was underwater as he moved to the fridge and grabbed the juice. The glass he poured stayed glued to his hand as he turned to look over the counter into the living room. From what Joey could see, the twins were tall and lean like Aaron, voices indistinguishable as they shouted at each other about the game. One of them jumped to his feet as the game-level ended. "Yeah."

The high scores came up. "Who the fuck is JDM?"

Joey put down the juice. "That would be me," he called.

The twins came around the couch at opposite ends and headed for the counter.

"Joey David Miller."

"Like I said," the twin without glasses who Joey guessed was Dylan spoke. "Who the fuck is Joseph David Miller?" He looked over at his older brother who was dishing up the eggs.

Aaron had left Joey out to dry, but he could see a twitch at the corner of Aaron's mouth that was the start of a smile. The twin in the eyeglasses, Darryl, watched Joey.

"It's Joey, not Joseph, says so on my birth certificate." He was pretty sure he knew how to handle Dylan. Joey had met lots of Dylans over the years.

"And I care why?" Dylan asked, still watching his older brother.

Joey looked around Dylan at the scores flashing on the screen. "Because Joey David Miller is the one who can totally kick your ass at GTA or Halo or anything else."

That dragged Dylan's attention back to Joey.

"Dylan, right?"

"How the—?"

"And Darryl?"

The twin in glasses nodded.

Dylan looked back at Aaron. "Why you puttin' me on blast for?"

"Shut up, Dylan," his twin said. "It's fucking pathetic when you try that gangsta shit. How's it go over at the Texas Culinary Academy?"

Joey had to suck in his lips to avoid laughing.

Aaron put the four plates of eggs on the counter, and Dylan came around to the kitchen side to pull out some silverware. Eyeing Joey more obviously than even the creepiest guy who'd ever cruised him, Dylan grabbed a fork for himself and his brother and went back to the opposite side.

"Damn, bro," Dylan said. "You know I ain't like that, but your boo's got a sweeter ass than a girl's. I'd so bust that ass up."

"Jesus Christ, Dylan." Darryl sounded a lot like his older brother when he was exasperated. "Like you get any at all."

Aaron leaned back against the counter edge between the fridge and the stove. Joey could tell he was hiding his smile in his coffee mug.

"I'll take it as a compliment, but no thanks," Joey said and watched Aaron choke on his coffee.

Aaron was blocking the silverware drawer, forcing Joey to hip him out of the way when he wouldn't move.

"So what are you doing here?" Dylan asked in between forkfuls of eggs.

That was the first thing Dylan had said that bothered Joey. He didn't want Aaron thinking too much about it, either. Going for the kill, Joey said, "I suck your brother's cock and take it up my ass. Any more questions?"

"Gross. Fuck no. Jesus." Dylan grabbed his plate and went into the living room.

"If you spill anything clean it up," Aaron yelled after him.

"Yeah, fine. Like your neat-freak shit wasn't my first clue you were a fag," Dylan muttered, but it was deliberately loud enough to be audible in the kitchen.

Darryl looked like he might want to apologize for his brother, and then simply pushed his glasses up his nose and started shoveling eggs and bacon into his mouth. He reached out for the glass of juice Joey had relinquished and downed it in a swallow.

Joey poured out the rest of the juice, and Darryl finished that too.

As Joey started on his own eggs, Aaron decided to offer an explanation, "I didn't know they were coming. They said they were too broke to do anything else for spring break so they caught a ride home."

"Where do you go to school, Darryl?"

"UT," Darryl mumbled around the food in his mouth.

"University of Texas. Full ride." The pride in Aaron's voice spread warmth all the way to Joey's stomach.

"With work study," Darryl added with an eye roll very much like Aaron's.

"Pays for the books, I bet. Do they have you running around the library?" Joey asked.

"Yeah. Did you do that?"

Aaron arched a brow. "Didn't Mommy and Daddy make enough?"

"I didn't get work study." Brendan, ex number two, did, but that was another topic Joey didn't particularly want to bring up right now. "I worked off campus."

"Where'd you go to school?" Darryl asked.

"USC."

"What for?"

"Masters in Counseling. Social work."

"Oh shit." Darryl looked like he wanted to crawl under the counter.

Joey had managed to figure out all by himself that Aaron's experiences with the Florida Department of Families and Children wouldn't be winning the agency any service awards, but he was still missing big pieces of the puzzle.

Aaron tossed the pans into the sink with enough force to snap Dylan's attention away from SpongeBob on the TV.

"What the fuck?" Dylan yelled.

"Shut up, Dylan."

Dylan flipped his brother off and went back to watching TV. Aaron turned the water on full blast.

"Um, Joey." Darryl looked over at his older brother's back. "How did you know which of us was which?"

"You guys identical?"

"Yeah."

Joey wasn't about to tell Darryl he'd figured him for the quieter one after having eavesdropped on Aaron yelling at them over the phone. "Lucky guess."

"Oh."

"Yo." Dylan came up behind his twin and shoved his plate onto the counter. "Let's go."

"Where?" Darryl asked, echoed by Aaron.

"Out."

Aaron went into his bedroom and came out with his wallet. He put a twenty on the counter. Dylan grabbed it.

"If you want to take the truck, get some groceries."

"Cool."

Aaron held up another twenty. "If you want this, you gotta come clean."

"About what?" Darryl asked.

"Don't bullshit me. Sheree sent you here. When's she coming?"

Darryl was able to pull off a look of confused innocence.

Dylan caved in a heartbeat. "She made us promise." He grabbed for the twenty.

Aaron held it out of reach.

"Fine. She said you were getting majorly old and it was your birthday so we had to show up."

"She'll be here Tuesday. She had an exam or something," Darryl added now that his brother had surrendered.

Aaron handed the twenty to Darryl who easily sidestepped Dylan's attempt to intercept the handoff. Aaron whipped the keys at Dylan who caught them easily.

"Make sure the place doesn't reek of spunk and ass when

178

we get back." Dylan made sure he was halfway through the kitchen door when he spoke.

"Will you shut the fuck up about it, Dylan? Jesus." The door slammed behind them.

Joey wished the twins hadn't taken off so fast. He wasn't sure how Aaron was going to react right now. He half-expected Aaron to suddenly remember that Joey out of the sling equaled Joey able to drive and toss him out the door.

Instead, Aaron slipped behind Joey where he was scraping the food left on the twins' plates into the garbage and rubbed his ass.

Joey sucked in a quick breath, not with pain, but with the sudden rush of want that hit as the sensitive skin tingled from the lightest touch.

"You ever gonna shower today?" Aaron draped his arms around Joey's waist.

"Sunday. I don't have any place to be."

"So you're going to spend all day smelling like sex?" Aaron's chin rested on the top of Joey's head. Had the sudden presence of his brothers turned Aaron into a cuddling softie?

"Hmm. What would your brothers think?"

Aaron shifted to hold him tighter, an arm over Joey's left shoulder and around his chest, and pulled him away from the garbage. "They can deal or crash somewhere else. Wish I'd had a camera for Dylan's face."

This was not what Joey had expected at all. Not Aaron dragging him into the shower. Not Aaron dropping to his knees and sucking Joey's cock into a hot, wet throat. Not the hoarse whispers of Joey's name as Aaron crouched to slide his cock between Joey's slick thighs.

And definitely not the way Aaron couldn't stop touching him.

Every time Joey thought he was starting to understand what Aaron wanted, needed, expected, everything shifted. After they toweled off, Joey ducked into Aaron's room to dress.

"They won't be back for awhile. They're making the

K.A. Mitchell

rounds," Aaron said as he grabbed a pair of jeans from his dresser.

"I'm sorry if I chased them off."

Aaron buttoned his jeans. "You didn't."

That didn't give Joey much to work with. "I don't have any brothers. Just three sisters. All younger."

"They get squirted into toilets too?" Aaron headed back for the kitchen.

Joey wasn't sure if it was a dismissal or an actual question. He followed.

Aaron picked up the carafe and poured another cup into his mug while Joey got a coffee for himself.

To the question in Aaron's raised brows, he said, "Someone kept me up late," and dug out the sugar.

"Don't remember a complaint. That or any other night."

"And you did promise."

"I did." Aaron blew on his coffee.

Joey took a deep breath. "My mom got pregnant with my sister Laura right after they brought me home. They thought she couldn't get pregnant, but she did."

"So poor little Joey is the odd one out?"

That wasn't it. Joey'd never felt that way because he was adopted. It was never a secret, and he was never treated differently—apart from having his own room since he was the only boy. "No, Laura was really premature. And sick for a long time. So—"

"Ahh, there's where we get poor little Joey. No attention from Mommy and Daddy. And you went into social work to save other families. How sweet."

That was the Aaron he knew. Why was Joey so disappointed? "One more time, Aaron, I'm not the social worker who fucked up your family."

"Well you sure as shit wouldn't be standing here if you were."

"And I'm not trying to fix yours."

180

Aaron slammed his mug on the counter. Coffee sloshed over the side and onto his hand. "Shit." He raised his knuckles to his mouth. "So there's something to fix? Fuck that."

Joey grabbed a dishrag from the sink and threw it at him. "No. Actually, you seem like a pretty un-fucked-up family."

"You sure you got a degree in this?"

"I mean now, Aaron. I don't know what happened before, but you've got three kids in college. The two I've met are happy and confident. What else matters?"

Aaron finished mopping the coffee off the counter and threw the dishrag in the sink. "Confident? I guess that's one way to describe Dylan."

"I can't imagine where he would have learned to be an arrogant prick."

"Well, you weren't around back then, but Sheree's still working on a tiara. The two of you in the same room is a terrifying prospect."

Aaron's words didn't trigger a slow warmth. It was a sudden hot prickle all over Joey's skin, heart so thick in his throat the air couldn't get around it. Because it sounded a whole lot like Aaron planned on having Joey "around" in the future.

Turning to the sink to hide the flush on his face, Joey started rinsing the breakfast dishes.

Aaron stepped up behind him, not touching, but close enough for Joey's skin to start buzzing. "You never back down, do you?"

If Joey turned around, everything he was feeling would be clear on his face. It wasn't backing down, just putting things off. He dug at a piece of egg stuck on the plate. "Not so far."

Joey did a few loads of laundry in between poking at the song he'd been working on since he moved to Jacksonville.

Sitting for any length of time was difficult, and when he thought about why, his blood pumped hard and fast to his dick and the notes in his head slipped away. Aaron had given him a long kiss before he left, lips finally moving to his ear and murmuring, "See you later?"

"Sure."

"With the kids here, I'm going to need to stop for some stuff on the way home, so I'll be late."

It wasn't quite late now, ten thirty, and Joey was dozing on the couch, curled up on his side, when he heard the twins come in.

He could have gotten up, let them know he was there. His parents had caught him eavesdropping frequently, but not as frequently as he got away with it. When he was younger, he had to listen to the it's-very-rude speech. When he got older, the lecture was on misinterpretation. No amount of time-out or parental lectures could ever convince Joey that careful listening without the speaker's knowledge wasn't a vital life skill. It was the only way to ever know what was actually going on.

The twins' conversation was punctuated by the removal of bottles from the fridge. Joey could give low odds on the bottles holding iced tea. The metallic flick of the caps on the counter confirmed that the twins were making their way through the six pack Aaron had in his fridge. If the boys headed for the couch, Joey knew he could pull off pretending to wake up—at least no one had caught him yet.

Joey might be able to tell the twins apart physically, but he couldn't distinguish their voices.

"Did Aaron seem different to you?"

"Like what?"

"I don't know...happy?"

Joey smiled against the cushion.

"Like he's getting laid?" That had to be Dylan.

"I guess." Darryl paused and then the bottle thunked back onto the counter. "So, like what would that guy be if he moved in here?"

"He'd be the guy our brother's fucking, what the hell?"

"They could go to California and get married."

In Joey's dreams.

"You're a freak, bro. He's just fucking him."

"He's never had anyone around before."

"That you know of. Dare, you think he wasn't getting laid all that time? C'mon."

"It's just weird."

That was surprising. Joey had thought Dylan was the one who had issues.

"You got a problem with him being gay? 'Cause Dad don't."

Where was Dad? From Dylan's last statement, it sounded as if Dad was still in the picture.

"You think Mom knew?"

"Fuck, Dare, you think that's why Mom left, 'cause Aaron's gay?" The fridge opened again, and two more bottles hit the counter.

"No."

"Mom left because she ran out of guys to fuck to get crack. Aaron didn't know we were coming, so that's why the guy was here."

"Then why's his car still here?"

"It is? Fuck."

"Jesus, Dylan, you are such a moron. And you didn't see them in the kitchen. The way they were looking at each other."

"You're worse than Sheree. She's been trying to fix him up since she hit middle school. Remember when she decided her history teacher was gay? The guy was so pissed he tried to fail me."

"Shoulda passed the class the first time."

"Fuck you."

"Fuck yourself. All the action you ever get."

"Like you do so much better. You couldn't even score with that slut at Manny's party."

There wasn't going to be much more useful conversation to overhear. Joey thought maybe it would be a good time to pretend to wake up. But then there was a sudden scuffle and feet thudding—away—and Joey was able to sneak into Aaron's room.

By the time Aaron had put away a hundred and fifty dollars' worth of groceries, it was one thirty. Joey's car was still in the driveway, but the house was quiet. All his beer was gone, which probably meant Dylan and possibly Darryl were sound asleep. He went into his bedroom and saw Joey faking sleep on one side of the bed. He had on a T-shirt and the pair of old boxers he'd scrounged. When Aaron had first seen them this morning in the bathroom, he'd started to say something. Sharing underwear was a little too weird, but then he'd remembered what they'd done. Joey's ass. The heat, skin red and white from the slap of his hand. Aaron's palm still tingled, and Joey'd been so sensitive this morning that every touch made Joey curl into him, dragged out a husky sigh. No wonder Joey was wearing something loose and soft.

On Joey, fake sleep was kind of cute. He was half on his side, ass tipped up invitingly. Aaron's lips twitched in a smile.

Tonight, he'd been impatient to get home. Not that he minded working. No one had died tonight—definitely not in Aaron's truck—and not to give Joey too much credit, but Aaron did love the adrenaline rush that came with working as a paramedic. But tonight he'd spent most of the shift wishing it was time to leave. Not like last night, dick aching and ready to give Joey everything they could handle.

No, tonight, even with the twins back in Jax where Aaron had to worry about what they were up to, home was where he wanted to be. Something he hadn't felt since the night when he went with Rafe to get Mom from the bar. The night everything went to hell.

Joey shifted and stretched like he was waking up.

"I know you weren't asleep."

The pretense fell away. "Huh? How?" Joey sat up.

Aaron sat on the bed and pulled off his boots. "Your body. Muscles aren't soft enough. What time they get back?"

"Around ten."

Aaron pulled off his jeans and shirt and leaned over to snap the waistband of the boxers on Joey's hips. "Run out of clean clothes?" Aaron knew why. But he wanted to hear it from Joey.

"No, these are just..." Joey looked up, tongue peeking out over his teeth. "They're softer on my ass." And then he flashed the same grin he gave before he took Aaron's dick into his mouth.

Aaron wrapped his hand around the back of Joey's neck and pulled him into a kiss. But Joey's response didn't match his grin so Aaron let him go.

"Why were you pretending to be asleep?"

Joey must've had to think about it, because he didn't answer. At least he didn't try to lie.

"If you don't want to fuck, just say so. Don't play games."

"It wasn't that. I didn't want you to think you had to. I mean with your brothers here."

"Even less reason. If I don't want to do something, trust me, you'll know."

"Like answering questions?" Joey's lips curved.

"Yeah, like that."

Joey turned and slapped his hands onto Aaron's shoulders, slamming him onto his back and straddling him in one fluid movement. "What makes you think you could fuck me without me being into it anyway?"

"C'mon, Joey." Aaron didn't want to hurt Joey's shoulder, but the idea of someone his size overpowering Aaron was ridiculous.

He shifted his shoulders under Joey's grip and when Joey

didn't let up, grabbed his wrists, twisted and flipped him.

But Joey's wrists snaked free before Aaron could pin him down and with two quick feints, Joey wrapped a leg around Aaron's for leverage, and flipped them back so that Aaron was underneath them, one arm over his head, the other twisted between his back and the bed. He tried to buck Joey off, but he stuck for a moment, long enough to show he could before rolling off, rubbing his shoulder and rotating it gently.

"Where the fuck did you learn that?"

Joey grinned. "Thought you didn't like questions." Joey straddled Aaron again. "Who's a princess now?"

Aaron twisted a hand in Joey's hair and pulled him down. "If the tiara fits..."

"Fuck you." But Joey moved the last inch on his own and kissed Aaron, no hesitation this time, deep strokes of his tongue in Aaron's mouth, their lips pressed hard against their teeth. Joey pulled back and sucked Aaron's bottom lip into his mouth, a tug that connected right to Aaron's dick.

When Joey lifted his head and pushed himself up with a hand on Aaron's chest, there was something going on behind those Bambi eyes.

"What?"

"Nothing." Joey's hand trailed down Aaron's sternum, gliding over his belly, fingers teasing below his navel.

For some reason, Aaron ignored the wail of protest from his dick and pinned Joey's hand before it reached its destination.

"Bullshit. Something's been on your mind since I got home."

Joey pulled his hand back and rested it on his thigh, still straddling Aaron's chest. "Where's their dad?"

None of your fucking business was the first answer that came to mind. And it wasn't. Joey didn't have any right to the information, and Aaron had no reason to give it to him. Joey'd probably been planning on springing the question on Aaron when he was all fucked out and half-asleep, the sneaky shit.

"What did they say?"

"Nothing. Just mentioned him. That's all."

Aaron watched Joey's face carefully. "Their father is in prison."

Surprise, but no disgust, no pity.

Joey's follow-up question wasn't what Aaron expected.

"How long?"

"Fifteen years. He's got one left."

"Do they ever see him?"

"Yeah."

And even though Joey didn't ask, Aaron found himself explaining. "He didn't do it. He's in for manslaughter, but he shouldn't be. The guy pulled the knife first." And fuck if he wasn't seeing the gravel parking lot, the crowd, the sudden glint of light on the blade.

"You were there."

It wasn't a question, but, "Yeah."

Joey rolled off and onto his back. "Shit."

Without having to look at Joey, the words slipped out more easily. "Our mom was a whore. She was better with Rafe. Mostly. But then she started drinking and shit again. One night Rafe went to get her from some bar and I went too—well, I hid in the car—and there was a fight." Aaron's own voice was unfamiliar—like when he heard it on voice mail, hollow and full of echoes. He could almost pretend he wasn't talking. "By the time I got out of the car, they were in the parking lot. Whole bunch of the other guy's friends there. They said Rafe had the knife."

Aaron swallowed back any more answers to questions Joey hadn't even asked. Aaron wasn't going to get into shit about the trial that didn't happen. About how the DFC worker fucked everything up. About what happened to Savannah. He didn't know how long he stared at the ceiling before turning to put his hand on Joey's shoulder. The light pressure was all the asking Aaron had to do. Joey pulled off his T-shirt before rolling onto his stomach.

Easing the waistband of the old boxers over Joey's ass,

K.A. Mitchell

Aaron inspected the skin for bruises. He didn't know whether to be relieved or disappointed that despite the heat still pouring off the skin when he pressed his palm against it, Joey's ass was unmarked. As Aaron ran a hand over it, Joey moaned and arched into the touch.

Aaron leaned toward Joey's ear. "Still get you hard?"

"Yes."

It got him hard too. The memory, Joey's response, fuck, lately even thinking Joey's name was enough to make Aaron's dick twitch. Sooner or later that kind of thing burned out, right? The need for one guy's smell and taste. His mouth. His ass. The feel of his skin. Unless Aaron really was like his mother and fucking Joey had become the crack pipe Aaron couldn't put down.

Aaron grabbed the new lube, working his hands across the sore cheeks while he stretched Joey with both thumbs. Joey arched up when they slid past each other, ground his hips down and whispered "Please" when Aaron used his thumbs to hold Joey open.

Another murmur of "Please" and Joey reached back, like he'd drag Aaron inside himself if necessary. Aaron rubbed the head of his dick over Joey's slick crack, and it wasn't until Aaron's nerves connected with his brain to tell him he was feeling the ripples in the skin and the twitch of muscle on his bare dick, that he realized he didn't have a rubber on.

"Fuck." He leaned back.

Joey's fingers dug into Aaron's thigh, pulling him back.

"Joey, wait. Gotta get a condom."

A breath and then, "Okay."

Was that a disappointed *okay*? A yeah-you'd-better *okay*? An are-you-fucking-nuts *okay*? Or a wish-we-didn't-need-one *okay*? Aaron's last negative test was two months ago. Joey— they hadn't talked about it—but Joey didn't seem like the kind of guy who wouldn't say something if he were positive.

But seconds away from fucking wasn't the best time to talk about it, especially not when he could still feel the way the muscle and soft skin had felt on the bare head of his dick. Not when Joey kept reaching back, trying to drag Aaron in, panting "Fuck me" in his husky whisper.

As soon as he had the rubber on, Aaron flipped Joey onto his back, because at that moment it wasn't enough just to get his dick inside Joey's body. Aaron wanted Joey all around him. Legs on his hips, arms on his neck. He wanted to swallow those moans in kisses and fall into Joey's eyes and not have to think about anything but staying inside him.

Aaron didn't even have to tell him. Joey knew, wrapped him up tight and dragged Aaron down to demand Aaron's dick in him. Now.

Aaron held his cock steady as Joey clamped around the head, almost painfully tight. He needed to relax, and Aaron wanted to pull back and give him a minute, but Joey held on and in a harsher voice than he'd ever used, grunted, "In. Now."

The same strength that had pinned Aaron flat was pulling him in and something got hot and loose inside his belly, and he shoved forward with a grunt of his own, releasing his cock and gripping Joey's hips for leverage.

The hot loose feeling turned dizzy, out of control, hydroplaning in his truck at rush hour on I-95 and there was nothing to do but grip the wheel and hang on. As Aaron rocked forward, got in deep and tipped his hips up to angle his thrusts, he managed to swallow back some of that sensation. "How's that, princess?" he muttered against Joey's mouth.

"More prick. Less smirk," Joey whispered back before sucking Aaron's tongue past smiling lips.

Aaron gave into the feeling and fucked away. If everything inside him wanted to go sliding around out of control, Joey would deal. And he did. Fist tight in Aaron's hair, other arm slung over his back, Joey locked his ankles until Aaron was barely stroking inside him, short stabbing thrusts until Joey spilled warm and thick between their bellies.

He still wouldn't let Aaron move or pull out, just gave him enough space to fuck harder, deeper, a soft hitch in Joey's breath every time Aaron bottomed out inside. He was kissing

Joey when it sparked in Aaron's balls, the only warning he got before it rushed through him in long deep spasms, twisting every last bit of him loose until he collapsed on top of Joey.

The pillow Aaron's face stuck to tasted like Joey. Moving had to happen sometime. Pulling out, ditching the condom, unsticking, but Aaron didn't want any of that. And he didn't want to look Joey in the eyes. What he was afraid of seeing there he didn't know, but he put it off until he pissed himself off and finally turned his head on the pillow.

Joey faced him. There was nothing there Aaron hadn't seen before. The same heavy-lidded, well-fucked expression. A trace of a grin at the corners of Joey's dark pink lips, one bleached strand of hair stuck to his forehead, the end tickling Aaron's nose.

Nothing he hadn't seen before, and everything he wanted to see.

Joey knew Aaron had the day off, but when he came out of the bedroom dressed for work, he was surprised to see Aaron and the twins gathered at the counter.

As he boosted himself onto a stool, he saw that Dylan was wearing Darryl's glasses.

"Pass the ketchup, please, Dylan."

Dylan looked up. "I'm Darryl, moron."

"No. You're Dylan. Your eyes are wonky from wearing your brother's glasses. Darryl is squinting and you are a terrible liar."

Aaron dropped some toast on a plate and made an exaggerated sigh.

"Besides," Joey went on. "You have that thing on your ear, Dylan."

Dylan's hand went to his left ear, squeezing a bump that might have been a scar.

Darryl's plate was an inch from his mouth. "Pay up," he mumbled.

Aaron and Dylan both dropped a ten on the counter.

"You bet against me?" Joey asked Aaron.

Aaron arched a brow. "They *are* identical. Fooled me more than once when they were kids."

"Easy money." Darryl slid the cash into his wallet.

"Next time, I want in," Joey said.

Darryl put down his plate, even though it was half-full. As Dylan shoved the ketchup in Joey's direction, Darryl downed a glass of juice and kicked away from his stool.

"Don't take off," Aaron said. "We're going to pay your dad a visit."

Darryl froze, so did Dylan.

For all their swagger, they were still kids. Kids who'd lost both parents. Kids who had nobody but Aaron.

"All of us?" Darryl asked.

"No. Joey's going to work."

"Did you tell him?" Darryl looked at his brother like Aaron had gut-punched him.

"Motherfuck," was Dylan's contribution.

Joey examined the pattern of ketchup on his plate.

Darryl took off through the garage door.

"Jesus Christ, Aaron. What the fuck are you doing?" Dylan demanded.

Joey gave his breakfast a longing look and spoke into the charged atmosphere. "I don't want to be late."

Aaron and Dylan ignored him. Joey'd have better luck trying to reason with two bull sharks.

He went out through the same door as Darryl, found him throwing a baseball hard into the cinderblock wall next to Aaron's Ducati. One bad bounce and the Ducati wouldn't be quite as shiny.

Darryl wasn't ready to talk. But he needed to. He wasn't like his brothers who wore their anger on the outside. He kept it stuffed down deep. With Aaron's opinion on psychology, Darryl'd probably never get a chance to deal with all the shit that had happened to him.

So Joey wouldn't talk to him, but he'd try to let him know he could. As Darryl's aim inched closer to throwing the baseball where it would bounce into the bike, Joey intercepted the rebound. The ball stung his palm as he caught it.

"Do you really want to have to deal with how pissed he'd be if you hit his bike?" Joey tossed the ball lightly and caught it again.

Darryl stared hard at Joey for a moment. The next time Joey tossed the ball, Darryl snatched it out of the air. He threw the ball so hard it scuffed a mark in the door to the kitchen. "What I want is for you to shove your Masters in Counseling degree up your ass. Leave me alone."

He took off down the driveway.

"Nice going, asshole." Dylan came out of the kitchen door and ran after his brother.

Aaron followed more slowly. "What the hell's going on?"

Joey walked over, picked up the baseball and put it in Aaron's hand. "I know you don't want to hear this—"

"You're right. I don't."

Joey blew out a breath between tight lips. "But Darryl isn't like you and Dylan."

"And he's still talking," Aaron said to the garage ceiling.

"You can't expect him to handle things the same way."

"Are you done?"

"I don't care if you think it's bullshit, you might have to suck it up for Darryl's sake."

Aaron's hand squeezed the baseball so hard Joey was surprised it wasn't dust and then whipped it into a bin. "When the fuck do you think I've done anything else? I've done everything for their sake for twelve fucking years. Longer." Aaron turned like he was going to go back into the house. "So that was bullshit what you said yesterday?"

"What?"

"About how happy they were."

"They are. But even happy people have issues sometimes. Like with their dad."

"Well, that's just the shit they've got to deal with. Not everybody gets to go from a toilet to a McMansion in the 'burbs."

But at least Aaron was listening, had been when Joey tried to tell Aaron how amazing it was that he'd managed it all on his own. He might have said his sister helped, but since no one mentioned her, Joey knew most of the responsibility had been Aaron's.

Joey walked toward him. "Toilet to a condo in L.A." He smiled. "Then the McMansion in Pasadena."

"Did I ask? Just stay out of it."

Joey didn't promise. He couldn't not help a kid like Darryl.

"I mean it. It has nothing to do with what's going on between us."

Joey'd had waves stuff his lungs full of sea water and had an easier time breathing. *And what is?* But he knew better than to ask a question with an answer he didn't want to hear. And Aaron's anger was so close to the surface now that even if he did know what was happening between them he'd never admit it.

Aaron hauled him in tight, and Joey thought blacking out from lack of air was a distinct possibility. And then he answered Joey's unspoken question anyway. "My dick, your ass. Remember?" Aaron grabbed Joey's ass with both hands.

Joey reached back and pulled Aaron's hands away. That wasn't all there was between them last night. Or the night before. Or why Aaron hadn't already told Joey to pack up and go back to his apartment. But Aaron wasn't ready to hear that.

"Sore?" Aaron's brow wrinkled.

"No. Late."

Aaron turned Joey's grip to a reciprocal wristlock and pulled him back. But the way Aaron threaded one hand through Joey's hair and rubbed against his cheek before kissing him lightly didn't have much to do with fucking.

"If you don't have plans, we could go out later." Aaron's tone suggested he didn't care about Joey's answer, but Joey almost lost his breath again. A date?

With Aaron—there wasn't any other word for it—*nuzzling* Joey's neck, he got bold enough to ask for it. "I'd love to go dancing."

"Pulse?"

"I thought it was full of pretentious assholes."

"248 has karaoke tonight. Unless you want to..."

Sing? In front of Aaron? Even if he sang something ridiculous, Joey was sure it would come out sounding like a declaration of undying love.

He shook his head.

Aaron kissed him again. "Pulse it is."

Chapter Thirteen

Joey went back to his apartment after work, packed another duffle, and headed over to Aaron's around nine. The twins were missing and so was the truck.

Aaron kissed him hello in the kitchen, then steered him back out the door. "Ready?"

As they crossed the garage to the Ducati, Aaron tossed Joey a helmet.

Joey loved riding, but as he swung his leg over the seat, the twinge in his ass reminded him why he'd been hoping they'd take the truck. Aaron couldn't hear Joey's quick intake of breath over the rumble of the bike coming to life. When they reached the main street, the bike idled, though there was no traffic.

Joey leaned to yell into Aaron's ear. "You want to go check on them, don't you?"

Under Joey's hands, Aaron's chest tightened then relaxed as he exhaled. "Yeah."

"So go do it."

Aaron turned and headed farther into South Jacksonville, eventually spinning the bike into a lot in front of a squat grey building with a half-lit sign. From the condition of the cars arranged haphazardly around, it was either the start of a junkyard or a dive bar. The rest of the street was nothing but graffitied warehouses.

Joey could already smell piss, smoke and beer over the bike's exhaust. Aaron pointed. If the twins' efforts at hiding the truck consisted of parking it between the bar and another building, they definitely weren't cut out for covert ops.

Aaron shut down the bike. "Shit."

Joey swung off as Aaron kicked down the stand.

"Stay here," Aaron said, already looking inside.

Joey stared down the dark street. Trash rustled ominously. "Because it feels so much safer out here?"

Aaron looked him over, and for once the inspection didn't make Joey's dick twitch. He glanced down at his tight T-shirt and jeans. "What? We were going dancing."

Aaron stripped off his leather jacket and handed it to Joey. "Here."

Joey shrugged it on. It was too big to even look silly on him. He could pass for a homeless person living out of Beverly Hills trash bins.

"Zip it."

Joey complied.

"That's actually worse. Fuck it. C'mon. Try not to do anything that requires a paramedic, okay?"

Joey followed Aaron into the dark, hazy bar. There were no steps, but Joey still felt like they were going down into something. Maybe the floor was uneven.

Men along the bar looked up as they passed. Joey kept a distance from Aaron and tried to project the straightest thoughts he could. After *Playboy* and bikinis, he was tapped out.

But even if it wasn't working, this place was as testosterone-laden as any gay bar Joey'd set foot in. At least at gay bars, there were usually some women around.

Aaron led the way to the back where the pool tables were.

Dylan was so intent on his game he didn't notice his brother come in. Darryl did. The widening of his eyes behind his black-rimmed glasses suggested he wanted to run first and warn Dylan after.

Back here, away from the door and closer to whatever

passed for a bathroom, the stench of the place was thicker. Joey'd smelled cleaner sex clubs in full swing. He resisted the urge to start breathing through his T-shirt, or better yet—through the rich scent of Aaron's coat—and assessed the guy Dylan was playing and probably trying to hustle. Big, but with the Hollister T-shirt and Abercrombie jeans, the guy was probably a college jock and not part of the regular clientele, most of whom would make excellent extras in a police lineup.

Joey knew enough about pool to use it to pick up guys, but that was it. He certainly didn't know what Dylan was trying to do, or whether or not he was any good at it. Joey drifted to the far side of the table, back against the wall where he could see all three of the brothers. Dylan finally noticed Aaron but to Dylan's credit, it didn't cause his aim to waver. He banked a shot around another ball, and despite Joey's lack of knowledge about the rules, it was clear Dylan had won. The Hollister guy slammed down a fifty on the rail.

Dylan swept it up. "Anybody else?" he asked, ignoring his older brother's glare.

"I'm in. Fifty?" Aaron stepped forward, steps a little uneven.

Joey was sure he was the only one who caught the look between the three brothers. Some kind of hustle was on. If Aaron was so intent on keeping the twins from hustling pool, why was he helping them?

"Fifty." Dylan and Aaron shook hands and started playing.

Aaron lost quickly and handed Dylan a fifty. "One more. I was just warming up." They shook hands again. As different as their appearance was, Joey could see the resemblance in the way they moved, the wry twist of their lips when they missed a shot. No one else appeared to notice.

After a brief conversation with one of his friends, Hollister guy said, "Side bet?"

"How much?" Aaron and Dylan asked.

"Twenty on him." Hollister guy nodded at Dylan.

"I'll cover it," Aaron said. "I'm gonna win this time."

Aaron made a few more shots, but still lost. He reached

into his pocket and handed Dylan another fifty, then paid off Hollister guy. Joey was starting to suspect it was the same fifty being passed back and forth between Aaron and Dylan whenever they shook on the bet.

"Easy money." Dylan laughed.

"One more." Aaron sounded angry. "I only missed that shot because you coughed."

"Nah, thanks, man."

"You took my money, you've got to gimme a chance."

Joey couldn't believe the college guys were falling for this.

"Okay." Dylan's reluctance was painfully forced.

Aaron staggered a bit as he went up to the table like he was drunk, but Joey could see the shimmer of excitement in his eyes. *Adrenaline junkie.*

"Cover another side bet?" asked Hollister guy.

"I'm gonna beat him this time," Aaron announced. "Hundred."

"You're on."

It looked for awhile like Aaron was going to lose. But then he made a tricky shot and looked surprised. Hollister guy looked pissed. When Dylan stepped up to make a game-winning shot, Hollister guy muttered, "Better not cost me, man."

"Don't sweat it." But when Dylan lined up, somehow the ball just missed the pocket.

Two more shots and Aaron was pocketing Hollister's hundred. Darryl had to cover for his brother, so Joey decided it was the same fifty passed between Aaron and Dylan.

"My table now. Time for kids your age to be in bed," Aaron said as he tucked the money away. It took a piercing icy-blue glare before Dylan gave in and let Darryl drag him away. They hadn't taken two steps before a wizened old man wandered up to the table and grabbed Aaron's arm.

"How come you don't stop by and see old Eddie? You too grown up for that now?" The fumes from the almost-toothless mouth made Joey's eyes water even from across the table.

The twins had stopped moving. Aaron's face was almost completely blank, but Joey was willing to bet it was a mask for panic. "Hey, Eddie, lemme buy you a drink, old man."

Aaron draped an arm around the hunched shoulders and started to steer him away from the pool table.

"These your boys, now? The brothers?"

Joey sometimes wondered if his life was on tape delay, since everything always seemed to follow a script. Right now, someone was filming in slow motion because it took forever for the next few seconds to unfold.

Hollister guy put it all together, quick enough to rule out Joey's initial assessment of an athletic scholarship.

Hollister guy turned and swung at Aaron who was trying to move old Eddie out of the way. The fist caught Aaron in the face, but it didn't stop him from blocking the next punch and getting in a few of his own. Hollister's friend went for Dylan, screaming something about two hundred and fifty bucks and then Joey wasn't sure how, but suddenly the entire back of the bar seemed like their whole new purpose in life was beating the crap out of all three of the brothers. A keg was blocking the back door, so Joey rolled it out of the way.

When he turned back, a guy who hadn't been anywhere near the pool game was going for Darryl with a broken bottle.

And Joey was back in Coach Gibson's sweat-soaked wrestling room, trying to get a takedown to finally end practice and hit the shower and it didn't matter how big the other guy was. *Leverage*, Coach shouted in his mind. Joey changed his level to drop under the bottle and hit a double-leg takedown that put bottle guy on his back.

The guy's head bounced off the concrete floor, and the bottle broke again before rolling out of his hand. Joey used his weight to keep the guy from getting up and drove bottle guy's head back with a punch to his chin, thought about what the bottle would have done to Darryl and hit the asshole again.

He landed a third punch before someone grabbed his arm and dragged him off. "Joey, man, c'mon, let's go."

Dylan and Aaron had fought their way to the door Joey had unblocked. Darryl pulled Joey toward it. "We gotta go. Now."

They hit the parking lot, Aaron holding his left arm tight against his chest, right eye almost swollen shut. "Darryl, take the keys from your brother and drive straight home."

Darryl released Joey and went over to help his brother toward the truck.

Aaron turned to Joey. "Can you handle the bike?"

Mark had let him take the Harley out alone a couple times. "Yes."

Aaron tossed him the keys, and Joey shrugged out of the jacket. There was no way he could manage the bike swimming in that leather. His shoulder ached and his knuckles throbbed like he'd punched a brick wall. As he climbed on the bike, he watched Aaron try to drag the jacket on quickly.

Something must have nailed him in the side, a punch, a kick or a cue stick. As Joey kicked the bike to start it, he hoped Aaron didn't have a cracked rib.

Aaron pulled himself onto the bike. "Let's go."

Unused to the Ducati, Joey kept it under twenty on the city streets.

At the sight of the truck in the driveway, Aaron sagged against Joey's back, puffing out a short sigh of relief.

Triage lasted until midnight. Dylan suffered a split lip, a cut over one eye, and the most troubling, a darkening bruise over his left kidney.

Aaron's fingers tightened on Dylan's arm as the boy turned to face him. "If you piss blood, tell me, or I swear—"

"You'll kick my ass, I know." Dylan pulled away.

It came as no surprise to Joey that Aaron wouldn't even put ice on his black eye until he'd checked both the twins over.

The eye wasn't bad, but something had hit Aaron's rib hard. Joey had managed to get him to sit on the couch, but still hadn't argued him out of his shirt when Darryl came back from the kitchen with an ice pack wrapped in a towel.

"Thanks." Joey took it from him and handed it to Aaron.

"Thank you," Darryl said sincerely.

"Dead ass serious, man, I thought that guy was going to cut Darryl up." Dylan met Joey's gaze and then shook his head. "And I couldn't get to him in time." Dylan gave a shove to Joey's shoulder he knew was meant to be full of camaraderie, but with the adrenaline still pumping through Dylan, the shove almost knocked Joey into Aaron's lap. "You really wailed on that dude."

The glare from Aaron's uncovered eye hit Joey's face like a high-beam headlight, but he couldn't figure out why, and Aaron's issues were going to have to wait until triage was complete.

"Are you giving up your shirt or do they hold you down while I rip it off?" Joey asked calmly.

"Too kinky for me, dude." Dylan smacked Joey again, this time a friendly clap on the back of his head. Joey's eyes felt like they popped in and out on springs. Aaron's one-eyed look turned mutinous, but he reached one hand down for the hem of his shirt.

"Don't be such a princess." Joey grabbed the shirt and whipped it over Aaron's head before he could protest.

"Fuck you."

"Don't piss the man off, bro. Dude's probably still looking for his brains on the floor of Cappy's. You can have my back any day, Joey."

"I'm hoping it's not going to be a habit." Joey studied the mark on Aaron's rib.

"It's not cracked," Aaron said. "I know what I'm doing."

"He does know," Darryl put in.

Joey frowned. "The last paramedic I—"

"Fucked?" Aaron suggested bitterly.

"I *saw*, Hector, the one who popped my shoulder back in, said you can't tell breaks without an X-ray."

"Yeah well, Hector's a moron. And he's only an EMT. And he's straight." Aaron muttered the last assessment under his breath. "It's my rib. It's not cracked. Now get the fuck off me." Dragging himself to his feet, Aaron went into the kitchen.

Joey couldn't quite call it a limp, but Aaron wasn't moving with his normal agility. He took a bottle of ibuprofen from a cabinet, shook some into his hand and swallowed them dry.

"Do not leave this house," he said to his brothers.

Dylan saluted him with the finger. Darryl nodded.

"Where are you going?" Joey asked.

"To bed."

Dylan and Darryl exchanged looks over Joey's head. It was just like being around Noah and Cameron. Joey needed to hang out with shorter people.

After giving Aaron a few minutes, Joey followed him into the bedroom, attributing the lack of vulgar comments from Dylan to a side-effect from the fight. Aaron had crawled into bed and lay on his uninjured side—on the half of the bed where Joey had been sleeping. There was a small space between Aaron's hips and the edge of the bed and Joey sat in it, looking down at Aaron's face.

"If you want to go to the hospital, I can drive you."

Aaron didn't blink.

"Or I can stay here with them and you can go."

"I said I'm fine." Aaron's breath was tight and quick, voice thin.

"So if you don't want them hustling pool, why did you help them?"

Aaron rolled away onto his back, staring at the ceiling. "Not now, Joey."

Joey swung his legs up onto the bed and waited.

"If you're looking to get fucked, I'm too sore."

"I'm not." Joey listened to Aaron's shallow breaths, tried counting them with an eye on the clock.

After twenty-eight short quick breaths in a minute, Aaron said, "I thought if Dylan was going to keep doing it no matter what, I could show him a game to run that he had do with someone who looked like a stranger, so he'd run it without Darryl." Turning his head to look at Joey, he pulled the ice pack down and said, "Thanks for getting there. I couldn't."

There was a lot more to that than Aaron was saying because he didn't look happy or grateful. He looked pissed, lips thin, eyes flat and hard. Everything sharp enough that Joey could cut himself if he wasn't careful.

"I'm glad I could do something."

"How is it you can barely walk without tripping and you're sitting here without a scratch on you?"

That wasn't what Aaron was angry about. But at least he was talking.

"Luck. And Coach Gibson's shark-bait drills."

When Aaron rolled back toward him, Joey settled down against him, holding the ice pack over Aaron's eye.

"Take that off me if I fall asleep."

"You got it. Aaron—"

"Joey, I mean it. Not now."

Aaron startled out of sleep and checked the bed. Empty. The clock. Six a.m.

Where the fuck did Joey go? Aaron started to get up, but sat back when everything from his waist up hurt. One of those assholes in the bar had even pulled on his hair like some big girl. He rubbed his scalp and that was a mistake. The bruised muscle over his rib screamed a protest.

Jesus. He had seriously fucked up. Almost gotten them all killed—or arrested. When he'd seen that guy go after Darryl with the broken bottle, Aaron knew he'd never get there in time. Trying had earned him the butt end of a cue in his ribs.

And then Joey. All the air had been sucked out of the room in the instant when Joey dove at the guy. And for that one way-too-long second, Aaron didn't know whether the terror crushing his heart was for his brother or that blond piece of ass who had managed to become something else.

203

Aaron had fallen asleep in his jeans, and he didn't bother with a shirt as he pissed and then made his way into the kitchen. Over the counter, he could see Dylan asleep on the recliner, Darryl's head just visible over the back of the couch. The credits for Grand Theft Auto were running on repeat on the TV.

When Aaron moved farther into the living room, he found Joey. He was slumped on the opposite end of the couch from Darryl, blond head resting against the sofa back, legs under Darryl's. Just a fucking part of the family. Aaron's gut tightened, and he took a deep breath in spite of the ache in his side.

Joey's eyes opened and he looked up at Aaron, a sleepy smile curving those full lips. Aaron's teeth ground together. He jerked his thumb in the direction of the kitchen. Joey eased out from under Darryl's long legs. The kid didn't even stir. Like he fell asleep on top of Aaron's—ah, fuck it—on top of his brother's boyfriends all the time.

Aaron went on out into the garage, and Joey followed.

As soon as Joey shut the kitchen door behind him, Aaron snapped, "What the fuck is going on?"

"We were all a little too wound up to sleep. So we played games and talked."

"What about?"

"I don't remember. Music. Movies. Whatever came up." Joey rolled his fucking eyes. "Don't worry. I didn't turn it into a therapy session."

How the fuck did Aaron get here? From finally being able to make decisions without having to think how it would affect the kids to this. To complications he didn't need, and for fuck-all certain he didn't want.

"So this is how you do it?"

"What?" Joey looked confused.

"Just move in. Manipulate things until you're already living there? Is this what you did to Tall Dude—Noah? All ten of 'em?" Aaron had hit something that time. He could almost see Joey flinch. Good. Aaron was tired of Joey's patient understanding, the way he treated Aaron like a kid having a tantrum. Let Joey get mad for once. Show the real man under all the psychobabble shit.

"You're the one who asked me to stay here."

"Because you were hurt. You're not now. So you can just go back to your boxes."

"I never asked you to take care of me."

The way Joey's voice broke a little made Aaron want to go over and pull him tight against his body. And then Joey had to go and fuck it all up.

"You know, just because your mother left doesn't mean—"

"Don't you start your counselor shit, or I swear I will drag you out and throw you in that car."

Joey didn't back down now. He crossed until he was standing inches from Aaron's chest. "You wouldn't hurt me."

"Really?" Aaron swatted his ass, barely enough to sting.

Joey flushed. "Not like that. Not when you're angry. You wouldn't."

Fucker was right. "No, I wouldn't."

And this close he smelled so good. He reached around Joey's neck to pull him in, but Joey ducked free.

"That's not happening." Joey was back in control now. And right now the look in his eyes, the look that Aaron had started to think meant that Joey knew what he was in for and wanted to be here anyway just pissed him off.

"What the fuck are you talking about?"

"Exactly what do you think is going on?"

Aaron rubbed his forehead with his thumb and index finger. "I told you, do not start that counseling shit with me."

"You have no idea how much counseling bullshit I'm holding onto. But we can make it all clear with one question."

Aaron waited, but he knew he wasn't going to have the right answer. Couldn't give Joey the answer he wanted.

"Do you want me here for any reason that doesn't have to

do with your dick and my ass?"

"And I'm guessing your mouth doesn't count?"

Joey turned and went back into the kitchen. Aaron thought about following, thought about the twins waking up to them arguing in the kitchen and stayed where he was.

When Joey came back out, he had all his stuff slung over his shoulder. So much for not backing down.

Aaron was trying to think of something to say, a perfect magical string of words to make things go back to the way they'd been when it wasn't so fucking complicated.

As he got to the garage door, Joey turned back. "Think about finding someone for Darryl to talk to, okay?"

This was not the way things were supposed to go. Joey was supposed to hate him. Slam the door, curse him out, be anything but okay with just leaving. Even the *fuck you* Aaron wanted to throw at his back wouldn't come.

"Bye, Aaron."

With that casual fucking dismissal Aaron found his voice. "So is this where I get on the list?"

Joey stepped back inside. "What list?"

"That list I told you to keep me off of. All your exes. What am I number eleven now?"

"Nope. You might actually have had to admit we were in a relationship first."

"Sorry I couldn't live up to your high standards in all of three weeks, princess."

"You're the one who told me to get out."

"Didn't take you long to pack. That why you live out of boxes? Always ready to pick up and move?"

Joey froze.

Aaron kept going. "How many cities are you up to now?"

"At least I'm not so emotionally stunted that I can't admit how I feel."

"And how do you feel? Have you mentioned it? Or am I supposed to be the one bringing you flowers and dropping to my knees to spout poetry?" Aaron stepped closer, watched Joey swallow hard. Aaron shoved his hands in his pockets to keep from reaching out for him. Those big, brown eyes played wounded so well. He shook his head. "You know, that's what makes you a princess, Joey. For someone so big on saving the fucking world, you're a selfish and manipulative bastard. And when you don't get your own way, you pull the poor-me routine and leave."

"I told you, you didn't get to treat me like shit after you got off."

"Well, guess what, I didn't get off, and I'm not treating you like shit. I'm just telling you the truth, and you don't want to hear it."

"Oh it's okay for me to hear it, but not for you? This from Mr. Not-now, no-questions-no-talking, my-dick-your-ass? Fuck you."

"Is that a new kind of therapist speech?"

"Yes, it's therapist speech for you're an emotionally stunted—"

"Said that already."

"Pissed off 'cause you got a raw deal, self-centered prick. I'm out of here."

Aaron had never been lucky, and he sure as hell wasn't now, because just as Joey turned back to the garage door, Sheree came in, dragging her suitcase. Joey and his bags tripped over the suitcase, and bounced off the wall, spoiling his dramatic exit.

Sheree caught him before he ended up on the ground. "I'm so sorry."

Joey didn't forget his nice McMansion manners. "No, my fault, sorry."

"I'm Sheree." The smile she beamed rounded her cheeks and sparkled in her eyes as she looked past Joey to Aaron. "Aaron's sister."

"I'm sorry. I was just leaving. Nice to meet you."

Sheree was a very sweet girl, but she hadn't made it as far

as she had in life without persistence. She could give Joey some lessons—especially since he was standing there with his bags all packed. She shot Aaron a glare and smiled again at Joey. "And you're—"

"Joey." He managed a polite smile. "I'm sorry. I'm going to be late for work. It was very nice meeting you, Sheree." He ducked out.

Sheree ran to give Aaron a hug, but he knew he wasn't getting off that easily. As soon as she released him she said, "No wonder you didn't want to meet anyone else. He's so cute. What did you do to him?"

"Me?" Aaron went over to get her suitcase. It almost pulled his arm out of the socket, which of course reminded him of Joey, and Aaron needed some fucking coffee. Now.

Ignoring the strain on his bruised oblique, he tried hoisting the bag and then had to drag the fucking thing. "Jesus, Sheree, you got bricks in here?"

"Textbooks. And don't change the subject. Who was he? What happened?"

"You're too young to know."

"If you don't tell me, I'll have to learn all about gay sex on YouTube."

"Christ, Sheree, that's— I don't even want to think about it."

"Then tell me."

Anyone who ever thought Aaron was in charge of this household had never met Sheree. From the time she was born she had them all wrapped around her finger.

Stalling for time, he took the bag down to her bedroom.

When he came back the twins were up, exchanging hugs and insults with their sister.

No one was making coffee.

"Where's Joey?" Darryl asked.

Aaron almost hit his head with the cabinet door as he got out the filter. "He went to work."

"Aaron did something to him," Sheree said.

"You didn't see anything gross, did you?" Dylan asked.

"No. Idiot. He made him leave or something."

Aaron put his mug down loudly enough to ensure everyone's attention. "I'm saying this once. He hurt his arm and couldn't drive so he was staying here. He's better now and he's back in his own apartment. That's the end of this discussion." He put every bit of authority he had in his look at his sister, but her smile, full of bright teeth, wasn't reassuring. Fuck. Getting them off to college was supposed to put an end to this parenting shit.

Chapter Fourteen

Joey thought that the most painful lesson he'd ever learned was that life-changing events, good and bad, never seemed to show up on the outside like they did on the inside. Even when he'd lost his virginity, when he'd felt like he'd been let in on the world's biggest secret, no one noticed. When Giles's emotional abuse left Joey wondering if he was worth the skin he was wearing, no one noticed.

Having Aaron—a guy Joey was sure he loved—rip him open like that ought to leave a visible mark, an end of the relationship stigmata, something like bleeding ulcerated stomach wounds. Instead, when he got into work, Vivian looked at the coffee cup in his hand and said, "Didn't sleep well?"

Caffeine could only do so much to replace six missing hours of sleep. Thank God he'd been cleared for field work again or he'd have fallen asleep on a pile of patchouli files, a fate even Aaron wouldn't wish on him—probably.

Joey only had time to send one pathetic text to Noah—*you were right*—before he went out on a call to a school. The teacher and nurse's concerns unfortunately were founded, the abuse severe enough to take seven-year-old Hannah Larsen and her eight-year-old brother Connor into emergency placement right from the school.

It was three before he sat down to type up the file and had time to check his phone. Nothing from Aaron, but Noah sent, *What about this time?*

Everything, Joey sent back.

The case was a painful reminder, enough to send fresh blood spilling from his imaginary wounds. The Larsen kids' dad was in prison. Mom had a new boyfriend who, given the welts on the boy's back and the cigarette burns on the girl's legs, really didn't like kids. Joey was just glad the boyfriend didn't like them too much. Joey wondered if the court would even consider giving the father custody when he got out of jail next month.

Aaron's brothers and sister were lucky to have had him. On this job, Joey had seen too much not to know how incredible it was that Aaron had managed to get all three of them safely to a chance at a successful adulthood. Too bad the experience had left Aaron so angry and defensive. Despite the internal bleeding, Joey still didn't want to believe that connection had been all in his head. He knew that if Aaron would stop trying to protect himself from everything, they'd be amazing together.

Joey's phone vibrated and skittered on the desk, and he checked the number before answering. Noah. He wasn't ready for an actual conversation.

There was one thing he was ready for. At least now he knew how to finish the song he'd been working on.

Having the kids home to worry about made for a couple nights of lousy sleep. Not being able to roll over and bury his face in a sunny, salty, sweet neck, to press against hot skin, maybe get a happy grunt or smile if he dropped a kiss on full lips, yeah, that didn't help either. Oh, and then there was the fact that he really needed to wash the sheets because sometimes he caught a whiff of Joey and got painfully hard with nothing but his hand to help out.

When the kids were gone, Aaron would go out and get laid. Not that they needed him home, but he felt better when he was. At least he knew what time the twins got in. And this week it was reasonable, nothing later than midnight, sober, and never reeking of smoke—legal or otherwise. They were more scared of Sheree than they were of Aaron.

By Thursday's shift he was tired enough to let Hennie drive. They pulled away from their usual convenience store stop and waited for the first of the rush-hour accident calls.

"Couch or curb?" Hennie asked.

One thing Aaron had loved about working with Hennie all these years was she never talked beyond what was necessary. At the sudden appearance of a personal question, Aaron choked and almost dumped his coffee down the front of his shirt. "What?"

"He kick you to the couch or the curb?"

"I got the reference, thanks. I just don't know why I'm having this conversation."

Hennie shrugged and started a slow cruise around Westbrook Park.

The silence was more annoying than the question. "What makes you think I didn't kick him out?"

"For weeks you've been unusually civilized. Something that used to take a triple espresso to bring out. When you're that happy, you don't kick him out."

Aaron hadn't kicked Joey out. He'd seen through Joey's attempts to turn what was going on between them into some look-now-I'm-part-of-the-family shit and called him on it, so Joey had left. So Aaron wasn't getting laid anymore. And he missed Joey singing in the shower, mocking Aaron's Xbox skills, the way Joey looked at him sometimes. Life sucked. What else was new?

"Do you want to get drunk tonight?" Hennie offered.

"No, thanks. Kids are in town."

She nodded and turned down Broadway.

"I'm always fucking civilized."

"I'd believe it if you used a different modifier."

He remembered that working an ambulance was Hennie's second career. She'd done twenty years in the public school system. Helped Dylan with some papers, including his application essay. Though why the fuck a cook needed to be able to write, Aaron couldn't figure out. He laughed. "Fucking English teachers."

"My point exactly."

Friday night, when Joey opened his door to a thumping that mimicked the forceful rhythm the police used and found Cameron scowling at him, Joey had one of those epiphanies. An ow-squint-at-suddenly-bright-sunlight realization that he should have done more than send a cryptic text in answer to all of Noah's voice mail and emails asking if he was okay.

"Where's Noah?" Joey asked.

"In our bed, probably. Where I'd be in an hour or two if I wasn't following orders."

"Noah gives orders?"

"The threat of withholding blow jobs is highly effective. I was driving back from St. Augustine. I worked my ass off this week so we'd have the weekend together, but he insisted I stop over and check on you."

"Want to come in?"

"Not particularly, but I also don't want to stand in the hall."

As Joey moved out of the doorway, Cameron followed.

"Okay. Choice A: You tell me what's going on. I tell you how to get your head out of your ass. I go home and enjoy my weekend. Choice B: I drag you to Tallahassee where Noah is looking forward to unloading a whole bunch of payback lectures and psychoanalysis on you, and since I won't be getting laid as much as I could be, I'm going to help ensure your weekend sucks worse than mine."

Joey considered being anywhere but here for the weekend, and then thought of being around Noah and Cameron, so perfectly in tune that Joey couldn't handle how sick he'd be with envy, because this time he'd been so close. He shoved his keyboard and laptop onto a box and flopped on the couch. "Choice A."

"That's my favorite." Cameron sat next to Joey and slapped his knee. "So tell me what I need to fix so you can call my boyfriend and tell him you're all better and then I can get blown."

"No pressure, thanks."

"You want pressure? I can be really persuasive."

Joey knew Cameron didn't like him. He almost never talked to him. Now Noah had really given him a reason.

Cameron opened the backpack he'd brought and pulled out a familiar white bottle of rum. "Or I could just get you drunk."

"Malibu?"

"Straight up or..." Reaching back in the bag, Cameron came up with a carton of pineapple juice.

"I— Thanks."

"Don't look so surprised, Joey. You lived with him for more than a year."

"I know." But Noah had remembered Joey's favorite drink. Told Cameron. Everything scabbed over by going back to the weekly routine was freshly bleeding again.

Cameron went out into the kitchen and came back with a mug. Joey was sure Cameron had poured some pineapple juice in there, but most of what Joey tasted was sweet coconut rum. He downed it fast enough that he could feel the heat hit his face. Another mugful—or was it two?—and he was nice and warm all over.

He looked over at Cameron pouring out another drink and decided he looked cuddly. The next thing Joey knew, Cameron was peeling Joey's arms off his neck and pressing the mug into his hand.

"I am so happy to be hours away from your hangover tomorrow, man. Now that you're sufficiently lubricated—"

That was funny.

"Okay, poor choice of words. Get off of me, Joey." Cameron moved away and sat on a box. Joey hoped it wasn't the one with his computer on it. Because he didn't want to lose the work on the song.

"You know," Joey said. "You'd think it would be blues, like Billie Holiday, but it's eighties dance music." He pointed to his head since Cameron didn't seem to follow. "Sylvester."

"I'm not equipped to deal with that statement." Cameron pulled the mug out of his hand. "So back to Choice A. You were telling me the story?"

"Where did I leave off?"

Cameron looked up like he was praying, but Joey didn't think Cameron was religious. Noah had never mentioned it. Or maybe he had and Joey was busy being a selfish princess.

"You told Noah you were staying with that guy since you couldn't drive after you hurt your arm. Which, by the way, nice work."

"What?"

"Moving in."

"Are you saying I dislocated my arm on purpose?" Wow, Cameron's eyes were really green. A hand on Joey's forehead pushed him back against the couch. "Are you saying that I'm manipulative? Does Noah think that? Shit, he does, doesn't he? But I don't—I didn't—"

He dove for Cameron's waist, but as Cameron tried to defend his virtue, Joey managed to grab Cameron's phone. After squinting at the buttons, Joey pushed number one on speed dial.

"Noah? Am I a selfish manipulative bastard?"

Being able to feel the force of Noah's sigh from a hundred miles away was a testament to Noah's lung capacity—or the Malibu. "Is Cam there?"

Joey nodded.

"Joey, man, he can't see you," Cameron said behind him.

"Put him on, Joey." And hey, Noah could give orders.

Joey handed the phone to Cameron and tried to figure out what Noah was saying based on Cameron's answers.

Did you tell him he was a manipulative bastard? "Of course not."

Then why did he say that? "I don't know."

Things got harder when Cameron's answers shortened to a syllable.

"Yeah... Yeah... I don't know." Then things got interesting again. "Well, how was I supposed to know? He's not that scrawny."

Joey peered down at his own chest. "Nope."

"Joey, when did you eat last?"

Joey couldn't remember. "Lunch maybe?"

"No, babe, don't. Please. I've got it. I'll hold his fucking head when he pukes and whatever... He's fine."

Joey lunged for the phone and was so surprised when he managed to grab it that he could only stare at it for a moment. Then he lifted it to his chin. "Noah, I am so sorry. You were right. I'm always trying to idealize people and then I get disappointed and it's not fair—"

Cameron snatched the phone away again. "Babe, please. Look I'll call back in a few minutes." He slid the phone closed.

"He's going to come here anyway."

"I know," Cameron said with a sigh.

"He's a really good guy."

"I know."

"I'm sorry."

Cameron's sigh rivaled Noah's. Lifeguards and their lung capacity.

"And you hate me. I know." And with that brilliant insight, Joey passed out.

Waking up to puke wasn't the worst part of Joey's night. Almost. Not that he liked puking. He woke up and found a bowl next to his pounding head, but he made it to the bathroom anyway.

No, the worst part of the night was hearing Noah and Cameron in his bedroom. When Joey was running to the bathroom, he could hear them laughing and talking—broken by water-bed-sloshing silences that fed Joey's hyperactive imagination. Of course, it's not like they couldn't hear him in the bathroom. Joey's apartment was smaller than the closet in his sister's bedroom.

"Okay, Joey?"

"Yeah," he managed before he puked again.

There was a lot more sloshing, and then a "Shit" from Cameron as Joey made his way back to the couch. And then a sound that had him covering his ears.

Next to the bowl, there was a bottle of water and two Tylenol. He swallowed them and face-planted on the lumpy cushion. But he didn't go back to sleep. Something, other than the whole stomach and possibly liver trying to exit through his throat in an act of self-defense, had woken him up.

He looked at his phone. One missed call. No voice mail. But it was Aaron.

He was still trying to overcome the side effects of Cameron-administered Malibu enough to decide if that was a good thing when the phone rang again.

He didn't wait for Aaron to say anything. "You were right. I suck. I'm a manipulative shit. I'm sorry. I—I get this thing and then when— Never mind. Just. I want to fix things." There wasn't any answer. "I should have said something. Aaron. I love you." There was something off about the breathing of the person on the other end of the phone. A wave of nauseating embarrassment had him reaching for the bowl even as he checked the number. It was Aaron's phone all right. But...he put the phone back to his ear. "Hello?" Whoever had been on the phone had hung up.

✧

Aaron checked the couch cushions. He never lost his phone. He never lost anything.

"Are we ready yet?" Dylan yelled from the kitchen door.

Sheree had decided they'd kick off her version of celebrating Aaron's birthday by going to breakfast at IHOP. He was carefully not thinking of Joey drowning his pancakes and then his lips in syrup.

"Just a second. I can't find my—f—friggin' phone."

"Um...Aaron?" Sheree came into the living room.

"Have you seen my phone?"

She looked down. "I have a confession to make."

"As long as you're not pregnant, I don't care."

"I stole your phone." She held it out.

"What the hell for? I pay for yours."

"I know. That's not it."

"We're starving up in here." Dylan's bellow ended in an *oof* that Aaron attributed to Darryl's needle-sharp elbow. Dylan managed to get his breath back fast enough to add, "Are you checking the traffic reports again? You are such a f—frigging control freak."

"So go stuff your ugly faces. We'll be there in a minute," Sheree snapped back.

"It's on Hendricks, south of Emerson," Aaron reminded them.

"Like we haven't passed it a million times. Jesus. What I say? Control freak." The door slammed.

"So why did you steal my phone?" Aaron asked.

"I wanted everything to be right for today. And you know I only want you to be happy."

"Sheree..."

"So I waited until you were asleep and I took your phone and I called him."

"Who?" But Aaron knew.

"Joey."

Aaron covered his face with his hands.

"Why? What's so wrong about that? Even Dylan likes him," Sheree said.

"Honey, I know you mean well but you can't—" he was going to say manipulate, "—just make things the way you want them to be."

"But he loves you."

"You know this from a three-second meeting in the garage?" They wouldn't be leaving until Sheree said everything she wanted to, so Aaron surrendered his dream of those copper thermos pitchers at IHOP and started making his own coffee.

"No. He told me."

Aaron shut the cabinet door and turned around. "He told you?"

"Well, not exactly. He thought I was you."

Aaron spaced his hands apart on the counter and pressed down, glaring at his sister across the shining surface. "Whole story. Now."

"I wanted him to come over today. I had to call him when you were asleep and so I called at about one o'clock last night and he didn't wait for me to say anything, he just started talking. I think he might have been drunk." She paused for a quick breath. "But he said he was sorry and that you were right and did you call him a manipulative shit? And then he said he loved you."

It's not like it was bad news. He'd just rather have heard it from the source instead of his baby sister. Have heard it live and in person. Then maybe he would know how to handle it. Could have figured out what Joey meant. Because even if Joey believed in all that falling-in-love stuff, all the great sex they'd been having could confuse anyone. And Aaron liked the guy. But the whole I-love-you-let's-live-together-forever thing—no. Aaron wasn't interested in being responsible for someone else's happiness. He'd done his part.

"Do you love him?"

Yeah. He kind of did. But that wasn't Sheree's question.

She wanted to know if Aaron was in love. In love like the whole Disney-fairytale-Cinderella-wedding which worked great in cartoons with cute animals, but in real life, not so much. Not answering wasn't a lie.

"Then how could you call him a manipulative shit? He apologized. Go get him."

"We've got breakfast plans, remember? Courtesy of our little cruise director."

"Men are such idiots. I think I'll be gay."

Aaron put his arm around her shoulder. "At least then you won't get pregnant."

It was bright when Joey woke up. Very, very bright. And some people were under the illusion that they were whispering. Unfortunately, even Joey's heartbeat was deafening. In fact, he imagined his head looked like a lopsided overripe melon. Squishy, bruised and definitely about to make a mess.

"I didn't tell you to get him so drunk he passed out."

"Well how was I to know it would happen so fast?"

Joey closed his eyes, and remembering what Aaron had said about his muscles, relaxed everything as much as his melon head would let him.

"I know you love the guy, babe, and I do too, but isn't he a grownup? It's about time he put his own life together."

Joey heard Noah come closer, felt him peering over the back of the couch. Either Joey was better at it now, or Aaron was still the only one who could catch him faking.

"He's always so busy doing things for other people." God, Joey loved Noah. He was so sweet. Then Noah went on. "Of course most of what he does for other people is manipulate them into doing what he thinks they should to fit his scheme of world domination."

Joey was starting to feel like a lead in a Shakespeare

comedy. He'd swear Noah knew Joey was listening, but when he popped up off the couch and said, "I knew it," Noah jumped a foot in the air and yelped, "Jesus Christ, Joey."

From his spot by the bathroom door, Cameron folded his arms in front of his chest. His bare chest.

Joey remembered crawling into his lap last night. "Crap." He dropped his head onto the top of the sofa back.

"Didn't your parents ever tell you it's rude to eavesdrop?" Cameron asked.

Without lifting his head, Joey said, "They tried." It was better this way. Darker.

"I'm sorry, Joey."

"No, it's true. Well, mostly true. But not the whole world-domination thing." He blinked, eyelashes rasping painfully against the cotton-covered futon. "I think." He didn't want to control the whole world. Just his part of it. He slid back down onto the couch and folded his arms over his face. "Okay, since I'd already rather be dead, just tell me it all. Tell me how incredibly obnoxious I am. Just do it softly. Very softly."

"You're not obnoxious." Noah came around and sat on his legs until Joey twisted and flung them up the back of the couch. "You really do care about people. Cam?"

"Well...considering how you put up with this brat for more than a year, I'd say yeah, you're a good guy, Joey."

"You just—remember what you said when you left me? That you knew when you met me I'd break your heart?" Noah said.

"You said that? You should be writing for the soaps, Joey. It's got to pay better than the thankless shit you do now."

"Cam, go get breakfast or shut the fuck up. Joey, it's like you've got this script in your head—like your whole life has to follow some kind of movie. Like people are actors. And if they don't say the right lines, you get pissed. And leave. The state."

"Easy for you to say." Joey wasn't pouting. His head hurt too much to pout.

"Why?"

"You've always known who you wanted. Your whole life. And I just keep—"

"Is this that Cody thing again? Lost the love of my life at ten?" Noah asked.

"Jesus, did you guys fuck at all or did you spend a year in therapy together?" Cameron leaned over the couch.

"It was that trip to South Beach," Noah said.

"The car stereo broke long before Orlando." Joey peeked out from under his arms. "It was talk or kill each other."

"Sometimes you don't see the value in an option until it's too late." Cameron's smile looked like something drawn on a super villain in a comic book.

"So what do I do? I already apologized. I told him I loved him."

"You drunk dialed him?" Cameron asked.

"No. He called me. Last night. But it didn't sound like him. How do I make him see that—?"

"You don't make him anything, Joey. That's the point. That's manipulation." Noah looked like he was losing patience. He sounded like a freight train.

Joey squeezed his arms more tightly over his ears. "But—"

"Joey, do you remember what you told me about Cam? That I had to change the pattern?"

"Throw out the script, man." Cameron folded his arms on the top of the couch. "I get it. I had a plan for how I wanted things to go and this brat wasn't in it." He straightened and gave the back of Noah's head a light cuff.

"What if I do and it still doesn't work?"

"What would you tell me?" Noah pulled Joey's arms down.

He hated that Noah had gotten so smart.

Joey forced himself to consider what advice he would give to someone. "Then it wasn't ever going to work. Let it go."

"Right." Noah released Joey's arms.

Cameron squeezed Joey's ankle. "So man up. Go over to his house. And tell him sober." He grinned. "And by the way, it's scary as fuck to do."

"Can I throw up again first?"

"If you really think it will help." But Noah still got off the couch in a hurry.

Chapter Fifteen

Sheree had found a card table in the attic that probably had been left by the previous owners and set it up in the tiny backyard. Air conditioning, Florida weather and life experience made Aaron forget he had a backyard. He let the moss grow under the crepe myrtle and oaks and hacked down anything else with a weed whacker when he started getting looks from the neighbors. Sheree was going in and out with food, and had drafted Mike, Savannah's husband, into helping her carry out any piece of furniture that wasn't nailed down.

"Just let her have this." Savannah's reading of Aaron's expression was accurate as always.

"I'm smiling, aren't I?"

"You look like you did before you got that tooth pulled."

Her little boy, Ben, Aaron's nephew—the only one he'd have for a long time, please—obligingly showed his teeth and then went back to driving a car up his mother's legs.

Aaron wasn't sure which he hated more, that Savannah maintained as much distance as Sheree would let her get away with, or that Savannah's visits reminded him how much he missed having someone around who remembered the really bad times. Aaron couldn't blame her for not wanting to remember any of it. For seeing them all as reminders. Especially Aaron. He was the one who'd failed her.

It was a good thing Joey wasn't here. Savannah was the only person Aaron knew who hated the DFC more than he did.

One of the twins called Aaron's name in the volume and

inflection which usually meant someone was bleeding or about to be. Savannah almost beat him to the twins' bedroom door.

But no one was bleeding. The twins were on the computer in their room.

"Jesus, you scared the fuck out of me. What the hell?" Aaron demanded.

Darryl got up and dragged Aaron to the computer.

"Isn't that his car?" Dylan asked.

Aaron had the desktop they all used set with traffic alerts, so he'd know what was going on when he drove, or if he was going to get called in. Or, as Dylan said, because he was a control freak.

As Aaron fought the first wave of dizziness, he tried to tell himself that there were probably lots of puke green—*It's seafoam pearl*—Yarises in Jacksonville in addition to the one crumpled like paper on I-95. The one with cops and ambulances around it as viewed from the live traffic cam. On the same stupid sharp curve on the interstate that had killed the Howard family on their way to Disney World.

There wasn't enough detail to make out which ambulance had shown up to get the driver, if there was anything left of the driver to get. Just because Joey was a klutz, had been in one kind of accident or another since they'd met, didn't mean it was him.

But logic couldn't stop Aaron's fingers from squeezing the back of the desk chair to the point where his fingers bored through the cheap fuzzy covering.

"Aaron?" Savannah put her hand on his arm.

Savannah hadn't willingly touched anyone other than Ben or Mike since the night after Rafe's fight. But Aaron couldn't take the time to think about that now.

He turned away and grabbed his phone, pressing Joey's number. Straight to voice mail. He tried to remember any time he had gotten Joey's voice mail. "Fuck." He called their ambulance dispatcher.

Great. Monica. The bitch hated him. As soon as she

realized who he was the professionalism disappeared from her voice. "You know I don't have time for this, Chase."

"Monica, please. Just tell me whether you handled the accident on I-95. The Yaris."

Monica sighed. "Adult male. White."

"How old?"

"Don't know. Don't care. Gotta go." Monica hung up.

"Is it him?" Sheree was there now. Darryl must have gone out to get her.

Aaron tried Joey's number again. Voice mail. "I don't know." But Joey's phone was never off.

Dylan turned around. "So what the fuck are you still doing here?"

Aaron didn't trust himself on the bike, and the trip to Shands had never seemed longer. It wasn't Joey. Even though he still wasn't answering his phone. Except...

Aaron's luck had always sucked. And life sucked for the people he cared about. And if Joey were still staying at the house, Aaron would have known where the fuck Joey was, know if he had a reason to be that far north on 95. Sheree had said Joey was drunk when she called. What if he still was, even at eleven thirty?

Joey didn't pick up any of the other three times Aaron tried to call before abandoning the truck as close to the ER as he could without blocking the ambulance entrance. They could fucking tow him. At least the triage nurse didn't hate him.

"In surgery," she said in answer to his question. She couldn't tell him the patient's name, so Aaron didn't even bother to ask. At least she wouldn't with her supervisor in earshot.

Aaron went looking for anyone who could give him an answer. His first trip through the ER was pointless, but then Kim stepped out of the elevator leading to the OR floor.

"Early shift?" Kim asked.

"Were you here? Is it him?" Aaron grabbed his forearm.

"What the hell's wrong with you?"

"Joey. Was he in that accident? The one they just brought in."

"Your blond?" If Kim kept Aaron waiting, he was going to fucking punch him. "Wasn't him."

Relief cut the tendons at the back of Aaron's knees, but Kim shoved him onto a bench.

"What's going on?" Kim stood in front of him like he thought Aaron was going to pass out. Given how he'd been acting, Aaron couldn't blame him. Much.

"Nothing. Just a stupid coincidence."

"Good thing too. That guy's not going to make it."

It wasn't Joey. And still the news brought a wave of fresh dizziness. What if it had been? What if there wasn't a Joey to make up with or fight with, to make Aaron laugh? Aaron didn't deal in *what ifs*. What happened, happened. This was nuts.

He started to get up.

Kim's hand was surprisingly tight on Aaron's shoulder, pressing him back onto the bench. "I don't think I want you behind the wheel right now. All the trauma surgeons are busy."

"Thanks."

"Oh I don't give a shit about you. But you might kill someone else."

"You wouldn't give a shit about them either."

Kim paused to consider it. "Probably not. C'mon. Coffee. They've got hazelnut today."

"I hate hazelnut."

"I know."

Aaron was still just using the cup of hazelnut coffee the bastard had bought him as a hand-warmer when Kim walked him back out to the ER.

And there was Joey. Talking to the triage nurse.

So many things hit him at once the only thing he could deal with was anger.

"Why the fuck don't you answer your phone?"

Joey looked up. He should have been scared. He should

have been pissed. Instead, he ran over and hugged Aaron. The coffee splashed over his wrist.

Kim took the cup from Aaron's hand. "You guys are more fun than a Legionnaires' outbreak on a cruise ship. Go down to the locker room before you endanger innocent bystanders."

"With what? Hi, Jae Sun."

"By putting them into a diabetic coma. Go."

Aaron didn't want to keep his arms around Joey, but he couldn't seem to let go either. "I've got to call home."

"They all know. It's how I found you. I went there first."

"They could have fucking called me."

"Check your phone."

He didn't have it on. He must have tossed it somewhere in the truck after getting Joey's voice mail. Again.

Somehow they'd gotten to a staff elevator. As soon as the doors closed, Joey hauled Aaron down, or maybe Joey climbed up, because they were kissing, and Aaron didn't have any idea how he'd gotten close to Joey's lips.

The kiss was sweet and hot, but all Aaron wanted was to bury his face in Joey's neck, in the sun, salt, sea taste of him. Press their bodies together so he could feel Joey warm and alive.

Aaron dragged Joey off the elevator, through the locker room and into one of the shower stalls. Slamming Joey into the tiled wall, Aaron bent and kissed his neck. "So why the fuck didn't you answer your phone?"

"I turned it off. After last night, I didn't want you to call and—I wanted to talk to you in person. So I drove over and then Darryl and Dylan came out and—"

Aaron kissed him to stop the rest of the story. "I can guess. That wasn't me, you know."

"What?"

"On the phone. Last night. It was Sheree."

"Crap." Joey drove his forehead into Aaron's chest.

"Ow. Still a little sore."

"Sorry."

"So what were you going to tell me that you drove over?"

Joey looked up. His brown eyes were more translucent than the glass at the hollow of his neck. He bit his lip once and then said, "I'm sorry. You were right. I was trying—I try—I want things so much that sometimes..."

Aaron thought about letting Joey off the hook.

"I'm not always honest about what I'm doing. And I should have said something." Joey bit his lip again. "I love you."

"I know."

Joey's eyes darkened. "You know? You arrogant fucking prick. That's all you're going to say, I know? You were freaking out so much you came to the hospital to see if I was dead and you're just going to say 'I know'?"

Aaron wanted to laugh. "I wasn't freaking out. But Sheree told me. She told me everything you said. Then she ripped me a new one for being mean to you."

"So?"

"Manipulating again?"

"Like I can make you do anything."

Aaron held Joey's head between his hands, fingers sliding through his hair, over the tiny knot of scar tissue from that first night, and kissed him, tongue stroking everywhere in his mouth. Heat building between them, Joey kissed him back, tangling a hand in Aaron's short ponytail.

Aaron lifted his lips enough to murmur, "What do you want?"

"What can I have?"

"Don't. Just tell me."

"I want everything. I want the play-house, meet-the-family, go-to-bed-together-every-night-wake-up-together-every-day thing. And I want it with you."

"And if you can't have that, you just leave?" Aaron's ribs ached again, and not only because of the still black bruise from the cue stick.

"No. I'm not going to just leave. I love you."

"But?"

"But I can't wait forever. I know you're probably going to laugh..." Joey's face had never been easier to read, so honest, embarrassed, open.

"What?"

"I've never wanted this more with anyone. I swear."

"Really." But Aaron knew Joey meant every word. So how much time did that buy Aaron? How much time before Joey decided he was tired of waiting?

So what if Joey left and life went back to sucking? Aaron could have this. Grab hold of this. Now. He took Joey's mouth, lifted him up, needing to pull Joey inside him, fill himself up with all Joey's warmth and optimism and hope. "I love you."

Joey had been moving against Aaron like he was going along with those plans to get inside each other. Now he froze.

"But?"

"I don't know if I can ever mean it like you do."

"How do you mean it now?" Joey's feet slid to the floor. "Like you love your bike?"

"Stop being a princess. I mean, I don't know if I can believe in it."

"Like believing in Bigfoot?"

"Jesus fucking Christ. Listen to me. I love you. But it scares the shit out of me."

Joey grinned. Fucking grinned. And then he was wrapped around Aaron again, leg hiking up around Aaron's thigh. "I know. Isn't it great?"

"Are you kidding?"

"Poor baby." Joey pushed Aaron's hair off the side of his face.

"Fuck you." Aaron grinned back.

Joey arched an eyebrow and slipped a hand down between them, rubbing Aaron's dick from *yeah* to *oh fuck yeah* so fast Aaron thought Joey must have left it programmed to respond to him.

Joey went up on his toes to lick at Aaron's neck. "You do find some interesting places to fuck." Joey had Aaron's cock out of his jeans in less time than it took Aaron to find the button on Joey's fly.

"No lube," Aaron pointed out.

"You? I thought you were Mr. Never-Leave-Home-Without-It."

"No condom. No wallet."

"You were freaking out." Joey started to drop to his knees, but Aaron caught Joey under his arms and kissed him, hard—hard enough to say *got you, safe, mine*—before pushing him back against the tiles and dropping in front of him.

Joey smiled as Aaron worked the buttons on Joey's jeans. Not teasing anymore, but a smile as warm and sunny as his smell. Aaron kissed the head with a spit-filled mouth and took the whole length deep in his throat, sucking and bobbing and it wasn't because he wanted to get Joey off in a hurry, but Aaron didn't know what else to do with what that smile had pulled up, dragged up inside him. He grabbed Joey's thighs and gave him everything he could.

Aaron felt it first in the muscles of Joey's thighs and looked up to see Joey stuffing half of his hand in his mouth. The skin against Aaron's lips got harder, tighter, and Aaron wanted it, wanted the heat, the life, Joey falling as hard and fast into Aaron as he could make him. Joey grabbed Aaron's head, not yanking him forward, but a sloppy caress as the vein pulsed against his tongue and Joey jerked, coming thick and hot in Aaron's throat.

He leaned back, tonguing the head until Joey pulled away, the same smile curving his lips. In the nonstop fight that had been Aaron's life, he finally had someone on his side.

The last time Aaron had called in sick was when thirteen-year-old Darryl ran a hundred-and-four fever with the flu. He'd have enjoyed telling Monica what she could suck, but when he called she said she'd already gotten someone to fill in. "Some big family emergency if you've got all this time on the phone," she snapped as she hung up.

"Jae Sun," Joey said when Aaron told him. "He must have decided you needed some time."

"Yeah. I'm going to make some time for him." Aaron paused in his thoughts of revenge and steered Joey toward the truck when he would have gone to his Yaris. Ignoring the way Joey mouthed "so freaking out" at him, Aaron said, "I'll drive you over to pick it up tomorrow."

He tossed Joey the phone as soon as they were in the truck. "Let 'em know we're coming."

From the length of the conversation carried out in rapid-fire speech, Joey must have gotten Sheree. Aaron grabbed for the phone. "We'll be there in seven minutes. You can talk world domination then."

Aaron could feel Joey giving him an odd look. "What?"

"Why did you say that?"

"World domination?"

Joey nodded.

"Knowing the two of you and your persistence, the world better duck and cover when you guys are in the same room."

"Noah said something like that this morning. Oh shit. He's still in my apartment." Joey fumbled for his phone. "I forgot to call him."

Joey was a lot less friendless than Aaron had thought when he met him.

"Is this going to be a thing? Your exes popping up all the time?"

"They do sometimes, I guess. I'm still friends with almost all of them."

"Something to look forward to."

Joey punched his shoulder. "Not if I can help it. Um, without, you know..."

"Being a manipulative shit?"

"Yeah." Joey put the phone to his ear. "It's all fine. Go home and fuck Cameron before he decides on a way to murder me in my sleep... We worked it out."

The words were out of Aaron's mouth before he stopped to think about what he was saying. "Might as well have them over."

"Hang on a sec, Noah. What?"

"Wasn't that what you said? Family, friends? Besides, maybe I can find out what I'm getting into. He seems to have survived it."

Joey gave Tall Dude—Noah—the address and hung up as they pulled into the driveway. Aaron kept the engine running for the A/C. Joey gave him that look again.

Tapping the steering wheel, Aaron said, "Listen. I'm not telling you what to do, but you know I'm not a big fan of the DFC."

"You want me to quit my job?"

"No, but Savannah, my sister—she hates it more. And with a lot of good reasons."

"So if I talk about work I should be prepared to reach minimum safe distance?"

"Something like that."

"Okay."

Aaron sighed. "And you can ask all your social workery questions later."

Dylan came out of the darkness of the open garage, one arm covering his eyes dramatically. "Are you guys doing something gross?"

Joey opened the truck door and swung down. "We're going to save that for some time when we've taped your eyelids open."

"Joey, man, good to see you undamaged." Dylan gave Joey a slap on the back that launched him forward a couple of steps.

Sheree was in the backyard presiding over her chocolate ice cream cake, which was suffering under the spring sun. "Where the hell have you been?"

Aaron held up his hands in surrender—at least until they started singing "Happy Birthday", at which point he started muttering loudly about the cake melting and how it was going to be a mess and could we just eat already.

Joey's clear, strong voice beside him colored even the wheezing repetition with something warm. With Savannah smiling as she handed him a piece of cake, Aaron decided he could have one day to be a sap.

Tall Dude—Noah—and Cameron arrived as the twins were scraping the last of the cake puddles into their bowls. Sheree looked up from where she was helping Ben try to get a bit more before his uncles started licking the cardboard circle the cake had come on. Hopefully, getting sticky would satisfy any of Sheree's maternal instincts for awhile.

Joey introduced everyone. Even Dylan could respect Noah's height and build—or Dylan was so busy stuffing his face he couldn't get anything antagonistic past his ice-cream-coated lips. Aaron saw that while Noah immediately crouched down to greet Ben and flashed Sheree a smile that could have melted a statue, Cameron stood off to one side. Not aloof, just assessing. Mike joined him after a few minutes, and they talked quietly.

And Joey, he looked happy, talking with Sheree and watching Noah play with Ben. Aaron wanted that shine in Joey's eyes all the time.

After exchanging a look with Sheree, Savannah headed back around to the front of the house. Aaron followed, grabbing a dish towel as she filled the sink with water and suds.

After the third bowl she said, "I like him. That's what this is about, right? Following me in here?"

Aaron didn't know until then how much he wanted Savannah—wanted them all—to like Joey. But especially Savannah. The first person he'd ever told he was gay. The first person he'd ever loved. He knew why she kept her distance, but it still hurt. "Yeah."

"And y'all're gonna what—live together?"

"'Bout all we can do in Florida."

"Like you'd ever get married."

Aaron shrugged.

"Have you told him?"

"Not everything."

"Should. My therapist—"

There were no two stranger words he'd ever hear come out of Savannah's mouth. "What?"

"I know. Don't laugh. But...after Ben was born I started having these nightmares. Real bad. The crack houses. That night. And it kept coming back to Ben. I got so I was asleep on my feet. I was scared I was going to drop him or something. Mike, he even went with me for awhile."

"I didn't know. Sav, I'm so sorry. If you—"

"What were you going to do, fight my nightmares for me? It's better now, most of the time. So hey, maybe it's not all bullshit. You should tell him. Everything." She put a soapy hand on his cheek and then smiled. "You do realize between him and Sheree you are majorly screwed, right?"

Chapter Sixteen

Before Noah left he dragged Joey into a long hug, then smiled and kissed him lightly. "Don't fuck this one up, okay?"

"Me?"

"Yes, you. He's a good guy. Deserves better."

Noah and Savannah had disappeared for a few minutes, probably conferring about whether their respective charges were ready to be turned loose on each other. "Bite me."

"That's his job now, Joey." Noah grinned.

"Is this going to be one for old times' sake?" Cameron called. "Because then I'm going to get a beer and a front row seat."

Noah kissed Joey again before letting him go. "Don't drop off the face of the earth, okay?"

"Okay."

Savannah and her husband left next. While they stood in the garage saying their goodbyes, Ben made another grab for Joey's necklace, and he distracted the two-year-old with a tickle and quick game of peek-a-boo, which left Joey squinching his nose at Savannah and pointing to Ben's butt.

"Do you mind, Joey?" She handed him the diaper bag from her shoulder.

"Not at all."

He took the toddler and the bag into the living room.

Dylan came to stand over Joey while he had Ben on the living room floor.

"Dee," Ben gurgled at his uncle.

"Got you pretty whipped already?"

Joey blocked any further leakage with the fresh diaper while cleaning up after the last one. "I don't mind. I love kids."

"Love kids as in want kids?" Sheree was standing with them now.

"I don't know." Which was a lie. Joey had always wanted kids. But somehow, getting Aaron and a premade family didn't make the need so intense anymore.

"Conversation's getting a little girly for me." Dylan turned to leave.

"Don't think you're getting out of helping me clean up." Sheree smacked her brother with a dishtowel.

"I've got a paper due."

"And you had all week to do it."

Joey slipped Ben into his new diaper, refastened his little khaki shorts, and picked him up to carry him back out to the garage.

After Joey handed off the kid and the diaper bag, Savannah leaned forward and kissed Aaron on the cheek. For a split second the emotions were clear on Aaron's face, surprise and pleasure, and then everything went back to the amused arrogance he wore almost all the time.

Aaron slung an arm around Joey's neck as the car cleared the driveway.

"You know, Ben reminds me of Seth. He's only a year younger and almost as big," Joey said.

"Who's Seth?"

"That little boy. From the accident. If it hadn't been for Seth, we might not have met."

"Is this going to be a habit too? Random statements that require some romantic response?"

Joey turned to lean chest to chest. He grabbed Aaron's wrist, finger running under the bracelet from the fair. "You are a sap, Aaron Benjamin Chase. But if you blow me like you did earlier, I won't tell anyone."

"I think the kids need to go to the movies."

"We could go to my apartment."

Aaron made a face and pulled away. "To your waterbed?"

Joey followed Aaron into the kitchen, where he grabbed the dishtowel from his sister's hands. "I'll finish up."

"But it's your birthday."

"My birthday was a week ago. But the cake and the party were great." He pulled out a fifty from his wallet. "Who wants to go to the movies?"

Dylan threw down his towel and grabbed for the money. "Sure. Let's see what's playing at makeup-sex theater."

Joey used his fingers to hold his eyes open then pointed at Dylan. "Don't think your brother doesn't have access to that surgical tape."

Dylan gave a mock shudder, but then yelped in outrage because his sister was already tucking the bill into her jeans.

"Promise we don't have to go to some stupid chick flick."

"I promise something will blow up." She rolled her eyes in a perfect imitation of Aaron.

"Dare!" Dylan bellowed. "Movies."

As soon as the kitchen door closed behind the three teens, Joey jumped and hurled himself at Aaron, pushing him toward the bedroom.

"Are you trying to say you only love me for sex?" Aaron's smile used a lot more than just the corners of his mouth for a change.

"Do you really need to ask that with a dick like yours?"

"Flattery will get you fucked."

"That's what I'm hoping."

Aaron had Joey's pants off before they hit the bed. Well, down to his ankles, so that Joey tripped backward and bounced.

"See, if we were on your waterbed, that would have bounced you onto the floor."

"I'd get up."

"But if you got hurt, then there would be a delay in getting my dick in your ass."

"Don't want that." Joey peeled off his shirt. Which got complicated because Aaron was trying to kiss Joey and jack him at the same time and then the shirt was strangling him.

Aaron yanked the shirt off, and Joey was happily naked. "I'm glad you're coordinated enough not to have yanked off the wrong thing."

Lips turned in to prevent what Joey was sure was a laugh, Aaron tugged on Joey's cock, hard dry friction that made Joey gasp.

"Joey. Shut up and roll over."

Joey wanted this, their first time after everything that happened today, to be face-to-face. He wanted to learn every feeling Aaron couldn't mask when he pushed inside. But Joey was dropping the script. He hoped there'd be at least ten thousand more times for that. He rolled and tipped his hips up.

Aaron's slick fingers fucked Joey open, and he knelt and shoved back against Aaron's hand.

The deep groan in Aaron's voice made Joey's dick rub up against his belly. "Do it nice later, okay? Just gotta—" His mouth opened on the back of Joey's neck and he sucked a deep bruise as he pushed in, fast enough, hard enough to make Joey want to jerk away almost as much as he wanted to push back against the burn.

"Jesus, Joey." And then Aaron drove his hips forward all the way, deep, hitting all the spots inside Joey that turned the stretch sweet. Aaron grabbed Joey's hips, and he moved his legs close together to make it tighter, harder, and so they were gasping together with every one of Aaron's quick thrusts.

Aaron reached up for Joey's shoulder, pushing down while driving forward and after that Joey couldn't think beyond the flashes of heat spreading from his ass to his balls to his dick. He didn't want a slow build, he wanted it now. He grabbed his cock to finish himself off and just as the pleasure rolled through him, Aaron fell forward onto him, hips still pumping, soft wet kisses under Joey's ear.

"So glad it wasn't you." The words rode Aaron's harsh breaths but to Joey they were soft and sweet. "Scared the shit out of me, you big klutz."

Joey smiled into the sheet. He was glad he hadn't worried about the script, because Aaron would never have said that if they were face-to-face.

"I'm fine. I'm really resilient. Born in a toilet, remember?"

Aaron didn't answer, and Joey knew joking had been the wrong thing, but he didn't try to fix it. He waited.

"It's why I just don't know if I can," Aaron said at last.

Joey had to work to put the pieces of that together. Finally he unstuck himself and squirmed out from under Aaron enough to turn and face him. "Wait. You don't think you can believe in us because I'm a klutz and you're afraid something will happen to me?"

"No. You're totally a klutz. But that's not all of it."

"Then...oh." Joey got it. "So I'm the one who wants to save the whole goddamned world?"

Aaron rolled onto his back. "Not the world, just the part of it I'm responsible for."

Joey cut off Aaron's retreat by flopping onto his chest. "They're all adults. I'm an adult. We're all responsible for ourselves."

"If that isn't the biggest piece of new-agey psych crap—"

"Is that a step up from bullshit?"

"Maybe." Aaron's lips twitched.

"They're all fine. I'm fine."

"Yeah, Rafe's fine—in jail. Sav's fine—in therapy. Darryl needs therapy. I did great."

"You didn't put Rafe in jail."

"You don't know that."

"I know you were fifteen. How could you have done anything?"

Aaron rubbed the back of his fist against his forehead. "I did enough."

Joey put his ear against the thump of Aaron's heart and listened.

"When Rafe killed that guy, Mom got sent to rehab. The kids went into foster care, but me and Savannah got dumped in emergency placement. Like some shitty dorm full of rejects."

Some places were like that. No state Joey had worked in gave enough money to those kinds of facilities, places for the kids no one wanted. Not enough for upkeep, not enough for decent staff. And the staff they did have were often working extra shifts.

"I know the kind of place you mean," Joey offered.

"Don't." Aaron moved, rolling away to sit on the edge of the bed with his back to Joey. "Just don't say anything." He ran his hand through his hair, freeing it from the elastic band.

Joey sat cross-legged behind, hand tucked under his thighs to control the urge to touch the tense back, to rub away the tight set of Aaron's shoulders.

Aaron leaned forward, as if he knew what Joey was trying not to do. "Fuck. I wish I still smoked." Aaron's hands came to rest on the bed on either side of his hips. "So we were there one night, and then the next—it was coed, separate halls but—"

Joey was afraid he knew what was coming. No wonder Aaron hated the DFC.

"Some punk. He got to Savannah. The night staff must have been sleeping. She fought him. Enough so I could see the bruises on her at breakfast and I made her tell me who."

The muscles in Aaron's upper back twitched as his hands tightened on the mattress. "I got him alone so that I could get in some damage before anyone showed up. Took five staff to get me off him. And then he told me she asked for it and I went right back at him. Felt so fucking good to feel his cheekbone break. I might have killed him. Wanted to."

Joey was doing some calculating in his head. How many months in juvenile detention—baby county, the kids in the system called it—would Aaron have gotten?

"Some DFC worker picked me up from juvie to make the statement to the cops about Rafe. She was all about covering her ass and covering up for that shithole. The workers there knew why I'd beaten that motherfucker up, but they weren't going to let that get out, and Sav didn't want to press charges. The DFC worker told the cops about my 'history of violent outbursts' and 'anger management issues.' After that I could have told them where to find Jimmy Hoffa and they wouldn't have listened to me."

Joey's stomach sloshed like he'd finished an entire bottle of Malibu. And then anger put a layer of ice on the nausea. He'd known from the beginning someone had fucked up. Failed Aaron and his siblings. He didn't realize that someone probably still working in the same building he did had deliberately ruined so many lives. It wouldn't take much to find out who she was, but Joey couldn't be too sure he wouldn't do something completely unethical once he found her.

Aaron got up. "Rafe listened to his piece-of-shit lawyer and pled out to manslaughter. I only did six weeks since I was fifteen. By that time, Mom was back home and clean for the next month, enough time to convince a judge to get us all home again.

"I fucked up once. I wasn't going to do it again, so when she took off we lied to the workers until I was old enough to petition for custody. If I'd have been sixteen when it happened—"

"The records wouldn't have been sealed. Shit. I'm sorry."

Aaron turned and leaned against his dresser. "Not why I told you. And you're not the social worker who pissed in my cornflakes, wasn't that what you said?"

Joey wanted to lower his eyes, but now wasn't the time to back down.

"So yeah, I don't know if I can believe in happy endings. I want to, Joey. I wish I could be like you."

Joey got off the bed and stood in front of Aaron. "You don't have to be. That would be boring. I have sex with myself enough." Taking Aaron's hand, Joey pulled him back to bed. "But I get it."

"That the world is a fucked up place?"

"I already knew that. But it doesn't mean you can't be happy. You don't always have to..."

"What?"

"Be that guy."

"What guy? The one who lives up to your perfect ideals before time expires and you leave? Should I start the chess clock?" Aaron stretched out on one hip, long, casual arrogance on display.

It was calculated to piss Joey off, because Joey knew anger was the easiest thing for Aaron to deal with. Joey didn't want to give in, but it was hard as hell not to respond. "Start any clock you want. I'm not going anywhere. What I meant is you don't always have to be in control."

"Says the master manipulator."

Joey wanted to get up. He wanted to yell a few more variations on the just-because-life-sucks-doesn't-mean-you-get-to-take-it-out-on-me theme. He wanted to kiss Aaron hard enough they'd both believe this was going to work. "If I didn't think you'd call it manipulation, I'd prove it to you."

Joey's stomach dropped like he'd just gotten up on that killer wave because suddenly he knew one way he could, and from the steady hot stare in Aaron's blue eyes Joey knew Aaron was thinking it too.

"So prove it." Aaron rolled facedown.

Aaron looked back over his shoulder to see Joey's eyes widen in surprise before he got the stubborn set to his jaw. Aaron turned his own smile back into the pillow.

It wasn't that he never bottomed. Sometimes he met a guy he wanted to have fuck him. But when he went looking for it, and never at his usual places, he was looking for something hard and fast. Something to scratch an itch he couldn't get to any other way. And he didn't care if it hurt to get there.

That wasn't what he wanted now, wasn't what he was going to get from Joey. Not with Joey kissing his way down Aaron's spine, hot hands warming and relaxing the muscles on either side. Not with Joey's tongue sliding down the crack of Aaron's ass, with Aaron arching up to meet him. And definitely not with the slow deliberate flick of that pierced tongue around his hole.

Spreading him wide, Joey teased, dragging the ball on his tongue down to rub on the skin behind Aaron's balls, to lick and suck before moving back up, but the teasing didn't stop. Aaron didn't mind bottoming, but he did draw the line at begging for it like a bitch. He pulled his lower lip between his teeth and groaned, but he wasn't begging.

Joey wiggled a wet finger in and then slid his tongue alongside it. He'd better be able to back this up with his dick. Two fingers and then just his tongue, in and out, the piercing dragging on the rim and his lips sucking. Aaron wanted to lower his hips and hump the fucking mattress, and then he didn't because Joey worked three fingers in him and spit was not the same as lube, not when those knuckles were big. A twist and Joey rubbed his prostate, hard enough and long enough to get Aaron thinking about the mattress again before Joey pulled his fingers out and kissed his way up Aaron's back.

Joey grabbed a condom and the "most amazing space-aged substance in the universe" lube from the nightstand. The lube did feel good, made Joey's thumb almost like his tongue, fluid and hot as he rubbed it inside. Aaron had just about forgotten how long it had been since he'd had a dick in his ass, and how much he didn't want to whine in front of Joey when the sheathed tip of Joey's cock slid around Aaron's hole.

He didn't want it rough or hard. Fucking was fucking and it was going to need to get athletic to get good, but, "Slow, okay?"

"Yeah," Joey sighed.

And the blunt head pressed in for just a second before Joey backed off.

"I don't mean like the traffic on 95."

Joey's cock was right up against him, and Aaron could feel Joey's laugh vibrate through them both. "What's that about topping from the bottom?"

Aaron thought about pushing himself backward, getting this all over with. But he didn't want it to be over with. As weird as the thought was, Joey was taking care of him, a thrust that stopped as soon as it got too much, one hand stroking down Aaron's chest, the other rubbing just above Aaron's dick.

He had definitely been infected by Sheree's endless parade of romance movies. Because what they were doing was making love. And the realization didn't make him nauseous. He only wanted to concentrate on how it felt when the press went deeper and he opened around Joey, took him in. Hot, but no burn, Joey shifting his way in until his hips hit Aaron's ass.

He knew Joey was waiting, and he wanted that so-good friction, wanted Joey's lube-slick hand to fuck into. But for a second, he wanted to stay right here. For the one second where yeah, he didn't have to be that guy—much as he liked to be. The hand on his chest was slick with sweat, his own stinging his eyes until he rubbed them on his shoulder.

"Go," he whispered.

Joey started slowly, and if he topped as rarely as Aaron bottomed that was some impressive self-control. Aaron moved with him and that was the trigger. Joey held on and fucked him, hips slamming forward, the thick sound loud enough that Aaron spared a thought to hope that whatever movie they'd picked was as long as *Titanic*. Even if he wasn't sure his ass would last for three hours.

Bending down to lick and kiss at Aaron's shoulders, Joey wrapped his arm around Aaron's hips, fingers tight around Aaron's cock. Joey stretched forward and his cockhead started rubbing across Aaron's prostate. He was pretty sure the bed-shaking moan gave it away, because Joey kept going at exactly that angle, setting off a slow, steady build until Aaron's balls buzzed like he was on his bike, then hiked up, filling. He covered Joey's hand with his own, increasing the pace. It rolled out from his ass until the heat was too much, rushing out his dick as he groaned Joey's name.

Joey slowed and stopped, easing back.

"Don't pussy out now." Aaron forced the words out through his aching throat.

Joey started slamming forward even harder, and yeah, Aaron was starting to rethink that advice.

"Sorry," Joey murmured. And Aaron didn't know how Joey could tell about the sting, but it didn't matter because they were finishing this right. Aaron reached for Joey's thigh when he tried to pull back again and three hard, deep strokes later, Joey froze and shuddered before falling on Aaron's back.

"God, that was hard."

Aaron's chuckle was interrupted by a wince as Joey separated them.

Then Aaron rolled to look at Joey's face. "Was that your first—?"

"No, but it's been awhile."

"You're not rusty."

"Good to know." Joey stripped off the condom and then rolled back, tangling them in a sweaty, comey mess. "I love you. I'm not going anywhere."

Aaron wanted to believe it. Maybe if Joey kept saying it, proving it...

It still wouldn't matter. Because sooner or later it'd all get fucked up.

Chapter Seventeen

They had exactly ten days before the next fight, give or take a few hours. And of course it was just when Aaron had settled into a routine, just when he'd forgotten how quickly things could go to shit, just when some morning sex and then making Joey breakfast before he went to work was going to be the way he always wanted to start his day.

Breakfast. Who the fuck had an issue with breakfast?

"I don't need you to always make breakfast for me," Joey said, running a comb through his wet hair.

"I don't mind it."

"Well, I can take care of myself, Mom."

"What the fuck is that about?"

"I'm not a replacement for the kids." Joey threw the comb onto the kitchen counter.

"Yeah, I thought the fact that I just had my dick up your ass made that pretty clear."

"I'd just like to get myself a bowl of cereal one time."

Aaron looked down at the French toast in the pan. "So you can make a mess when you put sugar on Cocoa Puffs?"

"I left the sugar out once. God, you are such a control freak."

"Does that mean you need to fuck me again?"

"It's pretty clear sex isn't one of our problems."

"We have problems now?" Aaron resisted the urge to prove one of Joey's points by putting the comb back in the bathroom.

"I didn't say that."

"Yeah, Joey, you did."

"Well, I didn't mean it."

"What did you mean?"

"I just meant you don't have to make me breakfast every damned morning. You don't have to wait on me. Sleep in. Go out for coffee, whatever." Joey picked up his wallet from the bowl on the counter.

"Wow. Is this some kind of record for you? Ten days and you're already bored."

"I get that anger feels safe for you—"

"Jesus Christ." Aaron rolled his eyes.

"And fine. You win." Joey headed for the kitchen door.

"That's it? You're leaving?"

"I'm only going to work. But if you want me to spend the night at my apartment just say so."

"Yeah, I'm sure you miss your waterbed."

"So was that a yes?"

Joey was too smart not to figure out how hard he was pushing Aaron. But this didn't feel like another manipulation. He'd gotten mad, gotten Joey mad and now Aaron was screwed.

"Do whatever the fuck you want."

"I will." Joey slammed the door.

Aaron really didn't want to go to work. Well actually, he wanted to go to work, because it beat the hell out of being pissed enough to go out and do yard work, but he didn't want any more sage advice from Hennie, and he sure as fuck didn't want to see Kim. Aaron had been taunting Kim with it's-good-to-get-laid-regularly-how-long-has-it-been-for-you smirks. There was no guarantee Aaron would run into Kim. But because Aaron's luck was nothing if not consistent, as soon as he came out of the locker room, there was Kim.

Aaron gave him his usual smirk and then sipped his coffee.

"Ouch," Kim said. "So soon?"

Aaron could keep emotions off his face. He knew it. How else could he hustle pool and lie to the DFC for two years? So how the fuck did Kim read him like that?

"Still doing better than you." Aaron went out to the truck.

If Hennie noticed anything, she kept it to herself. They made their usual stop at the QwikStop on Eighth Street just before rush hour, but before Aaron went in to get his coffee, they got a call.

"481 Van Buren, first floor apartment. Guy's pretty hysterical. All he said was an accident, lots of blood, and then a lot of *oh God*s."

"We're only two blocks away. We'll take it," Hennie radioed back.

The cops weren't there yet. They looked around the neighborhood. Four o'clock, but no kids around. No one came out to see what the sirens were for, but a couple of neighborly curtains twitched.

Hennie raised her eyebrows in question and Aaron nodded. They unloaded the stretcher and lifted it up onto the porch.

They knocked, but no one answered at first.

Aaron was getting an itch between his shoulder blades. He was about to tell Hennie that they should go back out and wait for the cops when the door swung open. A guy in his mid-thirties stood there in a blood-soaked dress shirt. "Please help."

They followed him back to the kitchen, and that warning tingle turned into a full-out alarm call all over Aaron's skin.

Hennie sucked in her breath.

The guy on the floor was still breathing, mostly, a whistling through the sucking hole in his chest from the fucking gunshot wound. The pistol was on the kitchen table, displayed as casually as a bag of chips.

"Is he going to die?" not-gasping-on-the-floor-guy asked.

They were screwed now. They could try to leave, but the gun on the table seemed to argue against that plan. Aaron knelt on the floor and looked at the wound while Hennie started the questions. "Mister?"

"Larsen."

"We're going to do everything we can, but can you tell us what happened?"

"It was an accident. I swear."

Fuck. They really should have waited for the cops.

"If he dies…I can't go back to jail."

Screwed was definitely an understatement.

And then the cops showed up.

And the gun was in Mr. Larsen's violently shaking hand.

"Why did you call the cops? I told you it was an accident."

Hennie lowered herself to the floor next to the victim. "We didn't, Mr. Larsen. The police always respond to a 911 call."

"I just want to see my kids. Do you know what this guy did to my kids?"

The pounding on the door did nothing to steady Mr. Larsen's arm. Fortunately, the gun wasn't aimed at either Aaron or Hennie. Unfortunately, there wasn't a lot of space in the kitchen where an accidental shot would miss them.

"I've got a gun," Larsen yelled.

Aaron shouldn't have argued with Joey about breakfast. If Joey wanted to make himself cereal, what the fuck difference did it make? Aaron could have let him bitch and moan about it and then kiss him senseless, fuck him over the counter. Tell him to forget about work so they could go back to bed.

At least the kids would get the insurance.

Twenty years in the Jacksonville public school system, Hennie had balls. "Mr. Larsen, if you really don't want him to die, we need to get him out of here."

"Do you think I'm stupid? They're going to take me right back to jail. No one's going anywhere until I see my kids."

"Peter Larsen." The sound of the bullhorn startled them all. But only Peter was holding the gun. Which went off.

$\diamondsuit$

Joey was going to go to Aaron's during lunch to apologize, or at least to talk and give Aaron an opportunity to apologize, but got called out to investigate something ridiculous and boring. No matter what the kid and the parent alleged, playing field hockey in full view of two gym teachers and twenty other students did not provide an opportunity for sexual conduct. Even if the sport was, in the mother's words, "An attempt to make my daughter gay."

He hadn't eaten all day so he stopped at a drive-thru on his way back. He could go home. By the time he got to the office, it would be four thirty. Not that Aaron would be home. But Joey would be there waiting for him, and maybe then Aaron would see Joey wasn't going anywhere. Not as long as Aaron wanted him to stay. And maybe even longer than that.

He flipped through the radio as he ate his burrito in the parking lot, searching for music, but even the FM stations were talking about a hostage situation downtown. Joey was about to switch to his MP3 player, but then he heard the word paramedic and froze. He punched in a news station that repeated the story again. Peter Larsen, recently released from the county jail, had shot his wife's boyfriend in their home and was now holding two paramedics hostage.

Joey called Carmen at the police station, but she said they didn't have the names of the EMTs.

Paramedic.

Whatever.

Aaron had given Joey the number for Shands dispatch, including a few choice words to describe the woman who worked the day shift. Aaron hadn't been exaggerating either, because despite the sweet smile in his voice that could usually get Joey anywhere, she assumed he was with the press and hung up on him.

Larsen. Oh shit. He called Vivian at the DFC.

"Could you check my files, founded allegation, kids into

care, April third. What was the last name?"

"You'd better be bringing me back Starbucks."

"Tomorrow morning, I swear."

She was back in two minutes. "Larsen."

Shit. "Thanks, Viv. Venti Macchiato I promise."

"Hey, Joey, is that the guy on the news?"

"Yeah. Viv, do you have it up on your computer?"

"Yup."

"Can you see the ambulance number?" Joey held his breath.

"Wait a minute, they're doing a zoom on the police surrounding the house. Yeah, it's 367."

Joey thanked Vivian again and hung up, put the car in reverse and drove toward the center of the city. There was no reason Aaron would always take the same ambulance out, except it was exactly the kind of thing he would do. And just because Joey thought being fucked in an ambulance was interesting enough of a life experience that his brain had randomly filed away the number still didn't mean Aaron was somewhere on Van Buren with a gun to his head.

Except that script or no, Joey's life was still on tape delay, like he was living two minutes ahead and he knew what was going to happen. Right now, he knew if he didn't do something, Aaron was going to die.

He parked a block away and walked, trying to pick out the negotiator. Moving around the barricades and under the police tape, Joey headed straight for the guys in suits.

Without waiting for the cop who faced him to ask what the fuck Joey thought he was doing there, he introduced himself, handing over his Department of Families and Children ID. "I'm the case manager for the Larsen children."

"Great, where are they?"

"Group home."

"Thanks. You've been a huge help. Now let the grownups get back to work." The guy turned away.

Joey moved so he was still facing the balding cop in the brown suit. "I'm the one who took the kids into care."

"Yeah."

"So maybe he'd take me instead. Like a hostage exchange."

"That's sweet, honey. Because what we really need is to add another victim to this clusterfuck. Not gonna happen. Asshole EMTs should've waited for us."

Joey knew the answer. He'd seen the coffee cup on the dash. But he still asked. "Who are they, the EMTs?"

"Fuck do I know? Some guy who looks like a tall Indian and an older black lady."

The confirmation washed over him in an icy wave. Joey had never been cooler or calmer in his life. Because he knew what he was going to do.

It was tape delay anyway. It didn't matter that it was wrong on so many levels, violated everything he believed in, every bit of ethics he had. The system did not get to screw Aaron again.

"If I could go get the kids, bring them here, could you guarantee their safety?"

The cop looked at Joey, really looked at him for the first time. "Well yeah, of course, but you want to tell me how someone on your pay grade gets to make that kind of a decision?"

"I'll get approval."

"You do that, honey."

The O2 tank ran out at five nineteen, and Aaron doubted Larsen was going to let them go to the truck for a fresh one. Aaron and Hennie had stopped the bleeding and kept the lung from collapsing with an occlusive dressing. The wound wouldn't necessarily kill the guy, provided they could keep him breathing until they got him into surgery.

Larsen's stray shot had taken out a chunk of the ceiling,

leaving all four of them covered in plaster dust and lead paint chips. He'd made Aaron push the kitchen table up against the back door after the cops started talking again, and everyone was cozily camped like Boy Scouts on the kitchen floor.

Hennie had tried the whole sympathy bit. *Yeah, your wife was wrong. Sorry about the kids. This bastard ought to be the one locked up. If someone did that to my kids...*

But Larsen wasn't budging.

Every time the cops called, all he asked was "Got my kids yet?" He never liked the answer and always hung up.

The guy wasn't a complete nutcase. Larsen knew his ass was headed straight back to jail, but he'd gotten this one idea and no amount of sympathy or reason was going to get a fresh concept into his skull.

Hennie'd taken the worst of the plaster shower, and the sweat rolling down her face made dark streaks through the pale coating. She kept the airway open, checking the pulse while Aaron worked the bag, the rhythm familiar and loud enough that Aaron didn't recognize the sensation right away.

His phone, buzzing on his hip. Fuck, he hoped Sav or the kids hadn't caught this on the news.

"What?" Hennie mouthed.

"My phone," he answered just as silently.

"Cops?" she suggested.

"What's going on?" Larsen and his pistol crawled closer. "Is the bastard dying?"

"Not yet," Aaron said. "My phone rang."

Larsen shrugged. "So answer it. I don't give a shit."

"My hands are a little full right now."

Larsen shoved the end of the pistol against Aaron's temple. "Don't try anything."

"I won't." It wasn't worth the risk. Not worth never seeing Joey or the kids again.

The gun pressed in deeper as Larsen reached for the phone at Aaron's belt. It hurt. Hard, warm metal shaking violently against his bone, boring in. If Aaron had anything but weary tension left in his body, he might have been scared.

Larsen opened the phone and put it to Aaron's ear, moving the pistol so it wavered in front of Aaron's face. Lucky for sucking-chest-wound guy, Aaron could work the bag blindfolded in the dark because he was going cross-eyed staring at that pistol.

"Yeah?" he said into the phone.

"Thank God you're all right. I am so sorry about this morning."

"Joey. It's not a good time." He felt Hennie's eyes on his face, but more than that, he felt the one-eyed stare from the end of the gun.

"Yeah, I guess not. Put Larsen on."

"What?"

"I know everything that's going on. I've got his kids with me."

Just when Aaron was pretty sure he was all out of panic, Joey had to say that. Aaron's temple throbbed like the gun was still digging at it, hot spikes of pain. "Joey, don't do this. Don't put those kids in the middle of this. Don't you get in the middle of this."

"We're all fine. Half a block away. Now put him on."

"What's going on?" Larsen asked.

Aaron pressed the bag again. "It's for you."

Larsen grabbed the phone.

The bag wheezed and expanded twice and then Larsen said, "Connor?... Connor. I missed you so much, son. Are you okay? You sure? Is Hannah okay?... Baby, Daddy just wanted to see you. It's okay, baby, don't cry. Honey, please don't be scared."

Larsen lowered the gun and his voice changed from soothing parent to someone who was almost dead. "Yeah. Okay. I know." He picked up the handset and called the cops. "I'm ready."

K.A. Mitchell

✧

Between getting the victim to surgery and filling out a metric ton of paperwork for the hospital and the cops, Aaron didn't get to finish making reassuring calls to Sav and the kids until after ten. When he finally managed to get Sheree to say good-bye it was ten thirty.

Joey was on his own phone, pacing around the living room, his side of the conversation consisting of one *I know* after another. Aaron sat on the couch and watched Joey get reamed out on the phone, stubborn tilt to his chin indicating he wasn't buying a word of it. After about the tenth *I know*, Joey said, "I understand," and hung up.

"Well?"

"The director—damn, you haven't been chewed out until you get the director on your ass at ten o'clock at night—said they were putting me on paid leave pending an investigation, but in the whole state of Florida, there is no one more fired than I am right now."

Joey wouldn't even need to invent a fight to walk out. He'd just find a job in New Jersey or something. Aaron used the last of his reserves to keep everything locked nice and tight and then asked as casually as he could, "So what are you going to do?"

"Sleep. I'm exhausted." Joey flopped onto the couch.

"No, I mean your job."

"Well, I'm guessing employment prospects are pretty dim for social work in the state of Florida. Maybe even the country if the story gets picked up."

Like he said, Joey wouldn't even have to try. Aaron arched a brow. "So where are you going to go?"

"Go?" Joey got up and stood over him. "What do you mean *go*?" His eyes got hard as he leaned down close to Aaron's face. "You son of a bitch. After everything today, do you really think I'm just going to hit the road?"

"Maybe if you didn't have more changes of address than

256

clean underwear, I wouldn't."

"God, what is it going to take for you?"

"Why did you do that today? Get those kids?" Because maybe if Aaron could figure that out he'd know why Joey was still there.

"I did it for you, you idiot. I'd never have risked their lives, but I wasn't going to sit on my ass and not save your fucking life. And I sure as hell wasn't thinking about my job."

"I thought you believed in all that shit, the system working."

"Fuck the system. It owed you."

Aaron snorted.

Joey straddled him and sat on his lap. "I wasn't going to get the kids at first. I tried to make the cops trade me."

"And I'm an idiot?"

But Aaron could breathe again, move again. He grabbed Joey's neck and pulled him down until their foreheads touched. Joey might be the worst klutz Aaron had ever met, but Joey had done it. Done what the Jacksonville police department negotiator couldn't. Joey had strolled into the middle of that mess and saved Aaron's life.

Joey wasn't just on Aaron's side, part of the tiny little faction that made up Aaron's fight against the whole sucky world, Joey was the one thing Aaron had never even imagined he'd have. Someone who put him first.

Aaron kept a hand on his neck and kissed him, tongue sliding inside like it was the only safe place he'd ever known. And it was.

"I love you."

Joey grinned against Aaron's mouth. "I know."

"You think so? Then listen to this, Joey Miller. I'm in love with you. And if you ever leave me, I swear to God I will come after you and drag you back."

"Really?"

Aaron hadn't thought Joey's smile could get brighter.

257

Mommy the dentist must have sent him special toothpaste. For an instant, Aaron felt sorry for all those other guys who'd let Joey go. And then he was glad they were all fucking morons. Because Joey was his.

"Worse than that. I'll send Sheree after you."

Joey made a kid's quick cross-my-heart gesture. "Not going anywhere. Except the bedroom. Unless you plan to fuck me on the couch. Again."

Joey got to watch Aaron's face as he pushed in this time, watch as something seemed to shift behind those pale eyes just before they closed. But he wasn't shutting Joey out, not with Joey's legs over his shoulders, cock driving so deep, so hard inside that every pulse of pleasure came with an equal ache. Joey only wanted to take him deeper, to pull Aaron all the way inside where he'd be safe. Because Joey got it. Aaron might need to protect his family, but he needed Joey to keep Aaron safe, especially from himself.

Aaron moved inside like he wasn't even flesh, just fluid heat, and there wasn't a part of Joey he wasn't touching. Tongue in his mouth, hands a bruising force on his hips and thighs. Joey knew he wasn't going to need a hand on his cock to come. Not when Aaron lifted his legs so high Joey couldn't catch his breath. Not when every stroke scorched like lightning on his nerves, pushed the heat from his ass until it welled through him like being lifted on a wave, but it was all around him, pouring through him.

Aaron didn't pull out when he came. He kept thrusting even though his dick had to be as wrung out and sore as Joey's ass. When Aaron stopped deep inside, his eyes opened and stared down into Joey's. "Don't want you to fuck other guys, okay?"

"Okay. But you know, with your dick in my ass, that might be considered manipulation."

Aaron gave Joey the quick almost smile that Joey would always be able to read. "It's negotiation. And I won't either."

"Then it's a deal."

Chapter Eighteen

Savannah called more often. And once, to Joey's delight and Aaron's dismay, left Ben with them for a weekend. At least when Aaron'd had to take over all the kids had been out of diapers. Two-year-olds were smelly and loud. He'd never been happier to get to work.

When Aaron got home that night, he could hear Joey singing over the choking snuffles of a two-year-old coming off a long screaming cry. He found them in the living room, Joey pacing around with Ben in his arms. His laptop played piano music while Joey supplied the words.

The song wasn't anything he recognized, not quite jazz or blues, not country, too soft for rock. But it was sad. Something about lying to yourself too many times. It made Joey's clear voice husky.

Joey looked up and Aaron leaned against the kitchen counter. "Another depressing song from that Gay-African American dude in the forties?"

Ben rubbed his face on Joey's shoulder.

"No." Joey stopped pacing. And then bit his lip. "It's mine."

Aaron couldn't keep the surprise off his face. He swallowed. "But..."

Joey smiled as he came toward him. "Yeah. I have to rewrite that last verse."

The smile warmed Aaron from the inside out. He lifted his nephew from Joey's arms, let the sleepy toddler's weight finish driving away the doubt jabbing under his ribs. "You'd better."

"I promise."

Dylan managed to not get tossed out of school, finished his last semester at the Texas Culinary Institute and promised to look for a job in Dallas if Aaron would cosign for an apartment for him and his brother. If Darryl had known he was going to be stuck with Dylan for life, Aaron thought maybe Darryl would have cannibalized his brother in the womb like those people who ended up with an extra eye in their skulls.

Sheree was home for three weeks at the end of the semester, and Joey's lease on his place to keep his boxes in was up in July. Joey had picked up some consulting work—with of all places the police department—but when Aaron told Joey he was welcome to move the boxes to the crawl space under the roof, Joey just gave him a weird look.

So maybe Aaron shouldn't have been surprised when he woke up to Joey's mouth on his cock the next morning. Not that part. Joey woke him up often enough with blow jobs that Aaron couldn't remember why living alone had seemed like such a good idea.

What he shouldn't have found surprising was that Joey pulled off just when Aaron's hands were fisting the sheets. A couple swirls with that pierced tongue and then Joey whispered Aaron's name. That's when he should have known he was in trouble.

But he still said, "Yeah?"

Joey took Aaron deep, sucking hard on the way back up, licking under the rim before he lifted his head, one hand maintaining a light steady stroke. Definitely in serious trouble.

"I was thinking." Another quick suck on the head and Aaron groaned. "Sheree said I could put the waterbed in her room."

"Uhn." But what he meant to say was *I never should have let the two of you meet.*

This time Joey swallowed around Aaron a few times before pulling off. "So I know you don't like fucking on it, but maybe we could sleep on it."

"Joey." Aaron grabbed his hair, hard enough to sting. "Didn't you promise not to manipulate?"

"It's not manipulation if you know I'm doing it. You call it negotiating."

Despite Aaron's grip, Joey leaned forward enough to lick precome out of Aaron's slit.

"Then no."

Taking Aaron to the back of his throat again, Joey slid tight wet lips up and down the hard shaft. Aaron loosened his grip, and Joey ran his fingers over Aaron's balls.

"How about two nights a week?"

"Joey." But there wasn't a lot of force behind the word when his cock was straining to get farther inside the guy who kept making sure Aaron's life didn't suck. But the good sucking, that could happen right now. *Please.* "Joey."

"And I want a dog."

They got a beagle-pug mix from the pound. Fucker had Joey's eyes.

About the Author

K.A. Mitchell discovered the magic of writing at an early age when she learned that a carefully crayoned note of apology sent to the kitchen in a toy truck would earn her a reprieve from banishment to her room. Her career as a spin control artist was cut short when her family moved to a two-story house, and her trucks would not roll safely down the stairs. Around the same time, she decided that Chip and Ken made a much cuter couple than Ken and Barbie and was perplexed when invitations to play Barbie dropped off. An unnamed number of years later, she's happy to find other readers and writers who like to play in her world.

To learn more about K.A. Mitchell, please visit www.kamitchell.com. Send an email to K.A. Mitchell at authorKAMitchell@gmail.com.

GREAT
cheap
fun

Discover eBooks!

THE FASTEST WAY TO GET THE HOTTEST NAMES

Get your favorite authors on your favorite reader, long before they're
out in print! Ebooks from Samhain go wherever you go, and work with
whatever you carry—Palm, PDF, Mobi, and more.

Samhain
Publishing, Ltd

WWW.SAMHAINPUBLISHING.COM

LaVergne, TN USA
26 February 2010
174366LV00003BB/12/P